中式英文面面觀

簡清國——著

英漢辭典主編用近 **1000** 則例句，
教你全面破解中式英文的謬誤

推薦語

中式英文Chinglish受母語干擾，不熟悉英語人士語言習慣，往往「倉頡造句」貽笑大方。本書協助我們一一破解，擺脫似是而非的陷阱。

——王安琪　東吳大學英文系專任教授

就好像數位改變世界，由0與1二元開始最快。

學好英文，由中式英文跟正確英文的二元對比最快。

——蔡淇華　暢銷書作家／惠文高中英文老師

推薦序一

在道地英文的呼喚中道別中式英文

余玉照　國立嘉義大學前副校長暨人文藝術學院院長

簡清國教授透過這本題為《中式英文面面觀》的新著，等於向學子們發出一個誠懇的呼籲：在道地英文的呼喚中，讓我們一起來道別中式英文吧！

他從開始關切中式英文這個嚴肅課題至今已長達四十多年，而他從動筆到完成這本書則花了十幾年。他為此深具創意和意義的重要工程，所展現出來的專業精神與恆心毅力，真是令人肅然起敬！我要誠摯恭喜他終於實現了長期以來念茲在茲的一個寶貴願望！我相信，這本書的出版將會引起同樣關心這個議題的讀者朋友們相當開心的歡迎、好奇和重視。

簡老師跟這個議題結下不解之緣，背後有個小故事。他在【前言】裡提到他「潛心研究中式英文四十多年，發現在學生習作錯誤中，除了冠詞和副詞之外，幾乎都有中式英文的影子。」無疑地，像他這麼熱心投入教學研究的老師，居然會因這個可貴的發現而「興奮良久，失眠三天」，乃是完全可以理解的。他進一步發現許多學生之所以覺得「英文程度停滯不前」的根本原因是他們在「母語的干擾」（mother-tongue interference）下，往往不自覺地習於說寫出中式英文來。他一語道破了中式英文的「元兇」：「透過中文的語言習慣，在說寫英文時生搬硬套，這就是造成中式英語的原因。」於是，為了有助於「提升讀者的寫作程度」，他實踐了一套創新務實的書寫策略。

本書共計十一章，外加兩篇附錄，核心內容就是將他彙整所得中式英

文之主要成因及其補救之道，分別作為各章之題旨，並藉由標示【正】、【誤】、【不佳】的三類例句，有系統地運用多元對照比較的方式給予簡明扼要的解說。基於本書展示的豐富內涵，我想至少可以歸納出以下三點特色：

一、目標鮮明，面面俱到：

《中式英文面面觀》讓人感覺其訴求目標相當明確引人，而且，中式英文一詞似乎給人強烈的新鮮感，同時帶有啟發性或警惕性的意味，所以容易激起讀者閱讀的興趣。另外，「面面觀」三字也能引發內容多元紮實的聯想。讀者明白此書的宗旨就是要幫助他們學習如何補救中式英文的缺失，從而可以踏上道地英文的學習之路，相信此一目標的價值將能獲得他們的讚賞。

此外，本書聚焦於改正中式英文的錯誤，雖然沒有論及有關其他包括英文發音、英文作文或演講等在內的課題，但卻在行文中引領讀者學習提升正確英文程度所需的各種基礎條件，包括加強字彙搭配的實力、機警防範母語之干擾、培養中英語法或慣用法之辨識及應用能力、乃至靈活運用簡老師用心研發推介的諸多學習訣竅等。換言之，儘管本書宣稱的目標是鎖定如何補救所謂中式英文的錯誤，然而，事實上，只要朝向這個明確的目標鍥而不捨地努力下去，也就等於不斷修練道地英文的實用功夫了。

二、分門別類，系統完整：

作者十分重視系統框架之建構在研究計畫推進的過程中佔有關鍵的位置，他對自己在中式英文「突破傳統」的研究表現頗覺滿意，即為現成的明證。

翻開本書的目錄，對作者如何利用周延的一套思維方法與步驟，將造成中式英文的種種因素及其補救方法加以系統地分類歸納，即可一目瞭

然，不待贅述。

如今，本書各章及附錄各有一明晰的主題，各主題之下又各設若干副題，而各副題之下亦視情況另設若干子題，依此類推，以便深刻探討各個相關層面值得或必須妥善處理的所有大小課題。

我之所以提到本書結構層層相連、井井有條之優點，目的在於指出此一結構上的特色帶來兩大好處。其一是作者可以徹底覺察並直探或深究所有相關課題。由此又帶來明顯的第二個好處，那就是讀者可以「一窺全貌」，一口氣讀完一遍，便能享有關乎中式英文及道地英文的全套入門心得

此外，每一章並附有與該章題旨密切相關的系列練習題，可以看出作者始終把握了盡量讓學生「做中學」的原則，並藉由適當例句，引導學生清楚理解中式英文跟道地英文之間的異同。無疑地，這種實作教學必然會為有心追求英語不斷進步的讀者如願爭取更多的收穫。

三、創意十足，獨樹一格：

作者講究創新教學，始終注重研採較好的方法以期收到更多更好的教學成果。他善用本書的書寫策略，就是現成的一個例證。他寫道：「本書搜集近千句常見的中式英語，以分類方式探討其成因，讓讀者迅速掌握訣竅，說、寫出正確而道地的英語。」他堅持井然有序的作風，他寧願設法另闢新路，獨樹一格。他指出：「坊間有關中式英語著作，大多零星散亂，缺乏系統。本書突破傳統，以分類方式剖析中式英語，讀者可以一窺全貌」由此可見，他滿懷熱誠想幫助學生學好英文的初衷是多麼積極。他為這本著作付出了非比尋常的創意才智，進而使他在中式英文研究領域裡獲得了作為一位先鋒或倡導者的可喜成就。

作者經過多年辛勤的鑽研細究，終於成功開發了一整套精湛實用的學術資源，不僅能藉以精確診斷中式英文的複雜成因，而且能針對當今中式英文所面臨的各樣症狀，施予真正具有療效的各種處方，同時還能靈活參

酌字彙搭配法則、文法、英文慣用法與思維邏輯等多元評量觀點與造句評等標準，隨時提供有關追求道地英文所需既深刻又細膩的相關論述解說。凡此諸多建樹，便是作者在本書中最可貴的成就，更是到目前為止，在中式英文研究範疇裡，最具開創性的卓著貢獻。

在結束本文之前，我想談一下作者列出英文句子四級評等背後的意義。簡老師出於他的創意在本書中首創這個論點，依高下排列，即為：【正】句、【不佳】句、【誤】句、以及最低等，像「people mountain people sea（人山人海），green oil oil（綠油油），horse horse tiger tiger（馬馬虎虎）」之類「只是遊戲式的說法，沒有『資格』稱為中式英語」。屬於第三等的【誤】句是錯誤的中式英文，也上不了說／寫英文的檯面。至於屬第二等的【不佳】句雖不歸為【誤】句，卻只宜用作不正式、非書面語。如此一來，唯有標示為【正】的第一等句子才是正確的「道地英文」。

對英文句子的分類及其分級有了上述的概念後，我相信對引起或增強學習道地英文的動機應該會帶來正面的助益。

最後，我想引用簡老師在【前言】中特別鼓勵高中學生的一段話：「在學習英文的過程中，尤其在高中階段，由於缺乏英語文詞彙和文法結構不同的認知，常有犯了中式英文而不自知的現象。這種錯誤如不及早改正，就是上了大學，以至出社會做事仍然會繼續再犯。」我相信，高中階段的的確確是開始為道地英文打基礎最好的時機，簡老師所提示的理由我深有同感。就從閱讀他這本書開始向中式英文道別，肯定是諸君日後回憶起來時，會深深覺得非常慶幸非常甜美的好事一樁！（寫於2020/12/31）

推薦序二

從中式英文到道地英文

林茂松　前國立臺灣科技大學英文教授兼人文社會學院院長、
　　　　東吳大學英文系教授兼外語學院院長

　　學習任何一種外國語文，都會有母語的干擾。以中文為母語的人士，學習英文的過程會受到母語與母文化的干擾，這種干擾在書寫能力方面尤其顯著，也就是寫出的英文不是道地正確的英文，而是受到中文語法結構影響，或基於中文思考模式寫成的錯誤英文。這種錯誤英文，一般稱為中式英文。

　　母語干擾可以經由訓練轉化為學習外語的助力，而不是阻力。藉由分析、歸納、比較兩種語言與文化的差異，熟悉這些相異之處，寫作時不但可以刻意避免，還有助於書寫道地正確的目標語。

　　例如，中文使用者想表示「我要實現我的夢想」時，他可能寫I want to carry out my dream，因為他先用中文思考，「實現」的相等語是carry out，因此他就寫出這樣的中式英文。正確的英文是I want to fulfill my dream，因為英文中dream最適當的搭配詞是fulfill。

　　上面的例子是中英文詞義與搭配詞的差異造成的錯誤中式英文。下面的例子是思考層面的差異造成的。中國人會寫Once a teacher, always a father 這樣的中式英文。這是不瞭解中文與英文思考方式的差異造成的錯誤。如果熟悉中文是跳躍的、間接的、感性的，英文是比較不跳躍、比較直接、比較理性的，就知道中文說「一日為師，終身為父」，是跳躍式的說法，把「像」跳過去了，省略了。用比較不跳躍的道地英文應該是Once a teacher, always like a father。

　　又如，中國人常寫The moon on the Mid-autumn Festival is the

brightest in a year。 對英美人士而言,這句話不合邏輯,是中式英文,因為一年中有好幾次月亮跟中秋節(的月亮)一樣亮(圓),用表示客觀事實的is ,以及唯一的最高級來講中秋節月亮的亮度,不合英文表達習慣。最好加個considered表示這是主觀的認定,不是客觀的事實:The moon on the Mid-autumn Festival is considered the brightest in a year.

　　簡清國教授是知名英文教授、辭典主編、作家。他旅居加拿大二十幾年,用畢生心力整理出中式英文的種類,分門別類說明條列,寫出這本《中式英文面面觀》,可說是嘉惠英文學習者的利器。讀者不必花時間自行探索中英文差異,只要依照本書章節研習演練,可早日登堂入室,寫出道地的英文。

林茂松
2020年歲末
於東吳大學英文系

推薦序三

英文如何表達才會道地自然？

——《中式英文面面觀》讀後感

陳東榮　前國立中央大學英文系教授兼系主任

在學習外語時，我們難免會受到自己母語的影響。國人在說、寫英文時，不時會出現中式英文（Chinese English or Chinglish）的錯誤或欠佳文句。例如「寫日記」該用keep a diary，但常被寫成*write a diary。「半熟水煮蛋」不是 *a half-boiled egg，應是a soft-boiled egg；沐浴時的「洗頭」不是*wash your head，應是wash or shampoo your hair。 上述例子顯示中式英文的產生與母語的干擾有密切的關聯。

英文易學難精，國人想要學會道地英文，首要之務是避免中文思維或中文句構的影響；換句話說，要盡量迴避中式英文的陷阱。

儘管坊間英文作文及翻譯的參考書籍琳瑯滿目，多不勝數，然而要找到一本有系統地探討中式英文的專書卻不容易。日前，我有幸讀到簡清國教授的新書《中式英文面面觀》文稿。閱畢之後，我有Eureka（我找到了！）的感覺。依我看來，這本新書將可協助去除中式英文的魔障，可使讀者的英文實力更上一層樓。

本書作者簡教授是位英文高手。移居加拿大之前，他早就是鼎鼎大名的英語教育工作者、翻譯名家和詞書編纂者。在臺灣的時候，除在大學任教之外，他一直筆耕不輟。市面上有多種英漢辭典係由他主編或合編，國內的報章雜誌也不時刊登他有關英語教與學的精彩好文。他與楊景邁、林茂竹、及其他教授合編或審定的工具書包括《文鶴英文用法字典》、《建宏多功能英漢辭典》、《當代英語搭配辭典》以及《建宏英漢六用辭典》。這些詞書的共通點就是強調字詞搭配的重要性。

《中式英文面面觀》是結合作者一生珍貴的知識和經驗所完成的實用好書。從高中時期開始，簡教授就不斷研讀英文，積累許多寶貴的知識。四十多年來，無論在臺灣或在加拿大，他都從事實際英語教學，從中擷取豐富的經驗。

　　為了讓讀者迅速掌握訣竅，說、寫出正確道地的英文，簡教授特別將批改前後的例句並列，附上解釋說明，指出錯誤成因，並提供解決之道。讀者詳讀本書的十一章和兩篇附錄之後，即可瞭解中式英文的由來；接著，實際演練每章後面的練習題，舉一反三，觸類旁通，當可大大增強學習效果。

　　本書的一大強項是作者費心搜集的那些頗具代表性的例句。除了提供可靠的準確文句，他又加上專業實用的點評與解說，使讀者知其然，又知其所以然，減少以後犯錯的頻率。

　　以下謹就書中內容分享一些讀後心得。對國人而言，英文動詞＋名詞的搭配最容易出錯，許多中式英文於焉產生。本書第一章的例句可以說明動詞＋名詞的搭配是如何困難和複雜。例如，我們可以用 raise a child / a protest / an issue / the rent / one's salary 等，但卻不能說 *raise a habit。要表示「養成某種習慣」，a habit 必須搭配其他動詞，如 foster / form / develop / acquire / get into 等。所以，「他養成了晚睡的習慣。」正確的說法是 He has got into the habit of going to bed late. 而不是 *He has raised the habit of going to bed late.

　　一般人看到中文「接受」，都會想到 receive 這個字，但並非所有的「接受」都可用 receive 表達，例如「接受手術」並不是 *receive an operation，而是 have / undergo an operation。「接受盲腸手術」應該是 have / undergo an operation for appendicitis。

　　不少人覺得介系詞和冠詞非常難纏，因為大都屬慣用語，是不合邏輯。例如「在校園」，到底要用 in the campus 或 on campus？ 本書第七章專門討論介系詞的誤用。簡教授特別將三個常見的介系詞 in, on, at 的用法歸納整理，好讓讀者容易理解和記憶。

此外，介系詞會受到中文思維的影響而被誤用，如：「他對我的態度已經改變了。」His attitude toward me has changed.「對……態度」的介系詞不是 to，而要用toward或towards。再者，一般人看到「的」就會想到 of，可是「她是林董的祕書。」不能說：*She is secretary of Chairman Lin. 必須說 She is secretary to Chairman Lin. 才對。

　　本書第九章談到誤用句型所造成的中式英文，內容非常豐富。其中第二節是關於動詞句型的普遍錯誤。例如，在表達中文的「……讓我……」或「……使我……」時，通常要用 make it easy / hard / difficult / possible / impossible / important / necessary for me to ...。 例如「網際網路使得人們購物和付帳單更加方便。」不可直譯為：*The Internet makes people easy to purchase goods and pay their bills. 應該說：The Internet makes it easy for people to purchase goods and pay their bills.

　　本書作者非常關心E世代年輕人學習英語的情況。由於網路上充斥各種資訊，讓人眼花撩亂，無所適從，他在「致讀者」中表達他的擔憂，並且提醒讀者在使用Google 或其他搜尋引擎時，務必要用對方法，慎思明辨。

　　我個人認為《中式英文面面觀》是一本值得大力推薦的好書。它不僅適合愛好英語的人士參考使用，並且適合各級學校選作英文作文或翻譯的教科書。

　　李安的電影《臥虎藏龍》有句意味深長的話：「劍，要人用才能活。」（ "A sword by itself rules nothing. It only comes alive in skilled hands.") 劍本身無法使力，惟有在劍俠手上，方能虎虎生風。英文亦然：惟有技藝高強的英文達人，才能將英文使用得道地自然。讓我們相互勉勵。

前言

　　許多人學英文多年後，往往發現自己的程度總是停滯不前，說、寫出來的不免夾雜著中式英文。苦惱的是不知道如何改進，因為文法、用法有書可查，正確、道地英文卻無規則可循。本書搜集近千句常見的中式英文，以分類方式探討其成因，讓讀者迅速掌握訣竅，說、寫出正確而道地的英文。

　　一提到中式英文，很多人便會聯想到people mountain people sea（人山人海），green oil oil（綠油油），horse horse tiger tiger（馬馬虎虎）等等大家耳熟能詳的例子。但是嚴格來說，這些只是遊戲式的說法，沒有「資格」稱為中式英文，稍具英文知識的人不會這麼用。

　　所謂中式英文，是指受中文思維影響，也就是語言學家所稱的「母語的干擾」（mother-tongue interference）而使用的不正確的英文。例如把「開燈」說成open the light、「開電視」說成open the TV、「開支票」說成open a check等等，都是典型的中式英文。使用中式英文，輕者會阻礙溝通，重者還可能造成誤會，不可不慎。

　　在學習英文的過程中，尤其在高中階段，由於缺乏英文詞彙和文法結構不同的認知，常有犯了中式英文而不自知的現象。這種錯誤如不及早改正，就是上了大學，以至出社會做事仍然會繼續再犯。

　　作者潛心研究中式英文四十多年，發現在學生習作錯誤中，**除了冠詞和副詞之外，幾乎都有中式英文的影子。本書首創以分類方式探討中式英文的成因，舉例說明，並提出解決之道。**

　　全書分成十一章，另加兩篇附錄，完全取材自學生的實際寫作錯誤範例，以正、誤句子呈現，並附以解釋說明。原稿都經加拿大籍英文老師修正，具有相當的準確性。兩位老師文字修養極好，且都擁有英文碩士學

位，任教英文數十年。衷心希望本書不僅成為愛好英文人士的參考書，也廣為各級學校採用的翻譯、作文教科書。

　　這本小書從執筆到定稿，歷經十多年。其間承蒙林茂竹、曾泰元、張華、李勝也、倪無言等學者、專家審校全部或部分文稿，提出一些改進意見，謹致謝忱。另外，旅居溫哥華的中國及臺灣留學生幫忙打字與整理文稿，其中出力最多者包括葉青、唐博一、胡凝、朱婷、劉孜融等五位，辛苦你們了。

　　坊間有關中式英文著作，大多零星散亂，缺乏系統。本書突破傳統，以分類方式剖析中式英文，讀者可以一窺全貌，然而疏失之處在所難免。讀者先進若有指教，請電郵：jian.education@gmail.com.

簡清國　謹誌

2021, 元月

中式英文面面觀　　目錄

推薦語　　　　　　　　　　　　　　　王安琪、蔡淇華　002

推薦文一　在道地英文的呼喚中道別中式英文　　余玉照　003

推薦文二　從中式英文到道地英文　　　　　　　林茂松　007

推薦文三　英文如何表達才會道地自然？　　　　陳東榮　009

前　言　　　　　　　　　　　　　　　　　　　　　012

致讀者　　　　　　　　　　　　　　　　　　　　　018

第一章　誤用詞彙搭配造成的中式英文　　　　　　020

　　　　　練習題　　　　　　　　　　　　　　　038

第二章　誤用文法搭配造成的中式英文　　　　　　044

　　　　　練習題　　　　　　　　　　　　　　　063

第三章　經由翻譯程序直譯造成的中式英文　　　　068

　　　　　練習題　　　　　　　　　　　　　　　095

第四章　誤用動詞造成的中式英文　　　　　　　102

　　　一、to be / to have　　　　　　　　　　　104

　　　二、動詞時態　　　　　　　　　　　　　　109

　　　　　a) 表示趨勢的動詞　　　　　　　　　109

b) 表示事實、真理、習慣的動詞　　　　111

c) 情態動詞　　　　112

三、幾個容易誤用的動詞／動詞片語　　　　114

四、主動態／被動態　　　　124

練習題　　　　127

第五章　因邏輯錯誤造成的中式英文　　　　132

一、由中文逐譯成英文造成的邏輯問題　　　　134

二、修飾語與主詞不一致造成的邏輯問題　　　　144

三、人稱代名詞it指涉不清造成的邏輯問題　　　　147

練習題　　　　151

第六章　誤用名詞／主詞造成的中式英文　　　　158

一、容易誤用的兩個名詞amount / number　　　　160

二、複合名詞（compound noun）　　　　162

三、使用動名詞片語當主詞　　　　165

四、主詞累贅　　　　170

練習題　　　　172

第七章　誤用介系詞造成的中式英文　　178

　一、介系詞in / on / at　　180

　二、當介系詞用的to　　182

　三、幾個容易誤用的介系詞　　188

　四、不定詞／介系詞for　　191

　練習題　　193

第八章　誤用形容詞造成的中式英文　　198

　一、修飾語誤置 (misplaced modifier)　　200

　二、表示必要性或迫切性的形容詞　　205

　三、修飾「人」或「事物」的形容詞　　207

　四、人稱代名詞＋形容詞　　209

　五、幾個容易誤用的形容詞／形容詞片語　　210

　練習題　　221

第九章　誤用句型造成的中式英文　　226

　一、雙名主詞　　228

　二、動詞句型think/ find/ make + it +形容詞　　230

　三、不能接受詞＋不定詞的動詞　　234

　四、形容詞句型　　236

　練習題　　239

第十章　誤用連接詞造成的中式英文　　244

一、 and / or　　246

二、 even/ even if/ even after　　252

三、not only... but also...　　254

四、no matter＋wh-clause　　256

五、 run-on sentences　　257

六、 than / compared to　　260

練習題　　262

第十一章　誤用所有格形容詞造成的中式英文　　266

練習題　　274

附錄一　代名詞it／指示代名詞this　　280
附錄二　容易誤用的副詞　　286

一、always / usually / often　　288

二、sometimes / sometime / some time　　289

三、especially / especially for　　290

四、關係副詞where　　291

練習題答案　　294

致讀者

　　語言乃約定俗成，中英文亦不例外。透過中文的語言習慣，在說、寫英文時生搬硬套，這就是造成中式英文的原因。作者以正、誤方式來討論英文句子，難免引起爭議。**本書以提升讀者的寫作程度為目的**，在判斷句子正、誤時，對於不正式、非書面語的表達方式，均列為【不佳】，而不歸為【誤】句，免得過於武斷。**讀者在書寫時，宜避免使用標示【不佳】的例子。**舉例如下：

1.　我脖子僵硬。
　　【正】：I have a stiff neck.
　　【不佳】：My neck is stiff.
　　【解說】：My neck is stiff. 顯然是由中文逐譯而成的中式英文。本書避免將它歸為【誤】句，主要是因為口語方面使用，尚能理解。然而英美人士會認為這不合乎慣用法（idiomaticity）。想要學好英文，一定要在慣用法方面下功夫。

2.　建核電廠的優點不計其數。
　　【正】：There are countless advantages to constructing nuclear power plants.
　　【不佳】：The advantages of constructing nuclear power plants are countless.
　　【解說】：【不佳】句顯然是由中文逐譯而成的中式英文。按countless作敘述形容詞（predicative adjective）和限定形容詞（attributive adjective）皆可，但本句雖然合乎文法的性能（grammaticality），卻不合慣用法而不能使用。其實，從語意觀

點來說，本句可謂頭重腳輕，言不盡意，因為聽話的人或看文章的人還期待你說Firstly（第一優點是……），Secondly（第二優點是……）。

3. 青少年看到電視上名人吸菸，他們自己可能也會吸起菸來。
   【正】：If teenagers see a celebrity smoking on TV, they may smoke as well.
   【不佳】：If teenagers see a celebrity smoking on TV, they may smoke themselves.
   【解說】：smoke themselves 是由中文逐譯的結果。雖然*Corpus of Contemporary American English* 也有類似的例句，但不宜仿習，例如「很多人抽菸，我自己也抽」不宜說：Many people smoke; I smoke myself. 正確的說法為：Many people smoke; I myself smoke. 或Many people smoke; I smoke as well.

4. 我們都知道健康很重要。
   【正】：We all know that staying healthy is very important.
   【不佳】：We all know that health is very important.
   【解說】：【不佳】句顯然是由中文逐譯過來的中式英文，雖然不會造成誤解，但就是不夠地道，也就是說，受過教育的英美人士不會這麼用。
   網路時代充斥著各種資訊，讓人眼花撩亂，無所適從。就以上一句「我們都知道健康很重要」來說，一上Google和Facebook，就有一大堆We all know that health is important. 的例句，讓人以為這是正確的英文，真是誤人子弟，莫此為甚。期盼讀者諸君慎思明辨：這種表達法口說尚無妨，書寫時一定要避免，因為不合乎慣用法。正確說法是：We all know that staying / being healthy is very important. 這種使用動名詞當主詞是華人學生的罩門。詳細說明請參閱本書第六章「使用動名詞當主詞」。

第一章

誤用詞彙搭配
造成的中式英文

本章重點：

詞彙搭配包括「動詞＋名詞」、「名詞＋動詞」、「形容詞＋名詞」、「動詞＋副詞」等等，其中以「動詞＋名詞」的搭配最為困難、複雜，而幾乎八、九成的詞彙搭配問題——也就是造成中式英文的元兇——都源於此。

中文裡同樣的動詞，英譯時要隨所接的名詞而變化，否則即不合慣用法，茲舉例如下：

例一：

1）提出問題：raise a question
2）提出辭呈：tender / hand in / send in one's resignation
3）提出證明：produce a proof
4）提出申請：file / make an application
5）提出建議：give / make a suggestion
6）提出警告：give / issue / serve a warning

例二：

1）提高待遇：raise someone's pay
2）提高嗓子：lift/raise one's voice
3）提高警覺：heighten one's vigilance
4）提高生活水準：better / elevate / raise one's living standard

例三：

1）開燈：turn on the light
2）開支票：write（out）/ make out / issue a check
3）開信用狀：issue / open a letter of credit
4）開門（開店、開火｛軍事用語｝、開帳戶）：open the door / a shop / fire / an account

例四：

1）接受禮物：accept a gift
2）接受軍事訓練：receive military training
3）接受手術：undergo an operation

以下是學生習作的錯誤例子：

1-1.　我們終於完成任務了。

【正】：We finally ***accomplished / completed / fulfilled*** our mission.

【誤】：We finally ***finished*** our mission.

【解說】：finish可與job / work搭配，但finish our mission是許多人容易犯的中式英文。

1-2.　他昨天接受盲腸手術。

【正】：He ***had / underwent*** an operation for appendicitis yesterday.

【誤】：He ***received*** an operation for appendicitis yesterday.

【解說】：「接受軍事訓練」說receive military training；「接受禮物」說accept a gift。請注意：receive a gift是「接到禮物」之意，例：I received a gift yesterday, but I did not accept it.（我昨天接到一個禮物，但我並未收下）；「接受教育」說acquire / gain / obtain / receive an education，但「接受手術」不能說receive an operation。

1-3.　送報生一大早送報。

【正】：Newsboys ***deliver*** newspapers early in the morning.

【誤】：Newsboys ***send*** newspapers early in the morning.

【解說】：send是「派人或經由郵局送」，deliver則是「親自送」，所以「送報紙」不能說send newspapers。

1-4.　老師送我們到門口。

【正】：The teacher ***walked*** us to the door.

【誤】：The teacher ***sent*** us to the door.

【解說】：「送某人到門口」是陪著某人走到門口，動詞不能用send，理由如上句，但也不能用deliver。

1-5.　我們都同意要幫他渡過難關。

【正】：All of us agreed to help him ***overcome / get over*** the difficulties.

【誤】：All of us agreed to help him **pass** the difficulties.

【解說】：pass作「通過，渡過，傳遞」解時，都指具體的事物，例：pass a ball（傳球）/ pass an exam/ pass a bill（通過法案）/ pass the customs（通過海關檢查）。difficulties為抽象名詞，不能與pass搭配。雖然坊間辭典列有pass difficulties的用法，但讀者不宜仿習，因為大部分辭典都找不到這種搭配。

1-6. **多吃水果可增進食慾。**

【正】：Eating more fruit can **improve / sharpen / excite** your appetite.

【誤】：Eating more fruit can **promote** your appetite.

【解說】：「增進瞭解」可說promote understanding，「促進和平」可說promote peace，「促進對外貿易」可說promote foreign trade，但「增進食慾」不能說promote appetite。

1-7. **此項新政策可能會給大部分中小企業帶來額外負擔。**

【正】：The new policy may **place** an extra burden **on** most small and medium-sized enterprises.

【誤】：The new policy may **bring** an extra burden **to** most small and medium-sized enterprises.

【解說】：「給……帶來額外負擔」說bring an extra burden to... 是中式英文。

1-8. **這個小孩太小，不會接電話。**

【正】：The child is too young to **answer** the phone.

【誤】：The child is too young to **receive** the phone.

1-9. **挖鼻子是不好的習慣。**

【正】：**Picking** your nose is a bad habit.

【誤】：**Digging** your nose is a bad habit.

1-10. 這隻狗看到主人就搖尾巴。

【正】：The dog *wags* its tail when it sees its master.

【誤】：The dog *shakes* its tail when it sees its master.

1-11. 我每次來上海都住那家旅館。

【正】：I *stay* at that hotel every time I come to Shanghai.

【誤】：I *live* at that hotel every time I come to Shanghai.

【解說】：stay是指短期的居留，live指長期的居住，「住旅館」該用
　　　　　stay at a hotel。

1-12. 手機給我們帶來方便。

【正一】：Cellphones are convenient.

【正二】：Cellphones make our lives easier.

【誤】：Cellphones *bring* us *convenience*.

【解說】：bring有兩個常用的意思：

ⓐ **帶來（具體的人或東西）**。例：I forgot to bring my cellphone.
／ Why didn't you bring your wife? 例句中的帶來「方便」
（convenience）為抽象概念，不能與bring搭配，但請注
意：「帶來和平」可說bring peace，「帶來快樂」可說bring
happiness，「帶來穩定」可說bring stability。然而「帶來麻煩」
不能說bring trouble，「帶來負面影響」不能說bring negative
influences，「帶來負擔」不能說bring a burden。可見一切都依
習慣用法，輕忽不得。

ⓑ **招致，引起（具體或抽象的事物）**。例：His speech brought an
angry reaction.（他的演說引起了憤怒的反應。）／April showers
bring May flowers.（四月驟雨帶來五月花。——北美諺語）／
The sad news brought tears to her eyes.（這悲傷的消息使她淚
流滿面。）

1-13. 某些電視節目會給小孩帶來不良影響。

【正】：Some TV programs *have* a negative influence *on* children.

【誤】：Some TV programs *bring* a negative influence *to* children.

【解說】：influence是抽象觀念，不能與bring搭配使用。另外，
influence to children也是中式英文。influence和effect後面
接on。

1-14. 我從林教授那裡學到了很多知識。

【正】：I have *acquired / gained / obtained* a lot of knowledge from
Professor Lin.

【誤】：I have *learned* a lot of knowledge from Professor Lin.

【解說】：「學到知識」直譯成learn knowledge是很普遍的中式英文。

1-15. 上下班尖峰時刻，駕駛人要多花時間等紅燈，那很浪費時間。

【正】：During rush hour, drivers have to *stop at* red lights longer. This
wastes plenty of time.

【誤】：During rush hour, drivers have to *wait for* red lights longer.
That wastes plenty of time.

【解說】：「等紅燈」直譯成wait for red lights邏輯不通，要改成stop at
red lights或wait at red lights。「那很浪費時間」直譯成That
wastes plenty of time的That應改成This。

1-16. 在得來速餐廳，可在車上取餐，不必下車。

【正】：People do not need to *get out of* their vehicles when they buy
food at a drive-in restaurant.

【誤】：People do not need to *get off* their vehicles when they buy
food at a drive-in restaurant.

【解說】：坐火車或公車等大眾交通工具，「上車」說get on，「下
車」說get off，但開私家車的「下車」要說get out of one's
vehicle。

1-17. **住在鬧市區生活方便，也使我更有安全感。**

【正】：Living downtown ***makes my life easier*** and enables me to feel more secure.

【誤】：Living in downtown ***makes my life more convenient*** and more secured.

【解說】：

(1)downtown可作副詞、形容詞與名詞用，但live downtown/go downtown/work downtown等等習慣用法，一定作副詞用，不作名詞，亦即不能說live in downtown。

(2)「讓我生活方便」直譯成make my life convenient是許多人容易犯的中式英文，convenient life是不通的英文。「手機給我們生活帶來方便」直譯成Cellphones bring our lives convenience。也是不折不扣的中式英文，因為bring convenience是錯誤的搭配。正確說法為：Cellphones make our lives easier。

(3)「使我更有安全感」說enable me（或allow me）to feel more secure。【誤】句中的make my life more secured不合習慣用法，而且secured一字的-d要刪去，因為secure也可當形容詞用。

1-18. **當你感到不舒服時，你應該好好休息。**

【正】：When you are not ***feeling well***, you should take a good rest.

【誤】：When you ***feel uncomfortable***, you should take a good rest.

【解說】：uncomfortable是指「東西使人感到不適或不舒服的」，例：an uncomfortable chair/dress。也可以指「人感覺不自在或不安的」，例：I feel uncomfortable among strangers.（在陌生人群中我感到不自在）。本句的「感到不舒服」應說are not feeling well才對。

1-19. **在以前，字體漂亮、拼寫正確是學生考試必備的兩個基本要求。**

【正一】：In the past, good handwriting and correct spelling were the two basic ***requirements*** that students had to ***meet*** when taking exams.

【正二】：In the past, good handwriting and correct spelling were the two basic skills that students needed when taking exams.

【誤】：In the past, having beautiful handwriting and correct spelling skills were two basic requirements that students needed to have on their exams.

【解說】：

(1)「字體漂亮」要說good / neat handwriting，不能直譯成beautiful。

(2)【誤】句中having作主詞的動名詞片語，後面動詞要用單數，不能用were，但是改成was two basic requirements 又不通。解決之道可把having刪去，用good handwriting and correct spelling當主詞。

1-20. **有些運動需要兩隊參賽者，例如美式足球、足球和籃球等。**

【正】：Some sports, such as football, soccer and basketball, *require* two teams of participants.

【誤】：Some sports *need* two teams of participants, such as football, soccer, basketball and so on.

【解說】：

(1)【誤】句中的動詞need要改用require，原因是need是一般的「需要」，如：We need your help. 而require則是帶有強迫性的要求，如：Driving requires your full concentration.

(2)such as連接的片語用來修飾sports，要放在sports後避免置於句尾。

(3)用such as舉例時，後面不可使用and so on。

1-21. **單親父母的缺點之一是，他們上班時無人陪伴小孩。**

【正】：One of the disadvantages of *being* a single parent is that there will be no one around to *keep the children company* when the parent goes to work.

【誤】：One of the disadvantages of a single parent is that there will be no one to *accompany* children when the parent goes to work.

【解說】：

(1)「單親父母的缺點」不能直譯成the disadvantage of a single parent，介系詞of的後面要用動名詞片語：the disadvantage of **being** a single parent。

(2)「陪伴某人」要說keep somebody company，例：I need to keep my parents company on weekends. 而accompany指伴隨某人去某地，例：I accompanied him to the train station.（我伴隨他去火車站）。

1-22. 假如優秀學生因為經濟因素無法接受大學教育，那是社會的損失。

【正】：If smart students are not able to **receive** a college education due to **financial** problems, this will be a loss for society.

【誤】：If smart students are not able to **accept** college education due to the **economic** factor, it is a loss for society.

【解說】：

(1)「接受大學教育」可說acquire/ gain/ get/ receive a college education，注意動詞不能用accept。

(2)「因為經濟因素」不能直接譯成due to economic factor，中文的「經濟問題」就是「財務問題」（financial problems），而economic problems指的是國家的「經濟問題」，不宜混淆。

(3)【誤】句中的it指代不清；用this才正確，因為this指由if所引導的子句這件事。

(4)【誤】句的it is a loss動詞用is不正確，因為if引導的子句用現在式，表示事情尚未發生，所以要用將來式will be。

1-23. 我想買一本字典，最好是英英字典。

【正】：I want to buy a dictionary, preferably an English-English dictionary.

【誤】：I want to buy a dictionary; it had better be an English-English dictionary.

【解說】：【正】句中的preferably是「最好是……，盡可能地……」之意，與ideally意思相當。【誤】句中的it had better be是由中文直譯而成。請注意：had better通常以「人」作主詞。

1-24. **過去三年來他學到了一些教書經驗。**

【正】：Over the past three years, he has *acquired/ gained/ obtained* some teaching experience.

【誤】：Over the past three years, he has *learned* some teaching experiences.

【解說】：「學到知識或經驗」，動詞不能用learn，應該要gain, obtain或acquire。（注意：句中的experience不加-s），但是「我們想向貴公司學習處理財務危機的經驗」，則可說We would like to learn from your company's experience in tackling financial difficulties.

1-25. **在享受網際網路給我們帶來方便的同時，我們也該注意個人資訊的安全。**

【正】：When we enjoy the convenience of the Internet, we should also pay attention to the safety of our personal information.

【誤】：When we enjoy the *convenience* which the Internet *brings* us, we should pay attention to the safety of our personal information.

【解說】：「帶來方便」說成bring us convenience是普遍的中式英文，很多人會不假思索的如此直譯，請讀者特別留意。

1-26. **教育使人學到知識，並訓練人們思考變得較有邏輯。**

【正】：Education/An Education enables people to *acquire* knowledge and *trains people to think* more logically.

【誤】：Education enables people to *learn* knowledge and *trains people's thought to become* more logical.

【解說】：

(1)「學到知識」動詞用learn 是錯誤的搭配。

(2)「訓練人們思考較有邏輯」應該說train people to think...，不是 train people's thought to become...。

(3)education前不一定要加不定冠詞an，視上下文而定。例：Education/An education is necessary if you want to find a good job. 但是「高等教育」（higher education）卻不可加a。

1-27. 開車的人每年做健康檢查，可以得知自己的健康情況。

【正】：Through annual physical checkups, drivers can **learn about** their health.

【誤】：Through annual physical checkups, drivers can **know** their health.

【解說】：「得知健康狀況」的「得知」應說learn about，避免用 know。由「聽或看而獲悉或得知某事」要用learn about。例： We learned about your new product on TV.（我們從電視上得知你們的新產品。）

1-28. 運動有許多種，像棒球、籃球、羽毛球等等，這些可歸類成團隊運動和 個人運動。

【正】：There are many kinds of sports, such as baseball, basketball, badminton, etc., and these can **fall into** two categories--- team sports and individual sports.

【誤】：There are many kinds of sports, such as baseball, basketball, badminton, and etc., and these can **be separated into** two categories--- team sports and individual sports.

【解說】：

(1)【誤】句中etc.前的and要刪去。

(2)「歸類成兩種」要說fall into two categories。

1-29. 三代同堂可帶來很多優點。

【正一】：Having three generations in the same house is advantageous to a family.

【正二】：There are many advantages to having three generations in the same house

【不佳】：Having three generations in the same house can **bring** many advantages to a family.

【解說】：

(1)「帶來優點」避免直譯成bring advantages。

(2)可把bring 改成have：Having three generations in the same house has many advantages.

1-30. 大部分青少年不懂得如何抗壓；他們經常選擇逃學、吸毒甚或自殺來對抗壓力。

【正】：Most teenagers have trouble handling stress; they often choose different ways to **deal with it**, such as skipping school, taking drugs, or even committing suicide.

【誤】：Most teenagers cannot **resist** their stress; they often choose different ways **to resist it**, such as skipping schools, taking drugs, and even committing suicide.

【解說】：

(1)「抗壓」說成cope with stress, deal with stress或handle stress皆可，說resist stress是中式英文；「抗拒誘惑」可說resist temptation，「與員警對抗」可說resist the police。

(2)「不知道，不懂得做某事」說cannot do something雖然正確，但用 have trouble/difficulty / problems doing something比較符合慣用法。

(3)「逃學」說skip school（school在這裡不能加-s）或play hooky皆可；「逃課」說cut class, skip class或skip classes皆可，但是說skip class比較普遍。

(4)and even 要改成 or even，原因是or用於選擇性，and用於全部。

1-31. **電腦給人的主要傷害就是視力問題。**

【正】：A major *harm* the computer can *do* to you is to cause vision problems / to give you vision problems.

【誤】：A major *harm* the computer can *make* to your body is your sight problems.

【解說】：

(1)「傷害某人或某事物」是do harm to，不能用make。

(2)「視力問題」說vision problems，不是sight problems。

1-32. **我反對當單親父母的原因是，他們會給小孩帶來很多負面影響。**

【正】：The reason why I object to people becoming single parents is that *it has* many negative influences *on* their children.

【誤】：The reason why I object to people become single parents is that it *brings* many negative influences *to* their children.

【解說】：

(1) object to的to是介系詞，所以後面要接名詞、代名詞或動名詞。

(2)「帶來負面影響」說bring negative influences是常見的中式英文，本書多處提及，請讀者留意。

(3) influence和effect一樣，與on連用，使用to也是中式英文。

1-33. **做整型手術可能引起嚴重後果。**

【正】：*Undergoing* cosmetic surgery may *have* serious consequences.

【誤】：*Doing* a cosmetic surgery may *cause* serious consequence.

【解說】：

(1)（醫師替某人）「做手術」說do surgery或perform surgery皆可。說某人接受手術時與surgery搭配的動詞要用have或undergo。

(2) surgery不加冠詞a，也不用複數。

(3)「引起嚴重後果」直譯成cause serious consequence也是中式英文，動詞可改成have, lead to或entai。另外，作「後果」解時，consequence一般習慣用複數。

1-34. 聰明人不吸毒，因為他們知道一旦碰了毒品就容易上癮。

【正】：Smart people do not **do** drugs because they know that once they try them, it is easy to become addicted to them.

【誤】：Smart people do not **eat** drugs because they know that once they try them, it is easily addicted to it.

【解說】：

(1)生病吃藥的「吃藥」不能說eat drugs或eat medicines，要說take medicine（注意用單數）；「吸毒」一般說do drugs，也可說take drugs，不能說eat drugs。

(2)【誤】句的it is easily addicted to it中的兩個it都錯，要改成it is easy to become addicted to them。原因是第一個it指代後面的不定詞 to become（【誤】句中沒不定詞）；第二個it 指drugs，所以要用 them。

1-35. 好廣告給我們生活帶來方便。現今許多廣告出現在各種媒體上，例如電視、報紙與網路。

【正】：Good advertisements **make our lives easier**. Today, many advertisements are found in various media, such as TV, newspapers and the Internet.

【誤】：Good advertisements **bring convenience** to our lives. Today, many advertisements are found in various media, such as TV, newspapers and Internet.

【解說】：

(1)「帶來方便」說bring convenience是中式英文，例如 「手機給我們帶來方便」要說Cellphones are convenient. 或Cellphones make our lives easier. 不能說Cellphones bring us convenience.

(2)【誤】句中的Internet 前面一定要加the。

1-36. **為舒緩交通擁擠，市政府可採取若干措施，包括課徵新車稅捐，鼓勵在上班場所附近購屋，以及在交通尖峰時刻禁行某類車輛。**

【正】：To **ease** traffic congestion, the city government can take several measures, including imposing taxes on new vehicle purchases, encouraging purchases of homes close to workplaces and banning certain types of vehicles during the peak hours.

【誤】：To **release** traffic jam, several measures can be taken by the city government, including imposing taxes on new vehicle purchases, encouraging purchases of homes close to workplaces and banning certain types of vehicles during the peak hours.

【解說】：

(1)「交通擁擠」可說a traffic jam或traffic jams，也可說traffic congestion，唯一區別是jam可加 "-s"，但congestion不能加 "-s"，所以【誤】句中的jam要加 "-s"。另外，release traffic jams是錯誤搭配，動詞要用ease。

(2)【誤】句中的several measures can be taken不是to solve traffic jams的行為主體，要改成the city government can take several measures才正確。

1-37. **我喜歡小組學習的原因是，它可以訓練我的溝通技巧。**

【正】：The reason why I like studying in a small group is that it can **develop** my communication skills.

【誤】：The reason why I like studying with a small group is that it can **train** my communication skills.

【解說】：

(1)「小組學習」可說study in a small group或study with a small group of people，注意介系詞的用法。

(2)「訓練我的溝通技巧」說train my communication skills不通，也就是

英文裡沒有train skills的搭配，動詞要改為develop。

1-38. 遺失信用卡會帶來麻煩。

【正一】：Losing our credit cards may be troublesome.

【正二】：Losing our credit cards, we may be in trouble.

【正三】：Losing our credit cards can *cause/create* trouble.

【誤】：Losing our credit cards may *bring* us trouble.

【解說】：bring trouble是錯誤的詞彙搭配。

1-39. 速食含有大量油脂，很容易使人體重增加。

【正】：Fast food *contains* a large amount of fat which *makes it easy* for people to gain weight.

【誤】：Fast food *includes* a large amount of fat which *makes people easy* to gain weight.

【解說】：

(1)「含有」要說contain，不用include。

(2)「使……易於」要說make it easy for somebody to do something，不能說make somebody easy to do something。注意：【正】句中的it指後面的不定詞片語。

1-40. 現今，很多大學畢業生面臨找工作的壓力。一張漂亮的履歷表能使雇主留下好印象。

【正】：Nowadays, many college graduates are suffering from the stress of finding a job. An *impressive* resume can make a good impression on *potential employers*.

【誤】：Nowadays, many graduate students from college are suffering from the stress of finding jobs. A *beautiful* resume can make a good impression on *employers*.

【解說】：

(1) graduate students是「研究生」，「大學畢業生」說college

graduates。

(2)「找工作」在此要用單數形的finding a job，因為每個人只做一份工作。

(3)「漂亮的履歷表」不能直譯成a beautiful resume。

(4)「雇主」在此要說potential employers。求職者應徵工作，雇主面談後如獲錄用，他才是你的employer，未獲錄用前要加potential，這是中英文的不同，也是許多人容易疏忽的地方。

1-41. 我贊成大學生應該在外獨居的原因是他們可以學會獨立。

【正】：The reason why I agree that college students should live by themselves is that they can learn to be independent.

【誤】：The reason why I support that college students should live by themselves is that they can learn to be independent.

【解說】：看到「贊成、支持」就本能地想到support，但是support後只能以名詞、代名詞或動名詞當受詞，不能接that引導的句子，改成agree即正確。

1-42. 他定期做運動以舒解壓力。

【正】：He exercises regularly in order to *relieve* stress.

【誤】：He exercises regularly in order to *release* stress.

【解說】：「舒解、舒緩壓力」是relieve stress或relieve pressure，動詞不能用release。「歌星發行新專輯」可說release a new album，「鬆開剎車」說release the brake，「釋放犯人」說release a prisoner。

第一章 練習題

選擇題：下列各題，請選出一個或兩個正確答案。

（ ）1. 手機在響，請幫我接一下。（請參考**1-8**）

    ⓐ My cellphone is ringing; please answer it for me.

    ⓑ My cellphone is ringing; please receive it for me.

    ⓒ My cellphone is ringing; please pick it up for me.

    ⓓ My cellphone is ringing; please talk it for me.

（ ）2. 你現在住在哪個旅館呢？（請參考**1-11**）

    ⓐ What hotel are you living now?

    ⓑ What hotel are you staying now?

    ⓒ Which hotel are you living now?

    ⓓ Which hotel are you staying now?

（ ）3. 遺失身份證會帶來麻煩。（請參考**1-12**）

    ⓐ Losing our identification card may bring us trouble.

    ⓑ Losing our identification card may be troublesome.

    ⓒ Losing our identification card may be in trouble.

    ⓓ Losing our identification card may bring about trouble.

（ ）4. 從這次車禍我學到了很多經驗。（請參考**1-14**）

    ⓐ I have learned a lot of experience from this car accident.

    ⓑ I have gained a lot of experience from this car accident.

    ⓒ I have acquired a lot of experience from this car accident.

    ⓓ I have learned a lot of experiences from this car accident.

( ) 5. 這條路交通信號燈很多，駕駛人要等紅燈久一點。（請參考 **1-15**）

    ⓐ There are many traffic signals on this street; drivers have to wait for red lights longer.

    ⓑ There are many traffic signals on this street; drivers have to wait at red lights longer.

    ⓒ There are many traffic signals on this street; drivers have to stop at red lights longer.

    ⓓ There are many traffic signals on this street; drivers have to await for red lights longer.

( ) 6. 住在校園讓我的生活方便多了。（請參考**1-17**）

    ⓐ Living on campus makes my life easier.

    ⓑ Living on campus makes my life more convenient.

    ⓒ Living on campus enables me to live convenient life.

    ⓓ Living on campus enables my life to be convenient.

( ) 7. 他身體不舒服，昨天未去上班。（請參考**1-18**）

    ⓐ He did not feel well, so he did not go to work yesterday.

    ⓑ He was not comfortable, so he did not go to work yesterday.

    ⓒ He did not feel comfortable, so he did not go to work yesterday.

    ⓓ He was uncomfortable, so he did not go to work yesterday.

( ) 8. 市政府已盡全力滿足公眾的需求。（請參考**1-19**）

    ⓐ The city government has tried its best to meet the requirements of the public.

    ⓑ The city government has tried its best to provide the requirements of the public.

    ⓒ The city government has tried its best to fulfill the requirements of the public.

d The city government has tried its best to answer the requirements of the public.

( ) 9. 開車必須全神貫注。（請參考**1-20**）

a Driving requires your full concentration.

b Driving needs your full concentration.

c Driving takes your full concentration.

d Driving necessitates your full concentration.

( ) 10. 父母親年紀很大，我得陪伴他們。（請參考**1-21**）

a My parents are getting old, so I need to keep them company.

b My parents are getting old, so I need to accompany them.

c My parents are getting old, so I need to keep their company.

d My parents are getting old, so I need to escort them.

( ) 11. 在現代社會，接受大學教育對每個人都很重要。（請參考**1-22**）

a In modern society, receiving a college education is important for everyone.

b In modern society, accepting a college education is important for everyone.

c In modern society, undergoing a college education is important for everyone.

d In modern society, acquiring a college education is important for everyone.

( ) 12. 當她得知父親健康情況時，突然哭了起來。（請參考**1-27**）

a When she knew her father's health condition, she burst into tears.

ⓑ When she learned about her father's health, she burst into tears.

ⓒ When she learned her father's health, she burst into tears.

ⓓ When she knew about her father's health conditions, she burst into tears.

( ) 13. 碰到任何問題，你可致電他們求助。（請參考**1-28**）

ⓐ As soon as you encounter any problems, you can call them for assistance.

ⓑ As soon as you meet any problems, you can call them for assistance.

ⓒ As soon as you come across any problems, you can call them for assistance.

ⓓ As soon as you meet with any problems, you can call them for assistance.

( ) 14. 他昨天接受肺癌手術。（請參考**1-33**）

ⓐ He had an operation for lung cancer yesterday.

ⓑ He underwent an operation for lung cancer yesterday.

ⓒ He received an operation for lung cancer yesterday.

ⓓ He performed an operation for lung cancer yesterday.

( ) 15. 雖然他病得很嚴重，但卻不肯吃藥。（請參考**1-34**）

ⓐ Although he was seriously ill, he refused to eat drugs.

ⓑ Although he was seriously ill, he refused to eat medicine.

ⓒ Although he was seriously ill, he refused to take medicines.

ⓓ Although he was seriously ill, he refused to take medicine.

( ) 16. 市政府實施此政策，以舒緩交通擁擠。（請參考**1-36**）

ⓐ The city government carried out the policy in order to relieve traffic congestion.

ⓑ The city government published the policy in order to release traffic congestion.

ⓒ The city government adopted the policy in order to release traffic jams.

ⓓ The city government published the policy in order to relieve traffic congestion.

( ) 17. 你應該多練習說英文，以便訓練口語技巧。（請參考**1-37**）

ⓐ You should practice speaking English more often in order to train your speaking skills.

ⓑ You should practice speaking English more often in order to develop your speaking skills.

ⓒ You should practice speaking English more often in order to practice your speaking skills.

ⓓ You should practice speaking English more often in order to build up your speaking skills.

※解答請見P.294

第二章

誤用文法搭配
造成的中式英文

本章重點：

文法搭配指名詞或形容詞與介系詞或其他文法結構的連用關係，包括「名詞＋介系詞」、「介系詞＋名詞」、「動詞＋介系詞」、「形容詞＋介系詞」等等，其中以前三項較為重要。

a) 名詞＋介系詞

1) **我接到一張五萬美金的支票。**

【正】：I received a check *for* US$50,000.

【誤】：I received a check *of* US$50,000.

2) **他是川普總統的外交政策顧問。**

【正】：He is an advisor *to* President Trump on foreign policy.

【誤】：He is an advisor *of* President Trump on foreign policy.

3) **她是林董事長的祕書。**

【正】：She is secretary *to* Chairman Lin.

【誤】：She is a secretary *of* Chairman Lin.

【解說】：

(1)以上三句介系詞不用of，原因是那是由「……的……」直譯而來的中式英文。

(2)「當某人祕書」secretary前不用a。

b) 介系詞＋名詞

1) **從你臉上的表情，我可以看得出你有了麻煩。**

【正】：I can see *by* the expression on your face that you are in trouble.

【誤】：I can see *from* the expression on your face that you are in trouble.

【解說】：【誤】句用from，是受中文「從……」影響。

2) **他自願做那件事。**

【正】：He did it *of* his own free will.

【誤】：He did it *by* his own free will.

C）動詞＋介系詞

1) **我們恭賀約翰弄璋之喜。**

【正】：We congratulated John **on** the birth of his son.

【誤】：We congratulated John **for** the birth of his son.

2) **老師稱讚他很勤奮。**

【正】：The teacher praised him **for** his diligence.

【誤】：The teacher praised his diligence.

以下是學生習作的錯誤例子：

2-1. **父母的行為對子女有深遠的影響。**

【正】：Parents' behavior has a profound influence **on** their children.

【誤】：Parents' behavior has a profound influence **to** their children.

【解說】：influence / effect / impact後均接on，【誤】句用to是由中文「對……影響」的「對」直譯而成的錯誤。

2-2. **老師對學生應該要嚴格。**

【正】：Teachers should be strict **with** their students.

【誤】：Teachers should be strict **to** their students.

【解說】：和上句一樣，看到「對……」，學生一成不變的就用to，不免犯錯。be strict with是固定搭配。「對……嚴格」還可以說be hard on，例：His parents are hard on him.

2-3. **這件處罰對我不公平。**

【正】：The punishment is not fair **to** me.

【誤】：The punishment is not fair **for** me.

【解說】：「對……公平／不公平」要說be fair / unfair to，介系詞不能用for。

2-4. **體育課對於增進學生的身體健康有幫助。**

【正】：Physical education is helpful ***in*** improving students' health.

【誤】：Physical education is helpful ***to*** improve students' health.

【解說】：be helpful in是固定搭配。【正】句亦可說：Physical education helps to improve students' health.

2-5. **他出生在富裕家庭。**

【正】：He was born ***into*** a rich family.

【誤】：He was born ***in*** a rich family.

2-6. **我今天從學校學到很多東西。**

【正】：I learned many things ***in*** school today.

【誤】：I learn many things ***from*** school today.

【解說】：

(1)【誤】句介系詞用from，顯然是受中文「從」的影響造成的錯誤。

(2)【誤】句另一個錯誤是learn用現在式。很多人誤以為副詞today時間點還是現在，所以用現在式，這是錯誤的觀念，因為既然已學到了，動作已經過去，就要用過去式。

(3) I learned many things from Professor Sun. 句中的from是正確的。

2-7. **a) 我們可以從網上下載很多資訊。**

【正】：We are able to ***download*** a lot of information ***from*** the Internet.

【誤】：We are able to ***download*** a lot of information ***on*** the Internet.

b) 我們可以從網上搜尋很多資訊。

【正】：We are able to ***search*** a lot of information ***on*** the Internet.

【誤】：We are able to ***search*** a lot of information ***from*** the Internet.

c) 我們可以從網上獲取很多資訊。

【正】：We are able to ***acquire/get/obtain*** a lot of information ***from*** the Internet.

【誤】：We are able to *acquire/get/obtain* a lot of information *on* the Internet.

【解說】：Internet前的介詞要隨著動詞而變化，亦即：*download* information *from* the Internet, *search* information *on* the Internet, *acquire/get/obtain* information *from* the Internet。

2-8. **竊賊好像是從窗戶爬進來的。**

【正一】：The burglar seemed to have entered *by* the window.

【正二】：The burglar seemed to have entered *from* the window.

【正三】：The burglar seemed to have entered *through* the window.

【誤】：The burglar seemed to have entered *by means of* the window.

【解說】：

(1)介系詞by表「經由……」之意，例：We flew to London by way of Paris.（我們經由巴黎飛往倫敦。）

(2)by means of是「藉由，藉著」之意，例如：He got the job by means of his father's influence.（他藉著父親的影響力得到那份工作。）【誤】句... entered by means of the window語意不清。

2-9. **地上蓋滿了雪。**

【正】：The ground is covered *with* snow.

【誤】：The ground is covered *by* snow.

【解說】：be動詞＋過去分詞一般都接by，例如John was fired by his manager.（John被經理開除。）但本句的be covered with是固定搭配，意為「蓋滿……，充滿……。」be covered by意思不同，例：The house is covered by insurance.（這棟房已保了險）／Shipping is not covered by the quotation.（報價中不包括運費）。

2-10. **幸福不是用金錢可以買得到的。**

【正】：Happiness cannot be bought *with* money.

【誤】：Happiness cannot be bought *by* money.

【解說】：介系詞with表「手段、工具」之意，例：eat with a knife and fork用刀叉吃／He caught the ball with his left hand. 他用左手接球。

2-11. **他在交通事故中喪生。**

【正】：He was killed *in* a traffic accident.

【誤】：He was killed *by* a traffic accident.

【解說】：in an accident是固定搭配，沒有by an accident的說法。【誤】句用by顯然是受be動詞＋過去分詞＋by的影響。「他被強盜殺死」要說He was killed *by* a robber.

2-12. **他為了自衛殺死強盜。**

【正】：He killed the robber *in* self-defense.

【誤】：He killed the robber *for* self-defense.

【解說】：

(1)介系詞in表「狀況，環境」之意，例：in despair（處於絕望之中）／in good condition（處於良好的狀態）。【正】句的in self-defense意為「在自我防衛的情況下」；【誤】句用for是由中文「為了」直譯而來。

(2)「他擁槍自衛」說He owned a gun for self-defense. 注意本句介系詞不能用in，因為for＝for the purpose of。

2-13. **課堂上學生應該專心聽課。**

【正】：Students should pay attention *in* class.

【誤】：Students should pay attention *to* class.

【解說】：pay attention to意為「專注於……，專心於……」，後面要接受詞，例：pay attention to my studies/ pay attention to the details。「在課堂要專心」要說pay attention in class，介系詞不能用to。

2-14. 銷售員向顧客介紹產品時要有耐性。

【正一】：Sales people should be patient *in* introducing their products to their customers.

【正二】：Sales people should be patient when introducing their products to their customers.

【誤】：Sales people should be patient *to* introduce their products to their customers.

【解說】：

(1) be patient後不接不定詞，如果接名詞時，介系詞可用with，例：He is patient with other people.／The teacher is patient with his students.

(2)【正二】句中的when introducing=when they introduce。

2-15. 乘坐捷運有許多優點。

【正一】：There are many advantages *to* taking / riding the MRT.

【正二】：Taking the MRT has many advantages.

【誤一】：There are many advantages *of* taking the MRT.

【誤二】：There are many advantages for you to take the MRT.

【解說】：「做……有許多優點」可說：There are many advantages / benefits to＋V-ing，後面不能接不定詞（因為to為介系詞）。

2-16. 現在速食很受青少年歡迎，它是很多青少年吃東西的首選。

【正】：Nowadays, fast food is very popular *among* teenagers; it is the first food choice of many teenagers.

【誤一】：Nowadays, fast food is very welcome by teenagers; it is the first food choice of many teenagers.

【誤二】：Nowadays, fast food is very popular *in* teenagers, it is the first food choice for many teenagers.

【解說】：

(1)「受歡迎」要說be popular among（或with），不能說be welcome。向人道歉，對方說「不客氣」才說You are welcome。

(2)【誤二】後半句it is the first food choice for many teenagers中的for要改為of。注意：the＋名詞＋of的句式。

(3)【誤二】是run-on sentence（即兩個獨立句子之間用逗號），it前的逗號要改成分號。

2-17. 這次地震造成十億台幣的財物損失。

【正】：The earthquake caused NT＄1 billion *in* property damage.

【誤】：The earthquake caused NT＄1 billion *of* property damages.

【解說】：

(1)【誤】句的of 是由中文「的」直譯而來。

(2)作「損害」解時，damage不加 "s"。

2-18. 美國已捐助五千萬美元的救濟物資。

【正】：The U.S. has contributed US＄50 million *in* relief goods.

【誤】：The U.S. has contributed US＄50 million *of* relief goods.

【解說】：【誤】句中的of是由中文的「的」直譯而來。

2-19. 有些雇主認為，支付受訓員工薪水對公司是個負擔，對其整體獲利也有害處。

【正】：Some employers believe that paying a salary to workers in training creates a burden *for* a company and is harmful *to* its overall profitability.

【誤】：Some employers believe that paying training workers a salary creates a burden *to* a company and is harmful *for* its overall profitability.

【解說】：

(1)「受訓員工」不能直譯為training workers，要說a trainee 或a worker in training；「對公司是個負擔」有如下各種說法：create a burden *for* a company／place a burden *on* a company／be a burden *to* a company。請注意：burden後的介系詞要隨著前面的動詞變化。

(2) be harmful後接to，不接for。

2-20. 開車到市中心的一個明顯問題就是會造成交通擁擠，尤以尖峰時刻為然。

【正】：One obvious problem *with* driving downtown is that it can cause traffic jams, especially during rush hour.

【誤】：One obvious problem *about* driving to downtown is that it can cause traffic jam, especially during rush hours.

【解說】：

(1)作「在……方面的問題」解時，problem與with連用，例：The problem with your English is that you have a limited vocabulary.（你的英文問題出在單字太少。）

(2) driving to downtown是中式英文，to要刪去，因為downtown在此是副詞。

(3)「交通擁擠」可說traffic congestion或traffic jam，但要注意congestion不能加-s，而jam若不加-s，就要用冠詞a，常說a traffic jam或traffic jams。

(4)「尖峰時刻」說during rush hours，during rush hour或in rush hour均可。

2-21. 禁止學生在學校使用手機不合理，因為如此學生就無法與家人和朋友聯絡了。

【正】：Banning the use of cell phones in schools is unreasonable because students will not be able *to contact* their parents or friends.

【誤】：Banning the use of cell phones in schools is unreasonable because students cannot **contact with** their parents and friends.

【解說】：【誤】句because後有兩個錯誤：

(1) students cannot要改成students will not be able to... 使用未來式是因為此事尚未發生；學校禁止學生使用手機後才會發生。

(2) contact是及物動詞，後不接with。但如果contact作名詞用則要接with，例：I finally got in/made contact with him in Japan.（我終於在日本和他取得聯繫。）

2-22. 根據一項研究，公立學校霸凌的比率要比私立學校高兩倍。

【正】：According to research, the percentage of bullies at public schools is twice as high as that at private schools.

【誤】：According to a research, the percentage of bullies at public schools is twice as much as at private schools.

【解說】：

(1)「根據一項研究」可說according to research（注意不用冠詞），也可說according to a study（注意要用冠詞）。

(2)「高兩倍」應說 twice as high as，high修飾percentage。

(3)【誤】句中缺少that，句子就變得不合邏輯了，that指代percentage。

2-23. 這種食品我們可以從麥當勞、肯德基或任何便利商店買到。

【正】：We can buy this kind of food **at** McDonald's and KFC, or any convenience store.

【誤】：We can buy this kind of food **from** McDonald's and KFC, or any other convenient stores.

【解說】：

(1)「麥當勞」是商店名，前面介系詞用at，不要受中文「從麥當勞」的「從」的影響，而譯成from。「我們從學校學到很多東西」直譯

成We have learned many things from school. 是典型的中式英文，要把from改成in。

(2)「便利商店」是convenience store，注意這是複合名詞，勿說成convenient store。

(3) any other 後接單數名詞，例：Vancouver is more beautiful than any other city in Canada. 請注意：【誤】句必須刪除other，因為McDonald's and KFC並不是便利商店。

2-24. 很多大學生課業壓力很大，修體育課可以讓他們舒解壓力。

【正】：Many college students are ***under*** tremendous pressure ***from*** their studies; taking physical education classes enables them to ***relieve*** this pressure.

【誤】：Many college students have huge pressure because of their study; taking physical education classes can enable them to ***release*** this pressure.

【解說】：

(1)「某人壓力大」要說Someone is under tremendous pressure，不能說have huge/strong pressure。請參考本書有關to be/ to have的用法。

(2) pressure與from或for連用，例：pressure for money（缺錢）／He changed his mind under pressure from others.（他受到別人的壓力而改變了主意。）本句的「課業壓力」要說pressure from their studies，注意用複數形式的studies。

(3)「舒解壓力」是ease/relieve pressure，不是release pressure。release有幾個常用片語：be released from prison（從監獄釋放出來）／release an album（發行唱片）／be released from debt（擺脫債務）／be released from duty（卸下職務；獲准離職；獲准放假；被解除職務）。請注意：「下班」可說be off duty／come off duty／get off duty／go off duty。不可以說be released from duty。

2-25. 自古以來，大部分人認為父母親是小孩的第一個老師。

【正】：***Throughout*** history, most people have believed that parents are the first teachers of their children.

【誤】：***From ancient to present***, most people believed that parents are the first teachers of their children.

【解說】：

(1)「自古以來」可說throughout history（注意不用the），in the history of humankind或from/since time immemorial。

(2)【誤】句中，動詞用過去式不對，應改為現在完成式。

2-26. 有些人習慣向朋友借點小錢，而忘了歸還。

【正】：Some people ***are in the habit of*** borrowing a small amount of money from their friends and then forgetting about it.

【誤一】：Some people ***are used to*** borrowing a small amount of money from their friends and then forget about it.

【誤二】：Some people ***form the habit of*** borrowing a small amount of money from their friends and then forgetting about it.

【解說】：「習慣做某事」要說be in the habit of doing something，【誤一】的are used to是「對某事感到很習慣或不以為苦」之意，例：I am used to getting up early.（我習慣早起。）意思是早起對我不是苦差事。【誤二】的form the habit of是「養成……習慣」之意，例：I have formed the habit of getting up early.（我已養成早起的習慣。）

2-27. 三代同堂的最主要問題是，家庭成員的生活習慣與作息不同。

【正】：Different lifestyles and schedules are the major problems ***with*** three generations living in the same house.

【誤】：The major problems ***of*** three generations living in the same house are their different living habits and schedules.

【解說】：

(1)「生活習慣」避免說living habits。

(2)「……的問題是……」要說the problem with，注意介系詞不用of。

例：The problem with your English is poor pronunciation.

(3)【誤】句中的their指涉不清。

2-28. **瞭解顧客的需求，對銷售員成功促銷產品有幫助。**

【正一】：Knowing what the customers need helps sales people *to* promote the successful sale of their products.

【正二】：Knowing what the customers need is helpful *in* successfully promoting sale people's products.

【誤】：Knowing what the customers need is helpful *for* sales people to sell their products successfully.

【解說】：【誤】句中的helpful後接for，這是許多學生容易犯的錯誤，應該接in，例：He was helpful in promoting peace between the two countries. 本句亦可說：He helped to promote peace between the two countries.

2-29. **近日大學生打工賺取學費很普遍；大學生未必非要出生在富有家庭才能接受大學教育。**

【正】：These days, it is common to see college students work part-time in order *to pay* their tuition; they do not necessarily have to be born *into* a rich family to obtain a college education.

【誤】：These days, it is common to see college students work part-time in order to *pay for* their tuition; they do not necessary have to be born *in* a rich family to obtain college education.

【解說】：

(1)「付學費」說pay tuition，不是pay for tuition. pay/ pay for許多學生經常混淆。pay後面接「錢」，for後面接付了錢所買的東西。例：「這台電腦我花了八百美金買的」說：I paid US$ 800 for the computer. 「這台電腦你付了錢沒有？」說：Did you pay for the computer?

(2)「未必……」說not... necessarily，注意用副詞necessarily，例：
Rich people are not necessarily happy.（有錢人未必快樂。）

(3)「出生在富有家庭」說be born into a rich family，注意介系詞用
into，不用in。

(4)「接受大學教育」說acquire/ gain/ obtain/ receive a college
education，注意要用冠詞a。

2-30. 由於油價上漲，物價隨著節節上升。

【正】：Commodity prices are getting higher and higher because of
the increase *in* oil prices.

【誤】：The market price is getting higher and higher because of the
increase *of* oil prices.

【解說】：「物價」是commodity prices; the market price指某種產品的
「市價」；「油價上漲」要說the increase *in* oil prices。

2-31. 雖然吃速食嚴重危害健康，但對許多學生來說，這是唯一的選擇，因為他們忙著學校的課業。

【正】：Although eating fast food can seriously damage a person's
health, many students have no choice because they are *busy
with* their schoolwork.

【誤】：Although eating junk food has serious damage on health,
many students have no choice because they are *busy on*
working their school projects.

【解說】：

(1)「嚴重危害健康」可說cause serious damage to a person's health/
seriously damage a person's health。注意：damage與to連用；另
外health前要加所有格形容詞a person's或one's或our。

(2)「忙於某事」be busy後接介系詞with/at/over，不接on，例：I am
busy with my homework. 如果接動詞，要用-ing式，例：I am busy
preparing for my exam.

2-32. **在現代社會，網際網路已經成為不同種族、性別、年齡的人，分享人生經驗的地方。**

【正】：In modern society, the Internet has become a place where people *of* different races, sexes and ages share their life experiences.

【誤】：In modern society, the Internet has become a place where people *from* different races, genders and ages share their life experiences.

【解說】：「不同種族、性別、年齡的人」要說people of different races, sexes（或genders）and ages，注意介系詞不能用from。

2-33. **限制人們使用槍支有助於社會安定，但槍支管制政策可能限制警員攜帶槍械。**

【正】：Restricting people's use of guns helps to keep our society stable, but a gun control policy may *restrict* police officers *from* carrying guns.

【誤】：Restricting people *to use* guns helps to keep our society stable, but a gun control policy may restrict police officers *to* carry guns.

【解說】：

(1) restrict後不接不定詞，只能接名詞。restrict people to use guns 和 restrict police officers to carry guns都是按中文句構直譯出的中式英文。可改為restrict people's use of guns或restrict people from using guns。

(2) 「槍支管制政策」說a gun control policy，不用controlling的原因是gun control是複合名詞，在此當形容詞用。

2-34. 現代社會，吃垃圾食品的人越來越多，因此人們變得不像以前那樣健康了。

【正】：In modern society, more and more people are eating junk food. Therefore, they are becoming *less* healthy *than* they were previously.

【誤】：In modern society, there are more and more people eating junk food. Therefore, people are becoming *unhealthy than* before.

【解說】：

(1)像more and more和fewer and fewer這樣的形容詞片語，常與現在進行式連用，例：Cell phones are becoming more and more popular. ／Fewer and fewer people are communicating with others by writing letters.

(2)【誤】句後半句的than 有問題，因為前面沒有more或less的比較級副詞，所以把unhealthy改成less healthy後面就可接than了。

2-35. 世上所有的人都不想變老，然而那是不可能的。

【正】：No one in the world wants to get old, but this is impossible.

【誤】：All the people in the world do not want to get old, but it is impossible.

【解說】：

(1) all和everyone一樣，不能接否定句，例：「每個人都不該忽略健康的重要」不能說：Everyone should not ignore the importance of health. 正確說法為：No one should ignore the importance of health.

(2)【誤】句中的it指代不清，要改成this，指「所有的人都不想變老」這件事。

2-36. 三代同堂有許多優點。首先，它對增進家庭關係有幫助。

【正】：Having three generations live together has many advantages. Firstly, this is *helpful in* improving family relationships.

【誤】：Having three generations live together has many advantages. Firstly, it is **helpful to** improve family relationships.

【解說】：

(1) helpful後不接不定詞，要接介系詞in。

(2)【誤】句的it指代不清，【正】句的this指前面的整個句子。其實後半句也可說：Firstly, this helps to improve family relationships. 用動詞help比較不易犯錯。

2-37. **他自從六十歲生日後就未曾做身體檢查；高齡駕駛未定期健檢會引起嚴重問題。**

【正】：He has not had a physical checkup since his 60th birthday. Not having physical checkups regularly may cause serious problems for senior drivers.

【誤】：He has not had a physical checkup since his 60-year-old birthday. Without physical checkups regularly may cause serious problems to senior drivers.

【解說】：

(1)「六十歲生日」要說60th birthday，不能說60-year-old birthday，因為60-year-old用於修飾「人」，例：a 60-year-old teacher。

(2)【誤】句中，without所連接的介系詞片語不能當主詞，要改成not having，如此，動名詞片語即可當主詞。

(3)【誤】句中problems後要接for。

2-38. **你在家排行老幾？**

【正一】：In what order were you born in your family?

【正二】：What birth order are you?

【誤一】：In which order were you born in your family?

【誤二】：In what ranking were you born in your family?

【解說】：

(1)「出生排行」是birth order，不是birth ranking，ranking是指企業、

富豪、名人等等的競爭排名。【正二】請比較：What sign are you?
（你是什麼星座？）

(2)【誤一】的which要改成what，原因是沒有選擇時用what，有選擇性
時才用which，例如：客人來訪，主人問：「你要喝點什麼？」要說
What would you like to drink? 此處不能用which，因為沒有選擇性。
但是如果主人問：「你要喝茶或咖啡？」則要說Which would you
like to drink, tea or coffee?

2-39. 大部分青少年花很多時間上網，那會造成各種健康問題。

【正】：Most teenagers spend *a lot of* time surfing on the Internet; this
can cause various health problems.

【誤】：Most teenagers spend *much* time surfing on the Internet; it will
cause various healthy problems.

【解說】：

(1) much和a lot of用法不同：much與否定句和疑問句連用，a lot of與
肯定句連用，例：Don't spend *much* time playing computer games.
／He spent *a lot of* time playing computer games.

(2)【誤】句的it指代不清，要改成this。有關it的用法，請參閱本書P.280。

(3)【誤】句中的will要改成can，此處的can是表示可能性很高的情態動
詞（modal verb）。

(4)「健康問題」要說health problems這是複合名詞。「健康的小孩」
說a healthy child。

第二章　練習題

選擇題：下列各題，請選出一個或兩個正確答案。

（　）1.　他父母對他很嚴格。（請參考2-2）

    ⓐ His parents are hard to him.

    ⓑ His parents are hard on him.

    ⓒ His parents are strict to him.

    ⓓ His parents are strict with him.

（　）2.　運動有助促進血液循環。（請參考2-4）

    ⓐ Exercising is helpful to improve your blood circulation.

    ⓑ Exercising is helpful in improving your blood circulation.

    ⓒ Exercising is helpful for improving your blood circulation.

    ⓓ Exercising helps to improve your blood circulation.

（　）3.　門鎖了，我只好從窗戶進來。（請參考2-8）

    ⓐ The door was locked, so I had to enter by the window.

    ⓑ The door was locked, so I had to enter from the window.

    ⓒ The door was locked, so I had to enter by means of the window.

    ⓓ The door was locked, so I had to enter throughout the window.

（　）4.　這條路上全是泥漿。（請參考2-9）

    ⓐ The road is covered with mud.

    ⓑ The road is covered by mud.

    ⓒ The road is covered in mud.

    ⓓ The road is covered into mud.

（　）5.　這吉普車車況很好。（請參考2-12）

ⓖ The jeep is in a good condition.

ⓗ The jeep is on a good condition.

ⓘ The jeep is in good condition.

ⓙ The jeep is on good condition.

（　）6.　你應專注你的功課。（請參考2-13）

ⓖ You should pay attention to your study.

ⓗ You should pay attention to your studies.

ⓘ You should pay attention in your study.

ⓙ You should pay attention in your studies.

（　）7.　住在都市有許多優點。（請參考2-15）

ⓖ Living in the city has many advantages.

ⓗ There are many advantages to living in the city.

ⓘ There are many advantages to live in the city.

ⓙ There are many advantages of living in the city.

（　）8.　這位英文老師很受學生歡迎。（請參考2-16）

ⓖ The English teacher is popular among students.

ⓗ The English teacher is popular with students.

ⓘ The English teacher is popular in students.

ⓙ The English teacher is popular for students.

（　）9.　颶風卡翠娜造成五十億美元的財物損失。（請參考2-17）

ⓖ Hurricane Katrina caused $5 billion in property damage.

ⓗ Hurricane Katrina caused $5 billion of property damage.

ⓘ Hurricane Katrina caused $5 billion in property damages.

ⓙ Hurricane Katrina caused $5 billion of property damages.

（　）10. 如有任何問題，請與我聯繫。（請參考**2-21**）

　　ⓐ Please contact with me if you have any questions.

　　ⓑ Please contact me if you have any questions.

　　ⓒ Please make contact with me if you have any questions.

　　ⓓ Please make contact me if you have any questions.

（　）11. 我們可以從這家店買到一些二手玩具。（請參考**2-23**）

　　ⓐ We can buy some second-hand toys at this store.

　　ⓑ We can buy some second-hand toys from this store.

　　ⓒ We can buy some second-hand toys through this store.

　　ⓓ We can buy some second-hand toys in this store.

（　）12. 他學校功課壓力很大。（請參考**2-24**）

　　ⓐ He is under tremendous pressure from his studies.

　　ⓑ He is under tremendous pressure on his studies.

　　ⓒ His pressure of schoolwork is huge.

　　ⓓ He has a lot of pressure on his study.

（　）13. 很多窮苦學生需靠打工賺取學費。（請參考**2-29**）

　　ⓐ Many students from poor families have to work to pay their tuition.

　　ⓑ Many students from poor families have to work to pay for their tuition.

　　ⓒ Many students from poor families have to work to pay off their tuition.

　　ⓓ Many students from poor families have to work to earn their tuition.

（　）14. 對於不同種族、性別、年齡的人，我們應該一視同仁。（請參

考2-32）

ⓐ We should treat people of different races, genders and ages equally.

ⓑ We should treat people from different races, genders and ages equally.

ⓒ We should treat people coming from different races, genders and ages equally.

ⓓ We should treat people out of different races, genders and ages equally.

※解答請見P.294

第三章

經由翻譯程序
直譯造成的中式英文

本章重點：

眾所周知，中英語文造句法差異很大。例如：「他偷我錢」要說He stole my money. 但是「他騙我錢」卻要說He cheated me out of money. 或He cheated money out of me. 而不能說He cheated my money.「他搶我錢」則要說He robbed me of my money. 再如把「我想換一部新車」譯成I want to change a new car. 信則信矣，但英文本身不合邏輯。正確說法為I want to change the old car for a new one. 可見中譯英時，不能經由翻譯程序逐譯。

以下是學生習作的錯誤例子：

3-1. 加拿大是個移民國家。

【正】：Canada is a country of immigrants.

【誤一】：Canada is an immigration country.

【誤二】：Canada is an immigrants' country.

【誤三】：Canada is a country for immigrants.

【解說】：【誤一】an immigration country不通，是中譯英逐譯造成的結果；【誤三】的a country for immigrants文法正確，但意思不通，加拿大不是「為移民而成立的國家」。

3-2. 根據我的經驗，他借錢從來不還。

【正】：Based on my experience, he never returns the money he borrows.

【誤】：According to my experience, he never returned the money he borrowed.

【解說】：according to是指根據報紙、雜誌、權威人士或研究報告等等的說法，例：according to China Times（根據《中國時報》報導）／according to a recent study（根據最近研究顯示）。

3-3. 醫師每天要面對痛苦的病人。

【正】：Doctors have to face patients in pain every day.

【誤】：Doctors have to face painful patients every day.

【解說】：painful patients不通，因為painful只能用來修飾事物，例如「數學多次考不及格，對我是個痛苦的經驗」可說Failing the math test many times was a painful experience for me.

3-4. 球打到我的時候，我並未感到疼痛。

【正】：I felt no pain when the ball hit me.

【誤】：I felt painless when the ball hit me.

【解說】：和painful一樣，painless只能修飾事物，例如醫院施行的「安樂死」——「善終」可說a painless death。

3-5. **有一部電影描寫一個人連續兩周三餐都吃麥當勞，結果送醫院治療。**

【正】：There is a movie about a person who ate *at* McDonald's three times a day for two weeks and who ended up in the hospital.

【誤】：There is a movie about a person who ate McDonald's three times a day for two weeks and he ended up in the hospital.

【解說】：「麥當勞」是速食店店名，說「吃麥當勞」在中文裡一點問題都沒有，因為中文比較簡潔，「吃麥當勞速食」的「速食」可省略，但英文一定要說eat at McDonald's（在麥當勞店吃東西）。另外，and he ended up ...的he要改成who，以與前面的who平行。

3-6. **根據我的看法，我認為一個人一生不應待在同一家公司。**

【正】：In my opinion, a person should not work for the same company all his/her life.

【誤】：In my opinion, I think a person should not work for the same company all his/her life.

【解說】：「根據我的看法」有如下各種說法：in my opinion/ from my perspective/ from my point of view。請注意：這個片語之後就直接敘述你的看法，不能加上I think或I believe。

3-7. **小孩容易感冒，一旦生病，他們會傳染給家人。**

【正】：Children can catch colds easily; when they get sick, they may infect other family members.

【誤一】：Children are easily to catch colds; when they get sick, they may infect to other family members.

【誤二】：Children are easy to catch cold; when they get sick, they may infect other family members.

【解說】：

(1)「容易……」說成are easily to是中式英文，說Children are easy to catch cold也不對，因為像easy, hard, possible, important, convenient等形容詞不能以「人」當主詞，應該以it當主詞。

(2) infect是及物動詞，所以後面to要刪去。

3-8. **住在市中心很舒適，因為所有交通工具都很方便，例如公車、火車、捷運等等。**

【正】：Living downtown is comfortable because all the means of transportation, such as buses, trains and Mass Rapid Transit, are very convenient.

【誤】：Living in downtown is comfortable because all the transportation tools are very convenient, such as buses, trains and Mass Rapid Transit.

【解說】：

(1)「住在市中心」要說live downtown或live in the downtown area，不能說live in downtown，因為live downtown的downtown是副詞。同理，He went downtown. 也不能說He went to downtown.

(2)「交通工具」說transportation tools是中式英文，tool是「器具」，例如A hammer is a tool. 要說means/ forms/ modes of transportation才正確。

(3) such as所引導的片語是舉例說明means of transportation的，所以要置於其後，避免按照中文句型置於句尾。

3-9. **上街購物沒有信用卡很不方便。**

【正一】：It is inconvenient for people to go shopping without credit cards.

【正二】：People are inconvenienced when they go shopping without credit cards.

【誤】：People feel inconvenient when they go shopping without a credit card.

【解說】：convenient或inconvenient不能以「人」當主詞（要用it當主詞）。類似的形容詞有：hard/ difficult/ easy/ important/ necessary/ dangerous/ possible/ impossible，例：他很容易生氣。【正一】：He gets angry easily.【正二】：It is easy for him to get angry.【誤】：He is easy to get angry. 但請注意：easy當「輕鬆，安逸，隨和」解時，可以用「人」當主詞，例：【正一】：He is easy to get along with.（他容易相處。）【正二】：I felt easy.（我感到輕鬆自在。）

3-10. 青少年看到電視上名人吸菸，他們自己也會吸起菸來。

【正】：If teenagers see a celebrity smoking on TV, they may try to smoke as well.

【不佳】：If teenagers see a celebrity smoking on TV, they may try to smoke themselves.

【解說】：避免說smoke themselves，【正】句中的they may try to smoke as well亦可說they may follow suit。

3-11. 現代人認為時間就是金錢，所以過著快節奏的生活。

【正】：Because of the idea that time is money, nowadays people are living fast-paced lives.

【誤】：Because of the idea of "Time is money", nowadays people are living fast rhythm lives.

【解說】：「快節奏的生活」不能直譯成fast rhythm lives。另外，「過著快樂的生活」可說live a happy life或lead a happy life。

3-12. 坐公車上學省我的錢，但是浪費我的時間。

【正】：Going to school by bus saves *me* money, but it wastes *my* time.

【誤】：Going to school by bus saves *my* money, but it wastes *my* time.

【解說】：「省我的錢」要說save me money，注意要用受格。「浪費我的時間」則說waste my time，要用所有格形容詞。

3-13. 父母親和老師的經驗比我們多．

【正一】：Parents and teachers have more experience than we (do).

【正二】：Parents and teachers are more experienced than we (are).

【誤】：Parents' and teachers' experience is more than ours.

【解說】：「比……有經驗」說be more experienced或have more experience均可，不要受中文影響，用所有格形容詞teachers' experience。

3-14. 像麥當勞和肯德基所賣的速食一般也叫垃圾食品。

【正】：Fast food like that sold by McDonald's and KFC is also called junk food.

【誤】：Fast food like McDonald's or KFC is also called junk food.

【解說】：McDonald's和KFC是速食店店名，所以fast food like McDonald's顯然不通；like後加上that sold by McDonald's就合邏輯了。另外，本句亦可說成Fast food like fries and hamburgers is also called junk food.但是意思不同。

3-15. 商人給人的印象就是錢財。

【正】：Business people convey/present an image of wealth.

【不佳】：Business people give people an impression of money.

【解說】：「給某人印象」避免說give people impression，「他給我很好的印象」可說He made a good impression *on* me. 或He left a good impression *with* me. 請注意：句中介系詞的用法。

3-16. 受全球金融危機的影響，許多公司行號倒閉。

【正】：Because of the impact of the global financial crisis, many businesses and corporations went bankrupt.

【誤】：Because of the impact of the global financial crisis, many companies and corporations had bankrupted.

【解說】：

(1)「公司行號」要說businesses and corporations或businesses，避免說companies and corporations。

(2) bankrupt可作形容詞或及物動詞用，所以【誤】句的had bankrupted要改成went bankrupt。

3-17. 我喜歡團隊運動的最主要原因是因為它有競爭性。

【正】：The most important reason why I like playing team sports is that they are competitive.

【誤】：The most important reason why I like playing team sports is because of their competitiveness.

【解說】：「……的原因是因為……」避免說the reason... is because，把because改成that是正式的用法。

3-18. 暑期打工學生可以學到一些學校學不到的東西。

【正】：Working part-time during summer vacations, students can learn something which they can't learn in school.

【誤】：Working part-time during summer vacations, students can learn something which they don't learn from school.

【解說】：【誤】句中don't learn 指「不要學」，要改成can't learn；另外，learn from是由中文直譯而成的錯誤。

3-19. 坐公車最大的優點是便宜。

【正一】：The greatest advantage of riding the bus is that it is inexpensive.

【正二】：The greatest advantage of taking the bus is its low cost.

【誤一】：The greatest advantage of taking the bus is low cost.

【誤二】：Cheapness is the greatest advantage of taking the bus.

【解說】：「做……的優點」The advantage of... is後可接that子句（如【正一】），亦可接名詞片語（如【正二】）。【誤一】缺少所有格形容詞its，是由中文直譯的結果，這是許多學生容易疏忽的地方。

3-20. **父母親富裕，可以資助子女上大學，當然有許多優點。**

【正一】：There are obviously many advantages to having wealthy parents who can support their children in pursuing a college education.

【正二】：There are certainly many advantages to having wealthy parents who can help their children to pursue a college education.

【不佳】：There are certainly many advantages if parents can support their children to obtain a college education.

【解說】：【不佳】句中受詞＋不定詞（support somebody to do something）的句型比較少用，宜避免。

3-21. **很多人迷上網際網路，因為他們可以在這虛擬世界裡找到快樂。**

【正】：Many people are addicted to the Internet because they can have a lot of fun in cyberspace.

【誤】：Many people are addicted to the Internet because they can have a lot of fun in this unreality world.

【解說】：「在這個虛擬世界」直譯成in this unreality world是中式英文，應該說in cyberspace, in virtual reality, in virtual space或in the virtual world。

3-22. **現在大部分家長都希望子女能夠進入好大學。**

【正】：Nowadays, most parents hope that their children will enter a good university.

【誤】：Nowadays, most parents hope their children to enter a good university.

【解說】：和support / affect 一樣，hope後面不接受詞＋不定詞，例：
【正】I hope that you will pass the exam.／【誤】I hope
you to pass the exam.

3-23. 擁有部落格方便人們結交新朋友。

【正】：Having a blog makes it easier for people to make new friends.

【誤一】：Having a blog makes people more easily to make new friends.

【誤二】：Having a blog is easy for people to make new friends.

【解說】：「方便人們……」要說make it easy（或possible）for somebody to do something，不能直譯成make people more easily to do something。

3-24. 小時候沒有兄弟姊妹，對我的性格造成不利的影響。

【正】：Having no siblings during my childhood had a negative influence on my personality.

【誤】：No siblings during my childhood had a negative influence on my personality.

【解說】：【誤】句意思是「小時候，沒有任何一個兄弟姐妹對我的性格造成不良影響」，語意與原句完全不同，這是由中文直譯的結果。把 No siblings改成動名詞片語Having no siblings（沒有兄弟姐妹這件事）就正確了。

3-25. 在現今社會，財富是用來衡量某人是否成功的標準。

【正】：In modern society, wealth is one of the criteria used to evaluate whether or not a person is successful.

【誤】：In modern society, wealth is the standard used to evaluate whether or not someone is successful.

【解說】：【誤】句中用standard來譯「標準」不正確，因為standard

是指界定事物的基準、水準或標準，常與high或low連用；criterion則指「價值」判斷的衡量標準或尺度，不能與high或low連用，例：What is the major criterion for judging a symphony?（衡量交響樂的主要標準是什麼？）

3-26. 網際網路使我們的日常生活變得方便了。

【正】：The Internet makes our lives easier.

【誤】：With the Internet, our daily lives are becoming more convenient.

【解說】：「生活變得方便」說成lives are becoming more convenient；「帶來方便」說成bring us convenience等都是中式英文。

3-27. 出國旅遊，人們常要面對飛行時差問題。

【正】：When traveling abroad, people often need to deal with jet lag problems.

【誤】：When traveling abroad, people often need to deal with time difference problems.

【解說】：「時差」不能直譯成time difference，應該說jet lag（飛行時差反應），例：Have you got over the jet lag?（你的時差克服了嗎？）time difference指不同的時區（time zone）造成的「時間不同」，例如 What is the time difference between New York and Tokyo?（紐約和東京有幾個小時的時差？）

3-28. 要想成功，努力是不可或缺的要素。

【正一】：Hard work is an indispensable element in achieving success.

【正二】：If you want to succeed, you have to work hard.

【誤一】：To be successful, hard-working is indispensable element.

【誤二】：To be successful, hardworking is a must-have element.

【解說】：

(1)表示目的之不定詞，後面主句中的主詞一定要是做這個動作的人，

不能以事物當主詞，例：【正】To pass the test, you have to study hard.【誤】To pass the test, it is important for you to study hard.【誤一】和【誤二】都是由中文逐譯造成的，主句中的主詞不是「人」，形成dangling modifier，如果改成：To be successful, you have to work hard. 即算正確。

(2) hard work是名詞，hardworking是形容詞。

3-29. 研究顯示，越來越多的家長喜歡把子女送到私校就讀。

【正】：Research shows / has shown that more and more parents are choosing to send their children to private schools.

【誤】：Research showed that more and more parents are liking to send their children to private schools.

【解說】：

(1)「研究顯示」這種流行的套詞，動詞用簡單現在式或現在完成式皆可，避免使用過去式。

(2) more and more... 這種句型後面接的時態視上下文而定，常用現在進行式，但應注意的是：像hate / like / prefer / love等動詞，不能用現在進行式。改用...are choosing to send或are sending即可。例：Nowadays, more and more people are preferring to live in the countryside. 句中的preferring也要改成choosing。

3-30. 現在許多嚴重的犯罪必然牽扯到槍械。

【正】：Nowadays, many serious crimes involve the use of firearms.

【誤】：Nowadays, many serious crimes are involved with firearms.

【解說】：

(1)involve當主動態時，意為「（必然）包含……」或「意味著……」，例：Winning the game involves both skill and fortune.（想贏得比賽既要技巧，也要運氣。）The exploration involves danger.（這次探險必然會遇到危險。）

(2) involve當被動態時，意為「把某人捲入某事件之中」，「連累」，

例：Some senators were involved in the scandal.（有些參議員捲入那件醜聞案。）

3-31. 現在汽車已經變成普遍的交通工具了。

【正】：Nowadays, cars have become a popular form of transportation.

【誤】：Nowadays, cars have become popular transportation tools.

【解說】：「交通工具」是a means of transportation或a form of transportation，不能說a transportation tool。許多學生一想到「工具」就一成不變的譯成tool。殊不知tool一般指an axe（斧頭）／a saw（鋸子）等「器具」。當然tool也可以指（工作所需的）工具或手段，例：Words are important tools for a salesperson.（語言對於推銷員來說是重要的工具。）

3-32. 在私校，不論在課堂上或課外，老師更能專注在每個學生上。

【正】：In private schools, teachers are able to pay more attention to each student both in class and after class.

【誤】：In private schools, teachers are able to pay more attention to everyone no matter in the class or after the class.

【解說】：

(1)「不論」可說regardless of或no matter，但是no matter 後一定要接wh-clause，即who, what, when, where, how等引導的子句，不能直接跟著片語。例：No matter what he says, I won't believe him.／No matter where you go, I will follow you. 事實上，「不論」並不一定要譯成no matter，可根據上下文而定，有時可譯成both...and...。例如【正】句中的both in class and after class。再如：We should be temperate both in eating and in drinking.（不論飲食喝酒都要有節制）。

(2)「在課堂上」說in class，「在課外」說after class，都不用定冠詞the。

3-33. 雞肉比其他肉類要有營養。

【正】：Chicken is more nutritious than other meats.

【誤一】：Chicken has more nutritions than other meat.

【誤二】：Chicken is more nutritional than other meat.

【解說】：

(1)「比……有營養」要說be more nutritious than...，不能說have more nutritions than...。就像「我心情不好」要說I am in a bad mood. 一樣，不能說I have a bad mood. 有關to be／to have的用法，請參閱本書第四章。

(2) nutrition 不能加 "s"。

(3) nutrition的形容詞nutritious意為「有營養的」，另一個形容詞nutritional意為「營養方面的」，例：nutritional information（有關營養方面的資訊）。

(4) meat 一般不加 "s"，但本句指各種不同的肉類,要加 "s"。

3-34. 大部分年輕人不關心政治，他們只想到玩樂或談男女感情。

【正】：Most young people do not care about politics; they are merely focused on having fun or seeking a relationship.

【誤】：Most of the young people do not care about politics; they only think of playing or falling in love.

【解說】：

(1) most of the young people中的of the要刪去，理由請參閱本書第八章。

(2)「想到玩樂」不能直譯成think of playing；think of是「想起，認為」之意，例：I think of my mom very often.「談男女感情」要說seek a relationship。

3-35. 那些無法支付學費的學生可向學校申請獎學金。

【正】：Those students who have difficulty paying their tuition fees can apply for scholarships provided by the school.

【誤】：For those students who have difficulties to pay for their tuition fees, they can apply for scholarships to the school.

【解說】：

(1) have difficulty/ trouble doing something，注意均用單數，不接不定詞，例：I have trouble solving the math problem.（我無法解這個數學題。）

(2)【誤】句的for those students..., they can...，是按中文句構直譯過來的。刪去for，以those students當主詞，同時刪除they即可。

(3)「向學校申請獎學金」說apply for scholarships to the school是中式英文。

3-36. **開車時要安全至上，不能貪圖方便。**

【正】：When driving, people should put safety before convenience.

【誤】：When driving, people should put safety in front of convenience.

【解說】：「安全至上，不能貪圖方便」說put safety before convenience（即「把安全擺在方便之前」）注意用before，不用in front of。

3-37. **現在越來越多人買彩券都希望能中頭獎。**

【正】：Nowadays, more and more people are buying lottery tickets, hoping to hit the jackpot.

【誤】：Nowadays, more and more people buy lotteries, hoping to win the first prize.

【解說】：

(1) more and more 句構，動詞習慣用現在進行式。

(2)「買彩票」說buy lottery tickets，「中彩票」說win the lottery，「中頭獎」習慣說hit the jackpot。

3-38. **三代同堂有個缺點，那就是代溝問題。**

【正一】：There is a disadvantage to having three generations living in the same house--- the generation gap.

【正二】：There is a disadvantage to having three generations living in the same house, and this is the generation gap.

【誤】：There is a disadvantage in having three generations living in the same house, that is the generation gap.

【解說】：

(1) there is a disadvantage後要接to，不能接in。

(2)「那就是代溝問題」直譯成that is the generation gap，與前面的主句連不起來。正確用法有二：使用破折號，如【正一】，或說and this is the generation gap，如【正二】，this指代前半句There is a disadvantage to ...這件事，注意不能把this改成it。

3-39. 小孩與單親爸爸或媽媽同住會不知如何與異性孩童相處，也無法培養健全的性格。

【正】：When living with a single parent, a child may have trouble learning how to get along with other children of the opposite sex and may not build a healthy character.

【誤】：When living with either his father or his mother, a child cannot know how to get along with the other sex children and may not build up a healthy character.

【解說】：

(1)「不知如何」說成cannot know how to... 不夠地道，應該說have trouble（或difficulty, problems）learning how to...。

(2)「異性孩童」要說children of the opposite sex，「同性孩童」說children of the same sex。

(3)「培養性格」說build a character；build up是「累積、建立、鍛煉」之意，例：build up one's fortune（累積財富）。

3-40. 打工不僅影響青少年的學習，也影響他們的日常生活。

【正】：Having/Taking a part-time job affects not only teenagers' studies but also their daily lives.

【誤】：A part-time job not only affects teenagers' studies but also their daily lives.

【解說】：

(1)【誤】句以job當主詞，不合邏輯，因為job本身不會影響青少年的學習。應以動名詞片語Having a part-time job 或 Taking a part-time job 當主詞。

(2)【誤】句中的not only應置於teenagers' studies之前；請注意：連接A和B的對等連接詞not only A but also B中，A與B的詞類必須相同，【誤】句中not only後面的A是動詞片語（affects teenagers' studies），而but also後面的B是名詞片語（their daily lives），因此明顯錯誤。

3-41. **長期睡眠不足的人會暈眩、頭痛，甚至生病。**

【正】：A person who lacks sleep for a long time will feel dizzy, have a headache, or even get sick.

【誤】：A person who is lack of sleeping for a long time will feel dizzy, headaches, even sick.

【解說】：

(1) lack當動詞用時是Vt，後不接of，例：「他缺乏常識」要說He lacks common sense. 不能說He is lack of common sense. 請注意：lack的形容詞是lacking，所以本句亦可說He is lacking in common sense. 另外，lack當名詞用時可接of，例：His lack of common sense annoys me.（他缺乏常識讓我很惱怒。）

(2) feel dizzy, headaches, even sick不通的原因是，動詞feel可搭配dizzy，但不能說feel headaches，也不能說feel sick，因為feel sick的意思是「感覺想要嘔吐或噁心」；另外，even是副詞，前面要加連接詞or，表示一系列的事情。

3-42. **青少年應該知道喝酒和吸毒一樣容易上癮。如果他們上癮了就很難戒掉。**

【正】：Teenagers should understand that drinking is as addictive as doing/taking drugs; once they are addicted to it, it is hard for them to give it up.

【誤】：Teenagers should understand that drinking is as addicted as doing drugs, once they are addicted to it, they are difficult to give it up.

【解說】：

(1)「某人做某事上癮」要說someone is addicted to something；「做某事容易使人上癮」要說doing something is addictive。例：He is addicted to drugs.（他吸毒上癮了。）／Doing drugs is addictive.（吸毒容易上癮。）【誤】句中的第一個addicted要改成addictive。

(2)有些形容詞，像difficult/ hard/ easy/ impossible/ important/ essential/ convenient等，主詞要用it，不能以「人」當主詞。

(3) once是副詞，非連接詞，所以once前要用分號，如用逗點，即成run-on sentence。（連寫句：即兩個獨立子句之間只用逗號，缺乏連接詞的錯誤。）

3-43. **每件事都有優缺點，互聯網／網際網路也一樣。**

【正一】：Everything has its advantages and disadvantages; the same is true of the Internet.

【正二】：Everything has its advantages and disadvantages; the Internet is no exception.

【正三】：Everything has its advantages and disadvantages, including the Internet.

【誤一】：Everything has its advantages and disadvantages; the same is true with the Internet.

【誤二】：Everything has its advantages and disadvantages; the Internet is similar to it.

【誤三】：Everything has its advantages and disadvantages, and so does the Internet.

【解說】：【誤一】the same is true with中的with要改為of。【誤二】the Internet is similar to it是由中文直譯造成的錯誤。【誤三】的and so does the Internet，表示Internet不屬於everything，邏輯不通。

3-44. 缺乏與人溝通的能力影響我交朋友。

【正一】：My inability to communicate with other people prevents me from making friends.

【正二】：My inability to communicate with other people affects me adversely in making friends.

【誤】：My inability to communicate with other people affects me to make friends.

【解說】：【誤】句中的affect 只能接名詞，不能接「人」再接「不定詞」，下題的support 也一樣。

3-45. 資助學生上大學有許多方式。

【正一】：There are many ways to support students who want to obtain a college education.

【正二】：There are many ways to support students in obtaining a college education.

【誤】：There are many ways to support students to obtain a college education.

【解說】：和affect一樣，support後面只能接名詞，不能接「人」，再接不定詞。請注意，college education前面一定要用不定冠詞a。

3-46. 媽媽開車讓我在麥當勞下車，然後就去上班。

【正】：My mom dropped me off at McDonald's, and then she went to work.

【誤】：My mom dropped me off at McDonald's, then she went to work.

【解說】：【誤】句把作副詞用的then當作連接詞，正確的說法要在 then前加上and。

3-47. 兩堂課間休息十分鐘，即使午休也只不過是一小時。

【正】：The break / recess between two classes is ten minutes, and even the lunch break is only about one hour.

【誤】：The break time between two classes is ten minutes, even the lunch break is only about one hour.

【解說】：和前句的then一樣，【誤】句中的even也是副詞，不是連接詞，所以要說and even，否則就成了run-on sentence。（連寫句：即兩個獨立句之間只用逗號，缺乏連接詞的錯誤。）這種錯誤非常普遍，都是受中文影響，由中文句型直譯過來。

3-48. 建核電廠的優點難以計數。

【正】：There are countless advantages to constructing nuclear power plants.

【不佳】：The advantages of constructing nuclear power plants are countless.

【解說】：「做……有優點」要說There are advantages to＋V-ing。【不佳】句直譯成The advantages of constructing nuclear power plants are countless. 不好的原因是頭重腳輕，言不盡意，人家還會期待你說**Firstly**（第一個優點是……），**Secondly**（第二個優點是……）。雖然countless作敘述形容詞（predicative adjective）和限定形容詞（attributive adjective）皆可，但實際應用時，還要看上下文而定。

3-49. 人們住在鄉下感到不便，是因為他們通勤很費時。

【正】：The reason why people find it inconvenient to live in the countryside is that they have to spend a lot of time commuting.

【誤】：The reason why people feel inconvenient living in the countryside is that they have to waste a lot of time to commute to the city.

【解說】：

(1)「（某人）對（某事）感到不便」直譯成「某人feel inconvenient」是中式英文，應該說某人find it inconvenient to do something。

(2)【誤】句中的waste a lot of time 後面要接動名詞，所以to commute 要改為commuting。注意spend time／waste time後要接動名詞或on＋名詞。

3-50. 他要求嚴格，為了小事動不動就發火。

【正】：He is very demanding and easily gets mad over a small issue.

【誤】：He is strict and is easy to get mad because of a small issue.

【解說】：

(1)「對人嚴格」說be strict with someone，例：The teacher is strict with his students. 單單說He is strict. 不好，改成demanding即無問題。

(2) is easy to get mad不對的原因是，像easy, hard, difficult, important, necessary, convenient, possible等形容詞，不能以「人」當主詞，要以it當主詞。例如「我容易感冒」不能說I am easy to catch cold. 可改為：It is easy for me to catch cold. 或I catch cold easily.

3-51. 在現代社會，公司行號總要聘用受過高水準教育的員工。

【正】：In modern society, businesses and corporations tend to hire people with a high level of education.

【誤】：In the modern society, companies tend to hire people with a high education.

【解說】：

(1)「在現代社會」說in modern society，不用定冠詞the；但「在現代世界」in the modern world，就要用the。

(2)「公司行號」說companies固然可以，但說businesses and corporations比較正式。

(3)「高等教育」要說higher education；「高水準教育」要說a high level of education。

3-52. **毫無疑問，有了知識，我們能夠做出正確決定，以及養成健康的生活習慣。**

【正】：There is no doubt that knowledge enables us to make the right decisions and to develop a healthy lifestyle.

【誤】：It is no doubt that knowledge makes us able to make the right decision and to develop a healthy living habit.

【解說】：

(1)「毫無疑問」是there is no doubt that，注意：主詞不用it。

(2) make us able是中式英文，【正】句中enables us也可用allows us或makes it possible for us。

(3)「做出正確決定」make the right decision中的定冠詞the不能省。「生活習慣」避免說living habits或life habits。

3-53. **更多的移民意味著來加拿大的技術工人會增加。**

【正】：Having more immigrants means having more skilled workers in Canada.

【誤】：More immigrants mean more skillful workers will come to Canada.

【解說】：

(1)「技術工人」skilled workers，不是skillful workers，很容易混淆。skillful是「靈巧的、精湛的」之意，例：He is skillful in fixing electrical appliances.（他精於修理電器用品）。skilled是指「經過

訓練而變得熟練的」之意。

(2)【誤】句有兩個動詞，是直接由中文逐譯而成的錯誤。正確說法應加上having而成為動名詞片語當主詞。

3-54. 上大學對我未來的一生有所幫助。

【正】：Attending college is good for my life in the future.

【誤】：Attending college is good for my future life.

【解說】：「未來的一生」要說life in the future；future life是「來世、來生」（next life）之意。

3-55. 雇主應該支付受訓員工薪水，即使他們並非正式員工。

【正】：The employer should pay a salary to workers in training, even if they are not regular workers.

【誤】：The employer should pay training workers a salary even they are not formal workers.

【解說】：

(1)【誤】句的「受訓員工」要說a trainee或a worker in training。

(2)【誤】句的even是副詞，要改成even if而成為連接詞。有關even／even if用法請參閱本書第十章。

(3)「正式員工」是regular workers，不是formal workers。

3-56. 鼓勵更多人搭乘公共交通工具，而避免開私家車，是解決交通擁擠問題的關鍵。

【正】：Encouraging more people to take public transportation instead of driving is the key to solving traffic congestion problems.

【誤】：Encouraging more people to take public transportation instead of driving their private cars is the key to solve the traffic congestion problems.

【解說】：

(1)「開私家車」不能直譯成drive a private car，英文沒有public car／

private car的說法。正確說法為instead of driving或instead of driving their cars。

(2) key to後要接動名詞，因為to在此為介系詞。

(3)「交通擁擠問題」traffic congestion problems不用冠詞。如果說「臺北的交通擁擠問題」就要用定冠詞：the traffic congestion problems in Taipei。

3-57. 許多人想要買車，因為他們認為擁有私家車可以讓他們的生活更方便。

【正】：Many people want to buy cars because they think that a car can make their lives easier.

【誤】：Many people want to buy cars because they think that personal cars can make their lives more convenient.

【解說】：

(1)「私家車」不能直譯成a personal car或a private car。

(2)「讓他們的生活方便」說make their lives convenient是中式英文，要把convenient改成easier才符合慣用法。就像「手機給我們帶來方便」多數人會不假思索的說Cellphones bring us convenience. 這樣的中式英文。正確說法為：Cellphones make our lives easier.

3-58. 由於網際網路當時尚未成為普遍的交流工具，寫信是他們唯一的聯繫方式。

【正一】：Because the Internet was not a popular means of communication at that time, writing letters was the only way for them to stay in touch.

【正二】：Because the Internet was not in widespread use at that time, writing letters was the only way for them to stay in touch.

【誤】：Because the Internet was not a popular communication tool at that time, writing letters was the only way left for them to contact with each other.

【解說】：

(1)「普遍的交流工具」不能直譯成a popular communication tool，就像「交通工具」不能說成a transportation tool一樣（應說a means of transportation）。「尚未成為普遍的交通工具」可譯成was not a popular means of communication或換個方式說「沒有被普遍使用」（was not in widespread use）。

(2) contact當動詞用時為vt，後面不接with，但是contact當名詞用時就要加with。

3-59. 癌末病人要接受化療，但化療有個嚴重的副作用，那就是病人會掉頭髮。

【正】：Cancer patients have to undergo chemotherapy, but it has a serious side effect : patients will lose their hair.

【誤】：Cancer patients have to undergo chemical treatment, but it has a serious side effect, that is, patients will lose hair.

【解說】：

(1)「化療」直譯成chemical treatment（化學治療）是中式英文。

(2)「那就是」直譯成that is沒錯，但that is是副詞，不是連接詞，後面不能接句子。例：He will quit the job next Monday, that is, February 10. 本句中的「那就是」其實不必譯出，用冒號 (:) 表示即可。

(3)「病人會掉髮」說Patients will lose their hair.句中的their一定要用。有關所有格形容詞，請參閱本書第十一章。

3-60. 選對公司做事，人們才會有動力。

【正】：Only by choosing the right company to work for can people feel motivated.

【誤】：Only by choosing the right company to work can people have motivation power.

【解說】：

(1)「在某家公司做事」要說work for或work at a company，注意介系詞不用in。【誤】句中的work後要加for。

(2) only置於句首時，主動詞要用倒置結構。

(3)「有動力做某事」直譯成have motivation power是中式英文。應該說can people be motivated，有關to have和to be的用法，請參閱本書第四章。

3-61. **研究顯示，能夠保持工作與娛樂適當平衡的人比較能成功。**

【正】：Studies show / have shown that people who can strike a proper balance between work and play tend to be more successful than those who cannot.

【誤】：Researches have shown that people who can keep the adequate balance between working and entertaining tend to be more successful.

【解說】：

(1)「研究顯示」可說studies show／have shown或research shows／has shown。注意research不用複數，也不用冠詞a。

(2)「保持平衡」可說strike（或maintain）a balance between...；請注意：keep the balance的balance指銀行帳目的「結餘」。

(3)「工作與娛樂」說work and play，兩字均可當名詞用，注意：entertaining是形容詞。

(4)【誤】句的tend to be more successful是由中文「比較能成功」直譯過來，語義不清，後面應加上than those who cannot（strike a balance）。

3-62. **工作的目的不應該純為賺錢，也應該是為了學習新技術以及獲得工作經驗。**

【正】：Working should not only be about earning money, but it should also be about learning new skills and gaining experience.

【誤】：Working should not only be about earning money, it should also be about learning new skills and experience.

【解說】：

(1)【誤】句it前要加上but，否則即成為run-on sentence（連寫句：即兩個獨立子句之間只用逗號，缺乏連接詞的錯誤）。注意：not only...but also...句構中的but不能省略。

(2)「學習新技術」可說learn new skills，但「學到經驗」動詞不能用learn，這是許多學生經常犯的中式英文，應該說acquire/gain /obtain experience。注意：本句的experience不加"s"。

3-63. **由於老年人數目增加，高齡社會的問題變得非常嚴重。**

【正】：With the increasing number of elderly people, the problems associated with our aging society have become very serious.

【誤】：With increasing old people, the problems of our aging society have become very serious.

【解說】：

(1)「老年人」說old people不太禮貌，應說elderly people。【誤】句的With increasing old people意思不清，應把number加上而成With the increasing number of...。

(2)「高齡社會的問題」譯成the problems associated with our aging society比較地道，be associated with 意為「與……有關」。

3-64. **在週末，許多人喜歡賴床多睡一點，因為平常上班日無法如此。**

【正】：During the weekend, many people want to sleep in because they are unable to do this on workdays.

【誤】：During the weekend, many people want to have longer-time sleep because they are unable to do it on work days.

【解說】：

(1)「故意賴床多睡」要說sleep in，也可說sleep late；注意：「睡過頭」要說oversleep；have longer-time sleep是不通的英文。

(2)【誤】句中they are unable to do it 的it指代不清，要改為this。

第三章　練習題

選擇題：下列各題，請選出一個或兩個正確答案。

（　）1.　根據我的經驗，這種健康食品可促進血液循環。（請參考3-2）
　　ⓐ　According to my experience, this health food helps to improve your blood circulation.
　　ⓑ　Based on my experience, this health food helps to improve your blood circulation.
　　ⓒ　From my experience, this health food helps to improve your blood circulation.
　　ⓓ　My experience told me that this health food helps to improve your blood circulation.

（　）2.　這個病人抱怨全身疼痛。（請參考3-3）
　　ⓐ　The patient complained that he was painful from head to toe.
　　ⓑ　The patient complained that he was in pain from head to toe.
　　ⓒ　The patient complained that he was painful the whole body.
　　ⓓ　The patient complained that he was in pain in the whole body.

（　）3.　依據我的看法，我認為住在都市比住在鄉下好。（請參考3-6）
　　ⓐ　From my point of view, I think living in the city is better than living in the countryside.
　　ⓑ　From my perspective, I believe living in the city is better than living in the countryside.
　　ⓒ　From my point of view, living in the city is better than living in the countryside.
　　ⓓ　From my perspective, living in the city is better than living in

the countryside.

（　）4.　學生很容易犯這種錯誤。（請參考**3-7**）
ⓐ Students make this kind of mistake easily.
ⓑ It is easy for students to make this kind of mistake.
ⓒ Students are easy to make this kind of mistake.
ⓓ Students are easily to make this kind of mistake.

（　）5.　他住在市中心，所以上班不必開車。（請參考**3-8**）
ⓐ He lives in downtown, so he does not have to drive to work.
ⓑ He lives downtown, so he does not have to drive to work.
ⓒ He lives at downtown, so he does not have to drive to work.
ⓓ He lives in the downtown area, so he does not have to drive to work.

（　）6.　現今沒有網路很不方便。（請參考**3-9**）
ⓐ Nowadays, people are inconvenient if they do not have Internet access.
ⓑ Nowadays, it is inconvenient for people not to have Internet access.
ⓒ Nowadays, people are inconvenienced if they do not have Internet access.
ⓓ Nowadays, people are inconvenient for not having Internet access.

（　）7.　學生住校園可以節省時間與金錢。（請參考**3-12**）
ⓐ Living on campus saves students time and money.
ⓑ Living on the campus saves students time and money.
ⓒ Living on campus saves students' time and money.
ⓓ Living on the campus saves students' time and money.

（　）8. 吃速食最大的優點是便宜。（請參考**3-19**）

⓪ The greatest advantage of eating fast food is that it is inexpensive.

⓫ The greatest advantage of eating fast food is inexpensive.

⓪⓿ The greatest advantage of eating fast food is its low cost.

⓿ The greatest advantage of eating fast food is low cost.

（　）9. 老師都希望我們畢業後能找到好工作。（請參考**3-22**）

⓪ Our teachers hope that we can find a good job after graduation.

⓫ Our teachers hope that we will find a good job after graduation.

⓪ Our teachers hope us to find a good job after graduation.

⓿ Our teachers wish that we can find a good job after graduation.

（　）10. 衡量一個好學生的標準為何？（請參考**3-25**）

⓪ What is the major standard for judging a good student?

⓫ What is the major criterion for judging a good student?

⓪ What is the major standard to judge a good student?

⓿ What is the major criterion to judge a good student?

（　）11. 考試要得高分，定期學習很重要。（請參考**3-28**）

⓪ To get high marks in exams, students have to study regularly.

⓫ To get high grades in exams, studying regularly is very important.

⓪ If students want to get high marks in exams, they should study regularly.

⓿ To get high grades in exams, it is important for students to study regularly.

( ) 12. 我們缺乏交通工具。（請參考**3-31 / 3-42**）

    ⓐ We lack means of transportation.

    ⓑ We are lack of means of transportation.

    ⓒ We lack transportation tools.

    ⓓ We are lack of transportation tools.

( ) 13. 明天不論晴雨，我們都會去游泳。（請參考**3-32**）

    ⓐ Rain or shine, we will go swimming tomorrow.

    ⓑ No matter rain or shine, we will go swimming tomorrow.

    ⓒ Whether it is raining or fine, we will go swimming tomorrow.

    ⓓ Regardless of rain or shine, we will go swimming tomorrow.

( ) 14. 住在校園有許多優點。（請參考**3-38**）

    ⓐ There are many advantages to living on campus.

    ⓑ Living on campus has many advantages.

    ⓒ There are many advantages of living on campus.

    ⓓ There are many advantages if students live on campus.

( ) 15. 他打電腦遊戲上癮，因為玩電遊容易上癮。（請參考**3-42**）

    ⓐ He is addicted to playing computer games because playing computer games is addictive.

    ⓑ He is addicted to play computer games because playing computer games is addictive.

    ⓒ He is addictive to playing computer games because playing computer games is addicted.

    ⓓ He is addictive to play computer games because playing computer games is addicted.

( ) 16. 任何事情都有優缺點，建核電廠也一樣。（請參考**3-43**）

    ⓐ Everything has its advantages and disadvantages; the

construction of nuclear power plants is no exception.

ⓑ Everything has its advantages and disadvantages, the construction of nuclear power plants is no exception.

ⓒ Everything has its advantages and disadvantages, including the construction of nuclear power plants.

ⓓ Everything has its advantages and disadvantages, and so does the construction of nuclear power plants.

（　）17. 市政府已竭盡全力資助這些窮苦人購買平價住宅。（請參考 **3-45**）

ⓐ The city government has tried its best to support these poor people to buy affordable housing.

ⓑ The city government has tried its best to support these poor people in buying affordable housing.

ⓒ The city government has tried its best to help these poor people to buy affordable housing.

ⓓ The city government has tried its best to finance these poor people to buy affordable housing.

（　）18. 學生睡眠不足，即使鑽研了所有課程教材，考試也不易取得高分。（請參考**3-47**）

ⓐ Without enough sleep, a student will not get a good grade in exams even he has studied all the course material.

ⓑ Without enough sleep, a student will not get a good grade in exams even if he has studied all the course material.

ⓒ Without enough sleep, a student does not get a good grade in exams even if he has studied all the course material.

ⓓ Without enough sleep, a student does not get a good grade in exams even he has studied all the course material.

（　）19. 在大學選擇正確的專業，對我未來的一生會有正面的影響。
（請參考3-54）

ⓐ Choosing the right major at college will have a positive influence on my future life.

ⓑ Choosing the right major at college will have a positive effect on my life in the future.

ⓒ Choosing a major correctly at college will have a positive effect on my future life.

ⓓ Choosing a major correctly at college will have a positive influence on my life in the future.

（　）20. 他在微軟公司服務二十多年了。（請參考3-60）

ⓐ He has served in Microsoft for over 20 years.

ⓑ He has worked for Microsoft for over 20 years.

ⓒ He has served at Microsoft for over 20 years.

ⓓ He has worked in Microsoft for over 20 years.

※解答請見P.294

第四章

誤用動詞
造成的中式英文

本章重點：

一、to be / to have

二、動詞時態

　　a)表示趨勢的動詞

　　b)表示事實、真理、習慣的動詞

　　c)情態動詞

三、幾個容易誤用的動詞／動詞片語

四、主動態／被動態

一、to be / to have

中文裡，表示「狀態、擁有」時，英文習慣用to be，不用to have。學生習作中，容易受中文思維的影響，該用to be時誤用to have，而造成中式英文。茲舉例如下：

4-1. **雞肉比其他肉類有營養。**

【正】：Chicken *is* more nutritious than other meats.

【誤】：Chicken *has* more nutrition than other meats.

【解說】：【誤】句用has顯然是由中文「有營養」直譯而來。

4-2. **一生當中，居住在不同地方要比住在同一地方有趣。**

【正】：Living in different places all one's life *is* more fun than living in one place.

【誤】：Living in different places *has* more fun than living in one place all one's life.

【解說】：【誤】句用has more fun顯然是由中文「比住在同一地方有趣」直譯過來的。【誤】句如果改用「人」當主詞，動詞就要用have：People who live in different places all their lives have more fun than people who live in one place. 也就是說，人＋has more fun／事、物＋is more fun。

4-3. **我教英文比他有經驗。**

【正】：I *am* more experienced in teaching English than he is.

【不佳】：I *have* more experience in teaching English than he does.

4-4. **癌末病人只要還有意識，就應有權決定何時結束自己的生命。**

【正】：As long as terminally ill patients *are still conscious*, they should have the right to decide when to end their lives.

【誤】：As long as terminally ill patients *still have consciousness*, they should have the right to decide when to end their lives.

【解說】：【誤】句的still have consciousness是由中文「仍然還有意識」直譯過來的錯誤。

4-5. **此項政策在改善交通擁擠方面不如其他方法有效。**

【正】：This policy *is less efficient* in improving traffic congestion than other methods.

【誤】：This policy *has less efficiency* in improving traffic congestion than other methods.

【解說】：【誤】句的has less efficiency是由中文「不如其他方法有效」直譯過來的錯誤。

4-6. **父母不准我紋身，我相信大部分青少年和我有同樣情況。**

【正】：My parents do not allow me to get a tattoo, and I believe most teenagers *are in similar situations*.

【誤】：My parents do not allow me to get a tattoo, and I believe most teenagers *have similar situations*.

【解說】：【誤】句的have similar situations是由中文「有同樣情況」直譯過來的錯誤。

4-7. **他有一隻腳跛了。**

【正】：He *is* lame in one leg.

【誤】：He *has* a lame leg.

【解說】：【誤】句用has a lame leg顯然是由中文逐譯造成的錯誤。
注意：【正】句亦可說：He is lame *of* one leg.

4-8. **遠距教學對於那些能夠自律、有動力的學生很適合。**

【正】：Distance learning is very suitable for those students who *are* self-disciplined and motivated.

【不佳】：Distance learning is very suitable for those students who **have** self-discipline and motivation.

【解說】：「他表現出自律」可說He displays self-discipline. 或He is self-disciplined. 注意：說He has self-discipline. 不合習慣用法。同理，「他很有動力」說He is motivated.比He has motivation. 符合習慣用法。

4-9.　**我心情不好。**

【正】：I **am** in a bad mood.

【誤】：I **have** a bad mood.

4-10.　**我對化學沒有興趣。**

【正】：I **am** not interested in chemistry.

【不佳】：I **have** no interest in chemistry.

4-11.　**我喜歡名牌產品的原因是，它們的品質一般都比較好。**

【正】：The reason why I like brand-name products is that they **are** usually of better quality.

【誤】：The reason why I like brand-name products is that they usually **have** better quality.

4-12.　**雖然他才35歲，健康狀況卻很不好。**

【正】：Although he is only 35 years old, he **is** in poor health.

【誤】：Although he is only 35 years old, he **has** poor health.

【解說】：【誤】句的has poor health不合慣用法。

4-13.　**現今大部分大學畢業生找工作的壓力很大。**

【正】：Nowadays, most college graduates **are** under enormous pressure to find a job.

【誤】：Nowadays, most college graduates **have** a high pressure to find a job.

【解說】：【誤】句除了誤用to have pressure之外，形容詞用high也不對，可改成enormous或great，因為high pressure是指電壓、血壓的高。

4-14. 擁有穩定、高薪的工作，人們的壓力就會減少。

【正】：With a steady and high-paying job, people will **be** under less stress.

【不佳】：With a steady and high-paying job, people will **have** less stress.

4-15. 我的處境和大部分的大一新生一樣。

【正】：I **am** in the same situation as most other college freshmen.

【誤】：I **have** the same situation as most other college freshmen.

【解說】：be in the same situation是固定搭配。

4-16. 假如你經常和朋友爭論，你就不會愉快。

【正】：You will not be happy if you **are** often in disagreement with your friends.

【誤】：You will not be happy if you often **have** disagreement with your friends.

4-17. 這件襯衫的尺寸和那件不同。

【正】：The two shirts **are** different in size.

【誤】：The two shirts **have** different sizes.

【解說】：本句也可說：The size of this shirt is different from that of that shirt. 但是這句合乎文法的句子卻不合慣用法，因為沒有人會這麼說。

4-18. 此項網上男女約會服務隱祕性很高。

【正】：The online dating service *is* very private.

【誤】：The online dating service *has* a high privacy.

【解說】：has a high privacy是由「隱祕性很高」直譯而成的，是不通的英文。

4-19. 大部分消費者面對許多功能與外表相似的產品時，都會感到茫然無助。

【正】：Most consumers tend to feel helpless when they face many products that *are* similar in function and appearance.

【誤】：Most consumers tend to feel helpless when they face many products that *have* similar functions and appearance.

【解說】：「A與B在某方面類似」要說A is similar in... to B。例如「金子的顏色與銅類似」要說Gold is similar in color to brass. 不能說Gold and brass have similar color.

4-20. 喜歡運動的男孩通常都很健康。

【正】：Boys who enjoy playing sports *are* usually in good health.

【誤】：Boys who enjoy playing sports usually *have* good health.

【解說】：to have good health不合慣用法。

4-21. 我沒有早起的習慣。

【正】：I am not *in* the habit of getting up early.

【不佳】：I do not *have* the habit of getting up early.

4-22. 你有麻煩了。

【正】：You *are* in trouble.

【誤】：You *have* trouble.

二、動詞時態

a) 表示趨勢的動詞

4-23. **手機變得越來越普遍。**

【正一】：Cellphones are becoming more and more popular.

【正二】：Cellphones have become more and more popular.

【不佳】：Cellphones become more and more popular.

【解說】：表示「趨勢」（trend）的動詞，用現在進行式和現在完成式均可，避免用簡單現在式。注意：本句前如加上recently，則一定要用現在完成式——Recently, cellphones have become more and more popular.

4-24. **現在的人越來越重視物質。**

【正】：Nowadays, people *are becoming* more and more materialistic.

【不佳】：Nowadays, people *become* more and more materialistic.

4-25. **在西方國家，越來越多的人選擇過單身生活。**

【正】：In Western countries, more and more people *are choosing to* remain single.

【不佳】：In Western countries, more and more people *choose* to remain single.

4-26. **現今越來越多的人沉迷電玩。**

【正】：Nowadays, more and more people *are becoming* addicted to computer games.

【不佳】：Nowadays, more and more people *are* addicted to computer games.

【解說】：【正】句的becoming也可改用being。

4-27. 在現今社會，越來越多的年輕人與父母分開住。

　　【正】：In modern society, more and more young people *are living* away from their parents.

　　【不佳】：In modern society, more and more people *live* away from their parents.

4-28. 世界上經受氣候變遷的國家越來越多。

　　【正】：More and more countries in the world *are experiencing* climate change.

　　【不佳】：More and more countries in the world *experience* climate change.

4-29. 大都市的生活費用變得越來越貴了。

　　【正】：The living cost in big cities *is becoming* higher and higher.

　　【誤】：The living cost in big cities *becomes* more and more expensive.

　　【解說】：【誤】句除了動詞時態外，還有一個搭配錯誤。中文可說「費用很高」或「費用很貴」，但英文cost不能與expensive連用，「東西」才可用expensive形容，例：The car is expensive. 但請注意：有些動詞，習慣不用現在進行式，例如：like, love, hate, prefer, happen以及care等。

4-30. 現今越來越多的人寧願住在小城鎮。

　　【正】：Nowadays, more and more people *are choosing* to live in a small town.

　　【誤】：Nowadays, more and more people *are preferring* to live in a small town.

4-31. 在現今社會，關心自身健康的人越來越多了。

　　【正】：In modern society, more and more people *are starting to care about* their health.

【誤】：In modern society, more and more people **are caring about** their health.

b) 表示事實、真理、習慣的動詞

4-32. 大部分中國人出生在中國。

【正】：Most Chinese people **are** born in China.

【誤】：Most Chinese people **were** born in China.

【解說】：【正】句用現在式are是因為表示「事實」，但「我出生在中國」要說I was born in China. 用過去式表示「動作」已過去。

4-33. 電腦在我們日常生活中扮演重要角色。

【正】：The computer **plays** an important role in our daily lives.

【誤】：The computer i**s playing** an important role in our daily lives.

【解說】：凡表示事實、真理、習慣的動詞用簡單現在式，不能用現在進行式。

4-34. 大部分人出生時視力都正常。

【正】：Most people **are born** with normal eyesight.

【誤】：Most people **were** born with normal eyesight.

【解說】：表示general truth（真理）時，動詞要用現在式。很多人一想到「出生」，就用過去式，這是不正確的概念。請注意；如是「特指」（specific），則要用過去式，例如：「我妹妹出生時視力很好」要說My little sister was born with perfect eyesight. 另請特別留意：eyesight前不能用冠詞 "a"。

4-35. 每個人都會老。

【正】：Everyone gets old.

【誤一】：Everyone will get old.

【誤二】：Everyone is getting old.

【解說】：「每個人都會老」是general truth，動詞要用現在式。但是「年輕人會變老」則要用將來式：Young people will get old.

c) 情態動詞

情態動詞（modal verb）亦稱情態助動詞（modal auxiliary），是指說話者的情緒及態度的助動詞，如will, may, can, shall, must等，其中will, may, can在學生習作中經常混淆，該用will或will be able to時，學生容易受中文思維影響而使用can，如4-36到4-39，這些也屬於中式英文。

4-36. 假如沒有很多人購買他們的產品，這些公司就無法生存。

【正】：If not many people buy their products, these companies **will** not survive.

【誤】：If not many people buy their products, these companies **cannot** survive.

【解說】：if引導的子句在此表「條件」，屬於尚未發生，所以主句要用will not.

4-37. 夜間未好好休息，第二天我就無法專注學業。

【正】：Without a good rest at night, I **will not be able to** focus on my studies the next day.

【誤】：Without a good rest at night, I **cannot** focus on my studies the next day.

【解說】：Without所引導的介系詞片語等於If I do not have a good rest at night。表示「條件」尚未發生，所以主句要用will not be able to。

4-38. 禁止學生在學校使用手機不合理，因為如此學生就無法與家人聯絡了。

【正】：Banning the use of cellphones in schools is unreasonable because students **will** not be able to contact their parents.

【誤】：Banning the use of cellphones in schools is unreasonable because students **cannot** contact their parents.

【解說】：students cannot要改成students will not be able to... 使用未來式是因為此事尚未發生：學校禁止學生使用手機後才會發生。以上三題，句中的「……無法……」，學生經常以cannot譯出而造成錯誤。

4-39. 有了良好居住環境，人的壽命會更長。

【正】：With a good living environment, people **will be able to** live longer.

【誤】：With a good living environment, people **can** live longer.

【解說】：With引導的介系詞片語等於If people have a good living environment。表示「條件」尚未發生，所以主句要用將來式will be able to。

4-40. 買彩券的人越來越多，他們都希望能中頭獎。

【正】：More and more people are buying lottery tickets, hoping that they **will** hit the jackpot.

【誤】：More and more people are buying lottery tickets, hoping that they **can** hit the jackpot.

【解說】：【誤】句的can要改成will的原因是，hoping 引導的子句中要用將來式。【誤】句用can可能是由中文「能中頭獎」直譯過來。

4-41. 想在一夜之間背下一本書，我覺得很困難。

【正】：It is difficult for me to memorize a whole book in one night.

【誤】：It will be difficult for me to memorize a whole book in one night.

【解說】：【誤】句用will be 不對是因為本句並非表示「條件」，不能用將來式。

4-42. **父母親經歷過困苦，對子女會比較嚴格，不許他們行為不端。**

【正】：Those parents who have undergone hardships tend to be strict with their children and *do not* allow them to misbehave.

【誤】：Those parents who have undergone hardships tend to be strict with their children and *will not* allow them to misbehave.

【解說】：【誤】句will not allow要改成do not allow，與tend to be平行。

4-43. **節食減肥是最安全的方法，因為對健康不構成威脅。**

【正】：Going on a diet is the safest way to lose weight because it *does not* pose any threat to people's health.

【誤】：Going on a diet is the safest way to lose weight because it *will not* pose any threat to people's health.

【解說】：【誤】句的it will not pose要改成it does not pose，以與主句中的is平行。

三、幾個容易誤用的動詞／動詞片語

a) **某些動詞後面可接雙受詞，如offer, charge，但某些動詞在雙受詞之間要加介系詞，如provide, rob, accuse, remind, deprive, cure, inform等，茲舉例如下：**

4-44. **我父母親提供我學費。**

【正】：My parents *provide* me *with* tuition.

【誤】：My parents *provide* me tuition.

【解說】：【誤】句provide後的雙受詞間要加with.

4-45. **他搶我的錢。**

【正】：He *robbed* me *of* my money.

【誤】：He *robbed* my money.

【解說】：「他搶我的錢」可說He robbed me. 但如果要加受詞，則要

在兩受詞之間加of。

4-46. 檢察官指控他受賄。

【正】：The prosecutor *accused* him *of* taking bribes.

【誤】：The prosecutor *accused* him taking bribes.

【解說】：【正】句的accused如換成charged，則介系詞要用with：
The prosecutor *charged* him *with* taking bribes.

4-47. 這讓我想起去年發生的一個悲劇。

【正】：This *reminds* me *of* a tragedy which happened last year.

【誤】：This *reminds* me a tragedy which happened last year.

4-48. 該監獄剝奪了囚犯的合法權利。

【正】：The prison *deprived* the inmates *of* their legal rights.

【誤】：The prison *deprived* the inmates' legal rights.

【解說】：【誤】句inmates'用所有格形容詞顯然是由中文直譯而成。

4-49. 搬到鄉下後，他的哮喘就好了。

【正】：Moving to the countryside *cured* him *of* his asthma.

【誤】：Moving to the countryside *cured* his asthma.

4-50. 請告知你的抵達日期。

【正】：Please *inform* me *of* your arrival date.

【誤】：Please *inform* me your arrival date.

4-51. 老師指派他點名。

【正】：The teacher *charged him with* taking attendance.

【誤】：The teacher *charged him to* take attendance.

但請注意：charge如當「徵收費用」或「索價、要價」解時，後面接的兩個受詞中間的with要刪去，例：

4-52. **人們移居他國，該國政府會徵收某些費用。**

【正】：When people emigrate to another country, the government of that country will ***charge them*** a certain amount of money.

【誤】：When people emigrate to another country, the government of that country will ***charge them with*** a certain amount of money.

4-53. **他向我索價一百美金。**

【正】：He ***charged me*** U.S. $100.

【誤】：He ***charged me with*** U.S. $100.

b) avoid / prevent

avoid和prevent意思很類似，學生習作中，該用prevent的地方，容易誤用avoid，例：

4-54. **癌末病人有權結束自己生命，以免忍受肉體痛苦。**

【正】：Having the right to end their lives can ***prevent*** terminally ill people ***from*** suffering physical pain.

【誤】：Having the right to end their lives can ***avoid*** terminally ill people suffering physical pain.

4-55. **以動物做醫學試驗，可以避免使用人體。**

【正】：Medical testing on animals can ***prevent*** drug testing on humans.

【誤】：Medical testing on animals can ***avoid*** humans from trying new drugs.

4-56. **課徵使用道路、圖書館和公園的費用，將使部分人無法享受這些設施提供的服務。**

【正】：Implementing user fees for roads, libraries and parks will ***prevent*** some people ***from*** enjoying the services at these facilities.

【誤】：Implementing user fees for roads, libraries and parks will **avoid** some people enjoying the services at these facilities.

4-57. **很多人相信，槍支管制可以防止人們犯罪。**

【正】：Many people believe that gun control can **prevent** people **from** committing crime.

【誤】：Many people believe that gun control can **avoid** people committing crime.

c) need / require

need和require均表示「要求、需要」之意，但need指一般、普通的需求，如：Our company needs 20 computers. 而require則表示需要某種技能或資格，且帶有強迫意味，如：Driving requires your full concentration. 學生習作中，該用require處，常誤用need，請看下例：

4-58. **在現代社會，大部分工作需要專業知識。**

【正】：In modern society, most jobs **require** professional knowledge.

【誤】：In modern society, most jobs **need** professional knowledge.

4-58. **打籃球講究協力合作。**

【正】：Playing basketball **requires** teamwork.

【誤】：Playing basketball **needs** teamwork.

4-59. **有些主修科目不要求學生寫論文。**

【正】：Some majors do not **require** students to write a thesis.

【誤】：Some majors do not **need** students to write a thesis.

4-60. **大部分公司都要求員工要有大學學位。**

【正】：Most companies **require** their workers to have a college degree.

【誤】：Most companies ***need*** their workers to have a college degree.

4-61. 當圖書館管理員或公車司機不需要有數學知識。

【正】：Becoming a librarian or a bus driver does not ***require*** knowledge of math.

【誤】：Becoming a librarian or a bus driver does not ***need*** knowledge of math.

d) lack / lack of

當「缺乏」解時，lack是及物動詞，等於be lacking in。「他缺乏常識」可說He lacks common sense. 或He is lacking in common sense. 很多學生會誤說成：He is lack of common sense. 請注意：lack當名詞時，後面才能接of，例：His lack of common sense annoys me.（他缺乏常識，讓我很惱怒）。

4-62. 在網上修課，學生與教授之間缺乏互動。

【正】：Taking a course over the Internet ***lacks*** interactions between students and professors.

【誤】：Taking a course over the Internet ***is lack of*** interactions between students and professors.

4-63. 他與同學關係不好。

【正】：He ***lacks*** a good relationship with his classmates.

【誤】：He ***is lack of*** a good relationship with his classmates.

4-64. 一個人缺乏專業知識，就很難找到好的工作。

【正】：It will be hard for a person to get a good job if he ***lacks*** professional knowledge.

【誤】：It will be hard for a person to get a good job if he ***is lack of*** professional knowledge.

4-65. 年輕人缺乏人生經驗。

【正】：Young people *lack* life experience.

【誤】：Young people *are lack of* life experience.

e) happen / break out

happen和break out均表「發生」，但用法有別：一旦發生（happen/ occur）後會擴散或蔓延出去的就用break out，例如：

4-66. 地震之後發生火災。

【正】：Fire *broke out* after the earthquake.

【誤】：Fire *happened* after the earthquake.

【解說】：火災發生後會擴散，所以用break out。

4-67. 那兩個國家爆發了戰爭。

【正】：A war *broke out* between the two countries.

【誤】：A war *happened* between the two countries.

【解說】：戰爭一旦爆發，會擴散或蔓延至鄰近地區，所以用break out。

4-68. 大洪水之後發生瘧疾。

【正】：Malaria *broke out* after the heavy flood.

【誤】：Malaria *happened* after the heavy flood.

【解說】：傳染性疾病發生後會蔓延至其他地區，所以用break out。

4-69. 這兩個男子發生激烈打鬥。

【正】：An awful fight *broke out* between the two men.

【誤】：An awful fight *happened* between the two men.

【解說】：發生「打架，打鬥」，可能波及鄰近地區，所以用break out。

f) destroy / ruin

4-70. 大火燒毀了那棟建築。

【正】：The big fire ***destroyed*** the building.

【誤】：The big fire ***ruined*** the building.

【解說】：destroy指具體、實質的（physical）破壞，例如：destroy a building / a city / a bridge。

4-71. 那場大雨使我們的野餐計畫落空了。

【正】：The heavy rain ***ruined*** our plan to go picnicking.

【誤】：The heavy rain ***destroyed*** our plan to go picnicking.

【解說】：ruin一般用於抽象的破壞，多用於借喻中（例如：ruin one's plan / ruin one's life），避免用於具體的破壞。

g) know / learn

4-72. 得知父親過世時，她嚎啕大哭。

【正】：When she ***learned*** that her father was dead, she burst out crying.

【誤】：When she ***knew*** that her father was dead, she burst out crying.

【解說】：learn除了當「學習」解之外，另可作「由聽或看而獲悉，得知」解，例：I learned that John had a car accident.（我獲悉John發生車禍）。此處不宜用knew的理由是，主詞I是聽別人說John發生車禍。

h) surpass / exceed

4-73. 他的構想比我的更具創意。

【正】：His idea ***surpasses*** mine in originality.

【誤】：His idea ***exceeds*** mine in originality.

【解說】：surpass指能力、速度、技術、構想勝過或超越某人。

4-74. **根據統計，去年的出口額超過進口額一百億元。**

【正】：According to statistics, export **exceeded** import by 10 billion dollars last year.

【誤】：According to statistics, export **surpassed** import by 10 billion dollars last year.

【解說】：指具體數字的超過要用exceed。

i) bring / fetch

4-75. **去學校把孩子接回家來。**

【正】：Go and **fetch** the child home from school.

【誤】：Go and **bring** the child home from school.

【解說】：bring指將人或物帶到或拿到說話者身邊的動作；fetch則是指「從說話者身邊去某處取回或帶回」的動作，例：The chair is in the garden; please fetch it in. 椅子在花園裡，請把它搬進來。

j) fill in / fill out

4-76. **我被要求填寫申請表。**

【正一】：I was required to **fill in** an application.

【正二】：I was required to **fill out** an application.

【解說】：fill in和fill out均可作「填寫文件或表格」解。

4-77. **我被要求填寫出生日期。**

【正】：I was required to **fill in** my date of birth.

【誤】：I was required to **fill out** my date of birth.

【解說】：填寫文件或表格中的某項資料（例如出生日期、出生地、國

籍等）要用fill in，不能用fill out.要用fill in 的原因可以理解為 *in* that box或*in* that space（在那個空格裡）。

k) beware of / watch out for

4-78. **在擁擠的公車上，要小心錢包。**

【正】：***Watch out for*** your purse on a crowded bus.

【誤】：***Beware of*** your purse on a crowded bus.

【解說】：beware of所接的受詞一般都指不好，或可能引起災害的人、動物或事物，例如：Beware of the dog.（提防那隻狗）／Beware of fire.（小心火燭）／Beware of pickpockets.（謹防扒手）／Beware of imitations.（謹防仿冒品）／Beware of that con man.（謹防那騙子）。【誤】句中的your purse 不屬於這類性質，所以不能用beware of，可用watch out for 或be mindful of。

l) hurry up / hurry in

4-79. **欲購從速，以免向隅。**

【正】：***Hurry in*** before they are sold out.

【誤】：***Hurry up*** before they are sold out.

【解說】：這是商家廣告推銷產品時，經常使用的套句。之所以用in的原因可以理解為hurry in the store，所以不能用hurry up。再舉一例：下大雨時，母親看到孩子在外面時說：Hurry in before you get wet.（趕快進門，免得淋濕）。此處的in可理解為in the house，所以不能用hurry up。

4-80. **我們要快一點，免得趕不上火車。**

【正】：We have to ***hurry up***, or we will miss the train.

【誤】：We have to ***hurry in***, or we will miss the train.

【解說】：催促別人加快步伐時，習慣用hurry up。

m) belong to / belong in

4-81. 這本書應該放在那個書架上。

【正】：This book ***belongs in*** that bookcase.

【誤】：This book ***belongs to*** that bookcase.

【解說】：

(1) belong作「屬於……，歸屬……」解，與to連用，例：The car belongs to me.／I belong to the tennis club.（我是這個網球俱樂部的會員）。學生一般都會運用自如，唯一要注意的是要用主動態，例如不能說The car is belonged to me.

(2) belong in意為「人或物適合在某地」，例：I feel that I do not belong in this place.（我覺得在此格格不入）／These chairs belong in the kitchen.（這些椅子要擺在廚房）。

n) interfere with / interfere in

4-82. 我們不允許任何國家干預我國內政。

【正】：We allow no country to ***interfere in*** our internal affairs.

【誤】：We allow no country to ***interfere with*** our internal affairs.

【解說】：interfere是不及物動詞，要與介系詞in或with連用，但意思不同：interfere in意為「干涉，干預」，後面的受詞一定是事物，而interfere with意為「妨礙，打擾」，後面可接人或事物，例：Don't interfere ***in*** other people's affairs.（別干涉他人的事）／My father always interferes ***with*** me.（父親經常打擾我）／The pillar interferes ***with*** the view.（這根柱子妨礙視線）。

四、主動態／被動態

英文動詞，絕大部分可用主動，也可用被動，但是有些動詞習慣用主動態，不用被動態，完全依習慣用法，沒有規則可循。

以下是學生習作常犯的錯誤。

4-83. 人類是由猿猴演化而來的。

【正一】：Human beings *evolved* from apes.

【正二】：Humans *have evolved* from apes.

【誤一】：Human beings *were evolved* from apes.

【誤二】：Human beings *have been evolved* from apes.

【誤三】：Human beings *evolve* from apes.

【解說】：

(1)當「進化，演化」解時，evolve要用主動態，所以【誤一】和【誤二】不對。至於【誤三】用現在式也不對，因為「演化」的事實已過去，要用過去式。

(2)「人類」可說human beings，也可說humans。

4-84. 我們從此次坦率的談話中獲益很多。

【正】：We *benefited* greatly by this frank talk.

【誤】：We *were benefited* greatly by this frank talk.

【解說】：【正】句中的by也可用from。

4-85. 我哥哥專攻化學。

【正】：My brother *specialized in* chemistry.

【誤】：My brother *was specialized in* chemistry.

【解說】：「主攻、主修」可說specialize in 或major in，均用主動態。

4-86. 這座橋倒塌是由大洪水造成的。

【正】：The collapse of the bridge *resulted from* the immense flood.

【誤】：The collapse of the bridge *was resulted from* the immense flood.

【解說】：result from（由……造成）和result in（導致某結果）均用主動態。本句亦可說成：The immense flood resulted in the collapse of the bridge.

4-87. 他在鄉下長大。

【正】：He *grew up* in the countryside.

【誤】：He *was grown up* in the countryside.

【解說】：「長大」要用主動態的grow up，但是raise和bring up要用被動態，例如本句亦可說：He was raised/ was brought up in the countryside. 但請注意：當「（把小孩）養育成人」解時，raise和bring up要用主動態，例：She raised/ brought up three children.

4-88. 考試到了，他專心課業。

【正】：With examinations coming, he *concentrated on* his studies.

【誤】：With examinations coming, he *is concentrated on* his study.

【解說】：【誤】句除了用被動態錯誤外，當「學習、課業」解時，study要用複數。「專心」亦可說be absorbed in.

4-89. 我們班有十個男生，十五個女生。

【正】：Our class *consists of* 10 male students and 15 female students.

【誤】：Our class *is consisted of* 10 male students and 15 female students.

【解說】：「由……組成」可說consist of（主動態），be composed of（被動態），be made up of（被動態）。

4-90. **隨著車輛廢氣排量的降低，市中心的環境將會改善。**

　【正】：With the reduction in the amount of waste gas produced by vehicles, the environment of the city ***will improve***.

　【誤】：With the reduction in the amount of waste gas produced by vehicles, the environment of the city ***will be improved***.

第四章　練習題

選擇題：下列各題，請選出一個或兩個正確答案。

(　) 1.　在電影院看電影比在家裡看要有趣。（請參考**4-2**）

　　ⓐ Watching movies at a cinema is more fun than watching them at home.

　　ⓑ Watching movies at a cinema has more fun than watching them at home.

　　ⓒ Watching movies at a cinema is more funny than watching them at home.

　　ⓓ Watching movies at a cinema contains more fun than watching them at home.

(　) 2.　雖然他在車禍中重傷，神志卻十分清楚。（請參考**4-5**）

　　ⓐ Although he suffered serious injuries in the car accident, he was perfectly conscious.

　　ⓑ Although he suffered serious injuries in the car accident, he had perfect consciousness.

　　ⓒ Although he suffered from serious wounds in the car accident, he was perfectly conscious.

　　ⓓ Although he suffered from serious wounds in the car accident, he had perfect consciousness.

(　) 3.　我的處境和你同樣困難。（請參考**4-7**）

　　ⓐ I have the same difficult situation as you do.

　　ⓑ I am in the same difficult situation as you are.

　　ⓒ I have the same difficult situation like you do.

ⓓ I am in the same difficult situation like you are.

（ ）4. 這些學生既不自律，也缺乏動力。（請參考**4-9**）

ⓐ These students are neither self-disciplined nor motivated.

ⓑ These students have neither self-discipline nor motivation.

ⓒ These students display neither self-discipline nor motivation.

ⓓ These students are lack of self-discipline and motivation.

（ ）5. 雖然我祖父八十歲了，健康情況仍很好。（請參考**4-13**）

ⓐ Although my grandfather is 80 years old, he still has good health.

ⓑ Although my grandfather is 80 years old, he is still in good health.

ⓒ Although my grandfather is 80 years old, his health condition is still good.

ⓓ Although my grandfather is 80 years old, he still enjoys good health.

（ ）6. 現代社會，大部分人的日常生活壓力很大。（請參考**4-14**）

ⓐ In modern society, most people have a high pressure in their daily lives.

ⓑ In modern society, most people are under huge pressure in their daily lives.

ⓒ In modern society, most people are under tremendous pressure in their daily lives.

ⓓ In modern society, most people have high pressure in their daily lives.

（ ）7. 他經常與同學爭論。（請參考**4-17**）

ⓐ He is often in disagreement with his classmates.

ⓑ He has often in disagreement with his classmates.

ⓒ He has often in a disagreement with his classmates.

ⓓ He is often in a disagreement with his classmates.

( ) 8. 他們提供食物和衣服給這些窮人。（請參考 **4-43**）

ⓐ They provided food and clothes for these poor people.

ⓑ They provided food and clothes to these poor people.

ⓒ They provided these poor people with food and clothes.

ⓓ They provided these poor people food and clothes.

( ) 9. 政府剝奪了他的公民權。（請參考 **4-47**）

ⓐ The government deprived his civil rights.

ⓑ The government deprived him of his civil rights.

ⓒ He was deprived his civil rights.

ⓓ He was deprived of his civil rights.

( ) 10. 我通知他父母說，他已安全抵達。（請參考 **4-49**）

ⓐ I informed his parents that he had safely arrived.

ⓑ I informed his parents that he already safely arrived.

ⓒ I informed his parents of his safe arrival.

ⓓ I informed his parents about his safe arrival.

( ) 11. 此項措施可以防止這些政府官員濫權。（請參考 **4-53**）

ⓐ This measure will avoid these government officials from abusing their power.

ⓑ This measure will prevent these government officials from abusing their power.

ⓒ This measure will stop these government officials from abusing their power.

ⓓ This measure will prevent these government officials to abuse their power.

(　) 12. 政府必須做個清楚明白的解釋。（請參考**4-57**）

    ⓐ A clear and lucid explanation must be required from the government.

    ⓑ A clear and lucid explanation must be required by the government.

    ⓒ A clear and lucid explanation must be needed from the government.

    ⓓ A clear and lucid explanation must be needed by the government.

(　) 13. 這些年輕法官缺乏人生經驗。（請參考**4-62/ 4-65**）

    ⓐ These young judges lack life experiences.

    ⓑ These young judges lack of life experiences.

    ⓒ These young judges are lack of life experiences.

    ⓓ These young judges are lacking in life experiences.

(　) 14. 我們終於得知那件事的真相。（請參考**4-72**）

    ⓐ We knew the truth about the matter at last.

    ⓑ We knew about the truth concerning the matter at last.

    ⓒ We learned the truth about the matter at last.

    ⓓ We learned about the truth concerning the matter at last.

(　) 15. 在百米賽跑中，他的速度與技術勝過我。（請參考**4-73**）

    ⓐ In the 100-meter dash, he surpassed me in speed and skill.

    ⓑ In the 100-meter dash, he exceeded me in speed and skill.

    ⓒ In the 100-meter dash, he overtook me in speed and skill.

    ⓓ In the 100-meter dash, he beat me in speed and skill.

（　）16. 他匆忙趕回來時差不多已經是傍晚了。（請參考**4-79**）

    ⓐ It was almost evening when he came hurrying up.

    ⓑ It was almost evening when he hurried in.

    ⓒ It was almost evening when he hurried up to home.

    ⓓ It was almost evening when he hurried in home.

（　）17. 他大學主修電腦工程。（請參考**4-85**）

    ⓐ He majored in computer engineering at college.

    ⓑ He was majored in computer engineering at college.

    ⓒ He specialized in computer engineering at college.

    ⓓ He was specialized in computer engineering at college.

（　）18. 這次車禍是他的疏忽造成的。（請參考**4-87**）

    ⓐ The car accident was caused by his carelessness.

    ⓑ The car accident was resulted from his carelessness.

    ⓒ The car accident resulted from his carelessness.

    ⓓ The car accident resulted in his carelessness.

（　）19. 我在鄉下長大，所以養成早起的習慣。（請參考**4-88**）

    ⓐ I was raised in the countryside, so I formed the habit of getting up early.

    ⓑ I was grown up in the countryside, so I formed the habit of getting up early.

    ⓒ I brought up in the countryside, so I formed the habit of getting up early.

    ⓓ I was brought up in the countryside, so I formed the habit of getting up early.

※解答請見P.294

第四章

誤用動詞造成的中式英文

第五章

因邏輯錯誤
造成的中式英文

本章重點：

造成句子不合邏輯的因素大致可以分為：

一、由中文逐譯成英文造成的邏輯問題

二、修飾語與主詞不一致造成的邏輯問題

三、人稱代名詞it指涉不清造成的邏輯問題

一、由中文逐譯成英文造成的邏輯問題

5-1.　強壯的體魄是成功的決定性因素。

【正】：Having a strong body is a decisive factor in a person's success.

【誤】：A strong body is a decisive factor in a person's success.

【解說】：verb to be所連接的左右兩個名詞，其意義應該相等才合邏輯，也就是說中間可以劃個等號。例：He is an idiot.（He ＝an idiot）這就是為什麼「這部車是白色」不能說This car is white color，因為This car≠white color。正確的說法是：This car is white.【誤】句不通是因為a strong body不等於a decisive factor。【正】句加上having，成為動名詞片語，Having a strong body就成為「事物」，事物便可以是一個factor。

5-2.　網路交友要小心。

【正】：One should be careful when making friends on the Internet.

【誤】：Making friends on the Internet should be careful.

【解說】：【誤】句中的主詞making friends 不能be careful，「人」才能be careful，造成【誤】句的主因是中文句子的主詞省去，英譯時要把主詞one或a person補上。

5-3.　無業遊民是每個大城市面臨的一大問題。

【正】：Homelessness is a big problem that every city is facing.

【誤】：Homeless people are a big problem that every city is faced.

【解說】：homeless people是「人」，不是problem，另外，「每個大城市面臨的一大問題」不能用被動態的is faced。

5-4.　**我不想從事像醫生這種忙碌的工作。**

【正】：I do not want to hold a job that takes up all my time, such as being a doctor.

【誤】：I do not want to hold a busy job like a doctor.

【解說】：

(1)「忙碌的工作」，直譯成a busy job是中式英文，不合邏輯，因為只有「人」才會busy，「工作」本身不會busy。解決之道，可說a job that takes up all my time（佔用我很多時間的工作）。

(2)誤句另一個問題是like a doctor，注意：a doctor是「人」，being a doctor是「工作」，例：Being a doctor is very tiring. 當醫生（這個工作）很辛苦。

5-5.　**現在大部分人都選擇在三十多歲生小孩。**

【正】：Nowadays, most people choose to have children when they are in their 30's.

【誤】：Nowadays, most people choose to have children in their 30's.

【解說】：【誤】句不合邏輯是因為in their 30's放在children後面（哪有小孩是三十多歲的？），這種錯誤叫misplaced modifier（修飾語誤置）。正確說法可在children前加上when they are。

5-6.　**獨自學習的學生比較能專心。**

【正】：Studying alone, students can be more focused on their work.

【誤】：Studying alone can be more focused for students.

【解說】：be more focused要以「人」當主詞，誤句不合邏輯，是因為它以「事」studying alone當主詞。之所以犯錯是由中文直譯造成的。

5-7.　**不論飲食、喝酒都要有節制，以免傷身。**

【正】：A person should be temperate both in eating and drinking in order to avoid damaging his / her health.

【誤】：Both eating and drinking should be temperate in order to avoid damaging health.

【解說】：be temperate in（在……有節制）要以「人」當主詞，不能以「事物」當主詞，所以【誤】句不合邏輯。

5-8. **我哥哥現在在美國讀博士學位。**

【正】：My brother is now studying for a Ph.D. degree in the U.S.

【誤】：My brother is now studying a Ph.D. degree in the U.S.

【解說】：「讀博士學位」直譯成study a Ph.D. degree不合邏輯的原因是，a degree（學位）是一張文憑，兩三分鐘即可study完畢。正確的說法如下：study for/ work for/ pursue a Ph.D. degree。

5-9. **太多人居住一起會很吵鬧、擁擠。**

【正】：Too many people living in the same house can be noisy and crowded.

【誤】：Having too many people living in the same can be noisy and crowded.

【解說】：【正】句的主詞是too many people，「人」才會吵鬧；【誤】句用having too many people 當主詞，就變成「事、物」當主詞，而「事、物」不會吵鬧，所以本句不合邏輯。如果說Having too many people living in the same house can be inconvenient.（許多人住在一起會很不方便）就說得通了。

5-10. **學校不該禁用手機的原因之一是，手機有字典和計算機的功能。**

【正】：One of the reasons why schools should not ban the use of cell phones is that cell phones have some functions, such as **being** a dictionary and a calculator.

【誤】：One of the reasons why schools should not ban the use of cell phones is that cell phones have some functions, such as a dictionary and a calculator.

【解說】：【誤】句後半句that cell phones have some functions, such as a dictionary and a calculator不合邏輯，是因為cell phones不是dictionary，也不是calculator，加個being就正確了。

5-11. 現代社會變得比以前要忙碌。

【正】：In modern society, people are getting busier than they were previously.

【誤】：Modern society is getting busier than before.

【解說】：「人」才能忙碌，所以【誤】句的society is getting busier不通。

5-12. 地震之後，這棟公寓暫時不能居住。

【正】：After the earthquake, the apartment is temporarily unsuitable for occupancy.

【誤】：After the earthquake, the apartment is temporarily unable to live.

【解說】：live 的主詞該是「人」，apartment不能live，所以要說unsuitable for occupancy。【誤】句犯錯誤的原因，是直接由中文逐字翻譯過來造成的邏輯錯誤。

5-13. 兒童過度肥胖在北美被視為一個嚴重的問題。

【正一】：Obesity in children is considered to be a serious issue in North America.

【正二】：The problem of obese children is considered to be serious in North America.

【誤】：Obese children are considered to be a serious issue in North

America.

【解說】：obese children是「人」，不是issue，所以【誤】句犯了邏輯錯誤。

5-14. **薪水是對辛勞工作的回報，而薪水多寡並不能代表工作的重要性。**

【正】：Salary is a form of compensation for those who devote their time and effort to their jobs. However, the *amount/size* of the salary does not reflect the importance of a job.

【誤】：Salary is the compensation for those who devote their time and effort to their jobs. However, the salary does not represent the importance of a job.

【解說】：【誤】句中的salary is the compensation... 不通，因為salary與compensation並不相等，改成salary is a form of compensation...（薪水是……的報酬方式）邏輯就通了。後半句的「薪水多寡」（the size of the salary）未譯出，而成the salary does not represent... 不通的英文。

5-15. **語言相通是我喜歡住在中國城的主要原因。**

【正】：Being able to speak the same language is the main reason why I like to live in Chinatown.

【誤】：Common language is the main reason why I like to live in Chinatown.

【解說】：【誤】句中common language is the main reason why... 不合邏輯，因為language不能成為一個理由。

5-16. **從事專業工作的人，例如醫生和律師，需要良好的職業道德。**

【正】：Those people who hold professional jobs, such as being doctors or lawyers, are required to have good work ethics.

【誤】：Those people who have professional jobs, such as doctors and lawyers, are required to have good work ethics.

【解說】：

(1) doctors和lawyers是「人」，不是job，所以【誤】句不合邏輯。
being doctors才是job，例：Being a doctor is very tiring.

(2)【誤】句中的and要說成or，因為一個人不可能又當醫師，又當律師。

5-17. 商場和餐廳等公共場所都禁止抽菸，史坦萊公園也不例外，園區內一概不准抽菸。

【正】：Many public places, such as malls and restaurants, have made rules that restrict people from smoking. Stanley Park is no exception, as smoking is banned in all the area it covers.

【誤】：Many public places, such as malls and restaurants, restrict people to smoke. Stanley Park is no exception, as it bans smoking in all the area it covers.

【解說】：

(1)場所（places）不能禁止（restrict），法律（laws）或規則、法規（rules）才能禁止。

(2)「禁止某人做某事」，restrict後接from，不接不定詞。

5-18. 醫生和律師很賺錢，所以現在越來越多家長希望子女從事這兩項職業。

【正】：Doctors and lawyers are among the most well-paid professionals, so nowadays more and more parents are encouraging their children to enter these professions.

【誤】：Doctors and lawyers are among the most well-paid professionals, so nowadays more and more parents hope their children to be in these jobs.

【解說】：

(1) 關於more and more 或fewer and fewer這種結構，動詞習慣用現在進行式或現在完成式，本書多處提及。

(2) hope後面不接受詞＋不定詞，可接that clause，所以【誤】句亦

可改成 ...more and more parents are hoping that their children will enter these professions。

(3)【誤】句中 ...children to be in these jobs邏輯不通，可改成 ...children to enter these professions或follow these professions。

5-19. 當發現新疾病時，醫生要想辦法找出根治之道。

【正】：When a new disease emerges, doctors have to find a cure.

【誤】：When people find a new disease, doctors have to find a cure.

【解說】：「人」（people）不能find a disease，但可以find a cure。【誤】句的find a disease邏輯不通，要改成When a new disease emerges（新疾病出現時）。

5-20. 醫生經常使用老鼠試驗新藥。

【正】：Doctors often use mice in their experiments of new drugs.

【誤】：Doctors often use mice to do their experiments of new drugs.

【解說】：【誤】句中的use mice to do... 不合邏輯的原因是，「老鼠」（mice）不會做實驗，「人」才會做實驗，所以to do改成【正】句中的in their... 就正確了。

5-21. 像公園和圖書館等公共設施該要求使用者付費，因為維護費用很貴。

【正】：Administrators of public facilities such as parks and libraries ought to require users to pay fees because maintenance costs are very high.

【不佳】：Public facilities such as parks and libraries ought to require users to pay fees because maintenance costs are very expensive.

【解說】：

(1) public facilities不能要求（require），「人」才能require，所以本句要以「人」（administrators）當主詞，避免以public facilities當主詞。

(2)「維修費用很貴」不能直譯成maintenance costs are expensive，因為cost只有高或低（high or low），「商品或東西」才會expensive，這也是邏輯問題。

5-22. 很多人喜歡買像炸薯條、可樂、漢堡等垃圾食品供作派對上食用。

【正】：Many people like to buy junk food, such as fries, cola, and hamburgers, to serve at their parties.

【誤】：Many people like to buy junk food at their parties, such as fries, cola, and hamburgers.

【解說】：

(1) such as fries, cola, and hamburgers是用來修飾junk food的，所以應置於其後。

(2) buy junk food at their parties邏輯不通，加個to serve（供作食用）at their parties意思就通了。

5-23. 捷運列車班次很多，假如我錯過一班，下一班五分鐘就來。

【正】：The Mass Rapid Transit runs frequently. If I miss a train, the next one will come in five minutes.

【誤】：There are many Mass Rapid Transit trains. If I miss a train, the next one will come in five minutes.

【解說】：說「公車多久一班」要說How often do the buses run? 請注意run字的用法。

5-24. 假如我中了樂透獎，我要把它存在銀行。

【正】：If I won the lottery, I would save the prize money in the bank.

【誤】：If I won the lottery, I would save it in the bank.

【解說】：「中樂透」要說win the lottery，「買樂透彩票」要說buy a lottery ticket。【誤】句不合邏輯，是因為I would save it中的it指lottery，「彩票」不能save，「錢」才能save。

5-25. 窮苦學生不該享有免費大學教育，主要著眼於公平性。

【正】：The main reason why a university education should not be free to poor students is that this will be fair to all students.

【誤】：The main reason why a university education should not be free to poor students is because of fairness.

【解說】：【誤】句的主句The main reason is because of fairness不通，因為fairness是「事物」，不是理由。

5-26. 我不贊成把垃圾傾倒在小城鎮，原因是會污染環境。

【正】：The reason why I disapprove of dumping garbage in small towns is that it may pollute the environment.

【誤】：The reason why I disapprove of dumping garbage in small towns is the environmental pollution.

【解說】：【誤】句的主句The main reason is the environmental pollution邏輯不通。

5-27. 像消防隊和醫院這樣的工會絕不該罷工。

【正】：Unions such as those in the fire department and the hospital should never go on strike.

【誤】：Unions such as the fire department and the hospital should never go on strike.

【解說】：【誤】句不合邏輯，是因為the fire department不是union，【正】句的those＝unions.

5-28. 交通方便是我寧願住在市中心的主因。

【正】：The ability to access convenient means of transportation is the major reason why I prefer to live downtown.

【誤】：Convenient transportation is the major reason why I prefer to live downtown.

【解說】：【誤】句的主詞convenient transportation是「事物」，不是

reason，所以不合邏輯。之所以犯錯是由中文逐譯造成的。

5-29. **政府應禁止暴力電視節目，最重要的原因是此類節目會提高犯罪率。**

【正】：The most important reason why the government should ban violent TV shows is that they may increase the crime rate.

【誤】：Increasing crime is the most important reason why the government should ban violent TV shows.

【解說】：【誤】句的主詞increasing crime是「事物」，不能成為reason, 所以不合邏輯。

5-30. **現今就業問題已成為熱門話題，即使當個銷售員，也得符合某些基本要求。**

【正】：Nowadays, the lack of employment has become a hot issue, and even to be a salesperson, you have to meet some basic requirements.

【誤】：Nowadays, the employment problem has become a hot issue, even to be a salesperson, you have to match some basic requirements.

【解說】：

(1)「就業問題成為熱門話題」直譯成The employment problem has become a hot issue是中式英文，因為邏輯不通——the employment problem不能成為一個issue。正確說法為：the lack of employment has become a hot issue或unemployment has become a hot issue。「缺乏就業機會」或「失業」才是問題。

(2)【誤】句中的even是副詞，不是連接詞，所以前面要加上and，以便連接兩個句子。

(3)「符合要求」動詞要用meet或conform to，用match是中式英文，是錯誤的搭配。

5-31. 他是個土木工程師，但父親建議他轉到電腦工程這行業。

【正】：He was a civil engineer, but his father suggested that he change his career to computer engineering.

【誤】：He was a civil engineer, but his father suggested that he change his career to computer engineer.

【解說】：

(1) computer engineering是「電腦工程」，computer engineer是「電腦工程師」，所以change his career to computer engineer邏輯不通。

(2) change用原形是因為前面省去should。

5-32. 這間教室空氣很悶。

【正】：The classroom is stuffy.

【誤】：The air of this classroom is stuffy.

【解說】：stuffy是指「（建築物）通風不良的，不透氣的」，主詞可用room / classroom / theater / building等。【誤】句以air當主詞，顯然是由中文直譯過來造成的錯誤：air不可能stuffy。

5-33. 沒有接受大學教育的人，通常都從事低薪工作，例如銷售員或服務生。

【正】：Those who do not obtain a college education usually work in low-salaried jobs, such as being a salesperson or a waiter.

【誤】：Those who do not accept a college education usually work in low-salary jobs, such as a salesperson or a waiter.

【解說】：

(1)「接受教育」要說acquire / gain / obtain / receive an education，注意動詞不能用accept。

(2)「低薪工作」是a low-salaried job或a low-paying job。

(3) such as 後要加being，否則邏輯不通，因為a salesperson是「人」，不是job。

二、修飾語與主詞不一致造成的邏輯問題

此類問題叫懸空分詞或不連結分詞（dangling participle），就是現在分詞與句子的主詞沒有文法、邏輯關係，例：Going up the hill, the statue of Lincoln struck my eyes.（在登上山的當兒，林肯的雕像引起我的注目。）Going up the hill本應修飾「人」，句中卻修飾the statue of Lincoln，造成不合文法、邏輯的句子。這種錯誤連西方人也常犯，國人尤其頻繁，請看下例：

5-34. **增加汽車稅捐，有些人可能就會放棄買車的念頭。**

【正一】：By increasing the tax on cars, the government may discourage people from buying them.

【正二】：Because of the increase in taxes, some people may give up the idea of buying cars.

【誤】：By increasing the tax on cars, there must be some people giving up on the idea of buying cars.

【解說】：【誤】句中的By increasing the tax... 應該修飾【正一】的the government，不能修飾there。另一個解決方法就是如【正二】的Because of the increase in taxes，如此即可避免邏輯問題。

5-35. **一天辛苦工作後，有必要找個安寧的環境。**

【正一】：After a hard day's work, I need a quiet environment.

【正二】：After working all day, I find it necessary to have a peaceful environment.

【誤】：After working all day, a peaceful environment is necessary.

【解說】：【誤】句中的After working all day，應該修飾「人」，不是environment。之所以犯錯是因為中文裡的主詞「我」省去，英譯時要加上。

5-36. 上班或上學，假如路途不遠，步行也許是個好主意。

【正】：When we go to work or to school, it may be a good idea to walk if it is not a long distance to get there.

【誤】：When going to work or to school, it may be a good idea to walk if it is not a long distance to get there.

【解說】：【誤】句中的going to work or to school應該修飾「人」，不是it，所以本句亦可說When going to work or to school, we may as well walk if it is not a long distance to get there. 句中的may as well是「不妨」之意。

5-37. 提供租稅減免，很多大公司就不會出走。

【正一】：By providing tax breaks, a country will attract many big corporations to stay.

【正二】：Having tax breaks, many big corporations will stay in the country.

【誤】：By providing tax breaks, many big corporations will stay in the country.

【解說】：【誤】句中的By providing tax breaks應該是修飾a country，不能修飾big corporations。如果主詞是big corporations，就要把By providing改成Having tax breaks，如【正二】。

5-38. 打完籃球後，我的心較易專注於課業。

【正】：After playing basketball, I can concentrate more on my studies.

【誤】：After playing basketball, my mind can concentrate more on my studies.

【解說】：【誤】句不通，是playing basketball修飾my mind，應該修飾I才對。之所以犯錯是由中文直譯造成的。

5-39. 學生出勤率高，學校給予獎品獎勵，如此學生會認為上學就是為了領獎品。

【正】：If schools reward students with gifts for good attendance, students may think that the purpose of going to school is to obtain gifts.

【誤】：By rewarding students with gifts for good attendance, students may think that the purpose of going to school is to obtain gifts.

【解說】：【誤】句以By引導的介系詞片語修飾主句中的主詞students 邏輯不通──因為成了學生獎勵學生。

5-40. 使用網際網路，人們隱私容易被侵犯。

【正】：When people use the Internet, their privacy may be easily invaded.

【誤】：When using the Internet, people's privacy may be easily invaded.

【解說】：【誤】句不合邏輯，是因為主詞privacy不會使用Internet。

三、人稱代名詞 it 指涉不清造成的邏輯問題

it 的用法大致如下：

a) 指前面提及的事物，不特別考慮性別的嬰兒、動植物等。

b) 指天氣、時間、距離等。

c) 作為形式上的主詞或受詞，代替不定詞、that子句、wh- 子句、V-ing 等。

d) 表示強調的句型：It is... that/ who/ which/ when... ，例：It was yesterday that/ when I met her.

除開以上四種用法外，使用it很可能犯了指涉不清的毛病，請看以下學生習作的錯誤。

5-41. **有才智的人因為付不起學費，而無法上大學，真是可惜。**

【正】：It is a pity for intelligent people to fail to attend college simply because they have no money to pay their tuition.

【誤】：It is a pity if people who are intelligent but cannot attend college simply because they have no money to pay their tuition.

【解說】：【正】句的It指後面的不定詞片語to fail to attend college。【誤】句的It指涉不清。

5-42. **每個人都想長生不老，但那是不可能的。**

【正】：Everyone wants to live forever, but ***this*** is impossible.

【誤】：Everyone wants to live forever, but *it* is impossible.

【解說】：【正】句中的this指Everyone wants to live forever這件事。

5-43. **有句中國俗話說：「金錢可買時鐘，但不能買時間」。這意味著說時間是有限的。**

【正】：There is a Chinese saying which goes, "Money can buy clocks, but not time." ***This*** means that time is limited.

【誤】：There is a Chinese saying which goes, "Money can buy clocks, but not time." *It* means that time is limited.

【解說】：【誤】句中的It指涉不清，用This正確是因為This指Money can buy clocks, but not time這句俗語。

5-44. **購買車子要付保險與汽油費，那是很大的投資。**

【正】：When people buy a car, they have to pay insurance and buy gas. ***This*** is a big investment.

【誤】：When people buy a car, they have to pay insurance and buy gas. *It* is a big investment.

【解說】：【誤】句中的It是由中文「那是很大的投資」的「那」直譯而來，但指代不清。

5-45. 學生獨自生活雖然有缺點，但對增進他們的生活技能與學習人生經驗卻有幫助。

【正】：Although there are disadvantages to students living independently, living on their own is beneficial to students not only for improving their life skills but also for gaining life experience.

【誤】：Although there are disadvantages to students living independently, it is beneficial to students not only for improving their life skills but also for gaining life experience.

【解說】：【誤】句中的it指涉不清。

5-46. 人與人之間的關係很複雜，尤其是男女關係。

【正】：The relationship between people is a complicated matter, and *this* is especially true when it involves men and women.

【誤】：The relationship between people is a complicated matter, and *it* is especially true when it involves men and women.

【解說】：【誤】句中的第一個it指涉不清，用this即可，是因為this指前半句。另外，【正】句中的when it involves men and women中的it指relationship。

5-47. 不論你如何隱瞞，人家遲早會發現真相的。

【正】：No matter how hard you try to cover up, people will find the truth sooner or later.

【誤】：No matter how hard you try to cover up, people will find it sooner or later.

【解說】：【誤】句中的it指涉不清。

5-48. 在動物園內飼養瀕臨絕種動物，可讓世人瞭解拯救這些珍貴動物的重要。

【正一】：By placing endangered animals in zoos, people will realize the importance of saving these precious animals.

【正二】：Placing endangered animals in zoos will make people realize the importance of saving these precious animals.

【誤】：By placing endangered animals in zoos, it will make people realize the importance of saving these precious animals.

【解說】：【正一】By placing... 是介系詞片語，修飾主句的people。【正二】的Placing endangered animals in zoos是動名詞片語，當主詞用。【誤】句中的it指涉不清。

5-49. 垃圾食品對健康不好，這是常識。

【正】：It is common sense that junk food is not good for health.

【誤】：Junk food is not good for health. It is a common sense.

【解說】：

(1)【正】句中的It指代後面的that子句；【誤】句中的It可能指代Junk food，也可能指代health，但二者均不對，因為本句的意思是「垃圾食品對健康不好，這件事是個常識」。

(2)【誤】句中的a common sense的a要刪去。

5-50. 如果全世界都能禁菸，對大部分人都有好處。

【正】：Banning cigarettes throughout the world would benefit most people.

【誤】：It would benefit most people if cigarettes could be banned throughout the world.

【解說】：【誤】句的it指涉不清。

第五章 練習題

選擇題：下列各題，請選出一個或兩個正確答案。

( ) 1. 固定的收入是買房子的重要考慮因素之一。（請參考**5-1**）

    ⓐ A steady income is one of the key factors to consider when buying a house.

    ⓑ A steady income is one of the key factors for consideration when buying a house.

    ⓒ Steady income is one of the key factors in considering buying a house.

    ⓓ Having a steady income is one of the key factors to consider when buying a house.

( ) 2. 在河裡游泳要小心。（請參考**5-2**）

    ⓐ Be careful when swimming in the river.

    ⓑ Swimming in the river should be careful.

    ⓒ In the river, swimming should be careful.

    ⓓ One should be careful when swimming in the river.

( ) 3. 失業人口是許多國家面臨的一大問題。（請參考**5-3**）

    ⓐ Unemployment is a big problem that many countries are facing.

    ⓑ Jobless population is a big problem that many countries are facing.

    ⓒ Jobless people are a big problem that many countries face.

    ⓓ Unemployment population is a big problem that many countries are faced.

（　）4.　我不想從事像垃圾收集工這種骯髒的工作。（請參考**5-4**）

ⓐ I do not want to hold a dirty job like a garbage collector.

ⓑ I do not want to do this dirty job like a garbage collector.

ⓒ I do not want to undergo a dirty job such as a garbage collector.

ⓓ I do not want to hold such a dirty job as being a garbage collector.

（　）5.　許多博士班畢業生在三十歲後才能找到工作。（請參考**5-5**）

ⓐ Many Ph.D. graduates do not find a job until they are in their 30's.

ⓑ Many Ph.D. graduates do not find a job after 30.

ⓒ Many Ph.D. graduates do not find a job in their 30's.

ⓓ Many doctoral graduates do not find jobs until after 30.

（　）6.　許多學生相信，一邊聽音樂，一邊做功課比較能專心。（請參考**5-6**）

ⓐ Many students believe that listening to music while studying can be more focused.

ⓑ Many students believe that listening to music and doing homework can be more focused.

ⓒ Many students believe that listening to music while studying can make them more focused.

ⓓ Many students believe that listening to music to study can make them more focused.

（　）7.　讀博士學位需要很長的時間。（請參考**5-8**）

ⓐ Studying a Ph.D. degree takes a long time.

ⓑ Studying for a Ph.D. degree needs a long time.

ⓒ Studying for a Ph.D. degree takes a long time.

ⓓ Learning a Ph.D. degree needs a long time.

( ) 8. 大量移民人口使得這城市非常擁擠。（請參考**5-9**）

ⓐ Having a large immigrant population makes the city very crowded.

ⓑ A large immigrant population makes the city very crowded.

ⓒ Big amount of immigrant population makes this city very crowded.

ⓓ A large immigration population makes the city very crowded.

( ) 9. 這棟舊房屋在全部整修完成前不能入住。（請參考**5-12**）

ⓐ The old house cannot be occupied before it is totally repaired.

ⓑ The old house cannot be lived before it is totally repaired.

ⓒ The old house is unsuitable for occupancy before it is totally repaired.

ⓓ The old house cannot move in before it is totally repaired.

( ) 10. 興趣相同是我們成為好朋友的主要原因。（請參考**5-15**）

ⓐ Same interest is the main reason why we become good friends.

ⓑ Similar interest is the main reason why we become good friends.

ⓒ Having the same interest is the main reason why we become good friends.

ⓓ A common interest is the main reason why we become good friends.

( ) 11. 雖然醫生和律師屬於收入最高的行業，可是他們未必是世界上最快樂的人。（請參考**5-18**）

ⓐ Doctors and lawyers are among the most well-paid

professions, but they are not necessarily the happiest people in the world.

ⓑ Doctors and lawyers are among the most well-paid professionals, but they are not necessarily the happiest people in the world.

ⓒ Although doctors and lawyers are among the most well-paying professions, but they are not the happiest people in the world.

ⓓ Doctors and lawyers are the most well-paying professionals, but they may not be the happiest people in the world.

（　）12. 當發現新疾病時，醫生必須為它命名作為識別。（請參考 **5-19**）

ⓐ When a new disease emerges, doctors have to give it a name for identification.

ⓑ When people find a new disease, doctors have to give it a name for identification.

ⓒ When a new disease is discovered, doctors have to give it a name for identification.

ⓓ When discovering a new disease, doctors have to give it a name for identification.

（　）13. 他是個電氣工程師，卻想轉到電腦工程這行業。這是不可能的。（請參考**5-31**）

ⓐ He was an electrical engineer, but wanted to change his career to computer engineering. This is impossible.

ⓑ He was an electrical engineer, but wanted to change his career to a computer engineer. It is impossible.

ⓒ He was an electrical engineer, but wanted to change to the career of computer engineer. This is impossible.

ⓓ He was an electrical engineer, but wanted to change his career to computer engineering. This is hardly possible.

( ) 14. 請打開冷氣，這房間的空氣越來越悶。（請參考**5-32**）

   ⓐ Please open the air conditioner. The room is getting stuffy.

   ⓑ Please turn on the air conditioner. The room is getting stuffy.

   ⓒ Please turn on the air conditioning. The air in this room is stuffy.

   ⓓ Please turn on the air conditioning. The air in this room is getting stuffy.

( ) 15. 接受過大學教育的人，起薪通常較高。（請參考**5-33**）

   ⓐ People who have received a college education usually have a higher starting salary.

   ⓑ People who have accepted a college education usually have a higher salary in the beginning.

   ⓒ People who have accepted a college education usually receive a higher starting salary.

   ⓓ Those who have obtained a college education usually have a higher starting salary.

( ) 16. 提供方便的公共運輸工具，有些人可能就會放棄自己開車的念頭。（請參考**5-34**）

   ⓐ By providing convenient public transportation, the government may discourage people from driving their own cars.

   ⓑ By providing convenient public transportation, some people may give up on the idea of driving cars by themselves.

   ⓒ By providing convenient public transportation, there must be some people giving up on the idea of driving cars by themselves.

   ⓓ Providing convenient public transportation may discourage

some people from driving their cars.

(   ) 17. 在海裡游完泳後，我的皮膚很癢。（請參考**5-38**）

    ⓐ After swimming in the sea, my skin was itching.

    ⓑ After swimming in the sea, my skin itched.

    ⓒ I had itching skin after swimming in the sea.

    ⓓ After swimming in the sea, my skin very much itched.

※解答請見P.294

第六章

誤用名詞／主詞
造成的中式英文

本章重點：

一、容易誤用的兩個名詞amount / number

二、複合名詞 (compound noun)

三、使用動名詞片語當主詞

四、主詞累贅

一、容易誤用的兩個名詞amount / number

amount 後面接不可數名詞，number後面接可數名詞，但是學生習作中，該用number的地方，習慣用amount，究其原因可能是受中文直譯的影響，例如：「馬路上車子的數量」應該說the number of vehicles on the street，但是一想到「數量」學生本能反應就是amount，而成the amount of vehicles on the street的錯誤英文。請看以下實例：

6-1.　**速食含有很高的熱量。**
　　　【正】：Fast food contains a high **number** of calories.
　　　【誤】：Fast food contains a high **amount** of calories.
　　　【解說】：「熱量」calorie為可數名詞，所以要說a high number of calories.

6-2.　**生存在那條河有五百年之久的一種魚，其數量已減少至原有的百分之一。**
　　　【正】：A fish species that had been living in that river for 500 years dropped to 1% of its original **number**.
　　　【誤】：A fish species that had been living in that river for 500 years dropped to 1% of its original **amount**.

6-3.　**大學畢業生找不到工作的數目逐年增加。**
　　　【正】：The **number** of college graduates who have trouble finding a job is increasing year by year.
　　　【誤】：The **amount** of college graduates who have trouble finding a job is increasing year by year.

6-4.　**由於乘坐大眾運輸工具的人越來越多，市中心的車輛就減少了。**
　　　【正】：As more and more people are taking public transportation, the **number** of vehicles in the city center has decreased.

【誤】：As more and more people are taking public transportation, the **amount** of vehicles in the city center has decreased.

6-5. **在2008年全球金融危機期間，很多工人被解僱。**

【正】：During the 2008 global financial crisis, a large **number** of workers were dismissed.

【誤】：During the 2008 global financial crisis, a large **amount** of workers were dismissed.

6-6. **熊貓圈養在動物園裡遭受傷害的機會較小，所以近年來其數量顯著增加。**

【正】：Living in zoos, pandas have **fewer** chances of getting hurt. Thus, the **number** of pandas has been increasing significantly in recent years.

【誤】：Living in zoos, pandas have **less** chance of getting hurt. Thus, the **amount** of pandas has been increasing significantly in recent years.

【解說】：【誤】句除了less要改成fewer之外，amount也要改為number，因為panda為可數名詞。

6-7. **大部分瀕臨絕種動物找不到足夠食物，這會大量減少這些動物的數量。**

【正】：Most endangered animals have trouble finding enough food to eat; **this** can greatly reduce the **number** of these endangered animals.

【誤】：Most endangered animals have trouble finding enough food to eat; **it** can greatly reduce the **amount** of these endangered animals.

【解說】：【誤】句除了amount要改成number外，代名詞it指涉不清，要改成this，指分號前的整個句子。有關this和it的用法，請參閱本書附錄一。

6-8. **現今有很多人移居他國。**

【正】：Nowadays, a large *number* of people emigrate to other countries.

【誤】：Nowadays, a large *amount* of people emigrate to other countries.

二、複合名詞 (compound noun)

顧名思義，複合名詞就是兩個名詞在一起的名詞片語，第一個名詞當形容詞用。要注意的是，第一個名詞要用單數，例如「蛀牙」要說tooth decay，不能說teeth decay。學生習作中，容易忽略複合名詞的概念，誤把第一個名詞變成形容詞，而造成邏輯不通的錯誤，例如「成功的故事」是a success story，不是a successful story，以下是一些常見的錯誤例子。

6-9. **他有很多工作經驗。**

【正】：He has a lot of work experience.

【誤】：He has many working experiences.

【解說】：

(1)【誤】句除了working要成work之外，experience作「經驗」解時，一般用單數，所以many要改成a lot of。

(2)「工作效率」說work efficiency，「工作態度」說work attitude，「工作環境」說work environment。這幾個複合名詞，學生習作中，經常誤用。在此特別提醒讀者，在求職寫履歷表時，「工作經驗」千萬不要寫成working experiences（但請注意：「工作條件」要說working condition）。

6-10. **他喜歡閱讀冒險故事。**

【正】：He likes to read *adventure stories*.

【誤】：He likes to read *adventurous stories*.

【解說】：「故事」本身不會「冒險」，所以【誤】句不合邏輯。

adventurous只能修飾「人」，例：He is an adventurous explorer.（他是個富有冒險精神的探險家）。

6-11. 這個病人已進入危險期。

【正】：The patient is in a ***danger period***.

【誤】：The patient is in a ***dangerous period***.

【解說】：period只有long或short，不能用dangerous形容。【誤】句犯錯，是由中文逐譯造成的。dangerous可修飾人或動物，例：a dangerous person/ a dangerous lion。

6-12. 這家工廠以其高安全標準出名。

【正】：The factory is famous for its high ***safety standard***.

【誤】：The factory is famous for its high ***safe standard***.

【解說】：standard只有high或low，不能用safe形容。safe可修飾「環境」，例：a safe environment / a safe haven（安全的避難所）。

6-13. 消費者對歐洲汽車的需求，過去五年來大約上升了百分之十。

【正】：***Consumer demands*** for European vehicles have risen about 10% over the past five years.

【誤】：***Consumers' demands*** for European vehicles have risen about 10% over the past five years.

【解說】：「消費者需求」要用複合名詞的consumer demands，consumer在此是名詞當形容詞用，不能用所有格形容詞consumers'。同理，「消費者信心」也要說consumer confidence。

6-14. 學生評鑒老師有助於改進教學品質。

【正】：***Student evaluation*** of teachers helps teachers improve their quality of teaching.

【誤】：**Students' evaluation** of teachers helps teachers improve their quality of teaching.

【解說】：「學生評鑑老師」與上題一樣，也要用複合名詞的student evaluation of teachers。

6-15. **本國的教育系統必須大加改進。**

【正】：The **education system** of our country leaves much to be desired.

【誤】：The **educational system** of our country leaves much to be desired.

【解說】：「教育費用」說educational expenses，但「教育系統」要用複合名詞的education system。

6-16. **本次遊行將會採取嚴格的安全措施。**

【正】：Strict **safety measures** will be taken during the parade.

【誤】：Strict **safe measures** will be taken during the parade.

【解說】：和「安全標準」要說safety standard一樣，「安全措施」也要用複合名詞的safety measures。

6-17. **街角邊有一家廉價商店。**

【正】：There is a **thrift store** near the street corner.

【誤】：There is a **thrifty store** near the street corner.

【解說】：thrift是名詞，thrifty是形容詞，很容易混淆。「廉價商店」要用複合名詞的thrift store，是因為store本身不能「節儉」，「人」才能「節儉」。就像「成功的故事」要說a success story一樣。

6-18. **許多政府花鉅款來改變罪犯行為。**

【正】：Many governments spend a great amount of money changing **criminal behavior**.

【誤】：Many governments spend a great amount of money changing ***criminal's behavior***.

6-19. 讓顧客滿意是我們的首要任務。

【正】：***Customer satisfaction*** is our first priority.

【誤】：***Customers' satisfaction*** is our first priority.

6-20. 有些學生覺得住在學生宿舍很無聊。

【正】：Some students find it boring to live in the ***student dormitory***.

【誤】：Some students find it boring to live in the ***student's dormitory***.

三、使用動名詞片語當主詞

　　國人學英文，習慣以人稱代名詞you, he ,I 當主詞。殊不知可當主詞的還包括：不定詞、動名詞、動名詞片語、名詞子句以及抽象名詞等等，其中學生最感困惑的是使用動名詞片語當主詞。學會使用動名詞片語當主詞最大的好處在於避免邏輯錯誤。以下是一些錯誤例子。

6-21. 三代同堂有優點也有缺點。

【正】：***Having*** three generations ***living*** in the same house has advantages and disadvantages.

【誤】：Three generations who live in the same house have advantages and disadvantages.

【解說】：【誤】句的主句Three generations have advantages and disadvantages. 邏輯不通。

6-22. 樂趣是選擇職業時考慮的主要因素之一。

【正】：***Finding*** enjoyment should be one of the main factors in choosing a career.

【誤】：Enjoyment should be one of the main factors in choosing a career.

【解說】：【誤】句有問題的原因是主詞enjoyment本身不能成為一個因素，finding enjoyment（得到樂趣）這件事才可能是個因素。

6-23. **體重超重是全球性的問題。**

【正】：***Being*** overweight is a global problem.

【誤】：Overweightness is a global problem.

【解說】：overweight可當動詞、形容詞與名詞用，沒有overweight-ness這樣的字。另外，being overweight才是個「問題」。

6-24. **強壯的體魄是成功的決定性因素。**

【正】：***Having*** a strong body is a decisive factor ***in*** a person's success.

【誤】：A strong body is a decisive factor in a person's success.

【解說】：【誤】句是由中文逐字翻譯造成的中式英文。a strong body和a decisive factor是兩碼事，不能用be動詞連接。加上having成為動名詞片語，就可以是個factor。

6-25. **更多的人乘坐公車可降低空氣污染。**

【正】：***Having*** more people taking buses can reduce air pollution.

【誤】：More people who take buses can reduce air pollution.

【解說】：【誤】句中的主句more people can reduce air pollution邏輯不通。

6-26. **一群學生在一起做功課比一個人做功課要有效率。**

【正】：***Having*** a group of students doing homework together is more efficient than doing it alone.

【誤】：A group of students who do homework together are more efficient than do it alone.

【解說】：【誤】句的主句A group of students are more efficient... 邏輯不通。

6-27. **體重過重會引起一些心理問題，例如缺乏自信。**

【正】：***Being*** overweight can cause some mental problems, such as lack of confidence.

【誤】：Overweight can cause some mental problems, such as lack of confidence.

【解說】：overweight本身不會cause problems, being overweight這樣的動名詞片語才會cause problems。

6-28. **一生住在不同的地方，比住在同一地方要來得有趣。**

【正】：***Living*** in different places all one's life ***is*** more fun than ***living*** in one place.

【誤一】：Living in different places all one's life ***has*** more fun than living in one place.

【誤二】：People living in different places ***are*** more fun than people living in one place all their lives.

【解說】：

(1)【誤一】的動詞has要改成is，因為「人」＋have fun，「事物」＋be fun，例：We had fun dancing all night. / Dancing all night was fun.

(2)【誤二】的are要改成have，因為主詞是people。

6-29. **家庭成員多，垃圾也就多了。**

【正】：***Having*** more family members means that more rubbish will be created.

【誤】：More family members mean that more rubbish will be created.

6-30. 體育課是讓學生輕鬆的很好方法。

【正】：***Taking*** physical education is a good way for students to relax.

【誤】：Physical education is a good way for students to relax.

【解說】：【誤】句中的physical education不能成為a good way，要加個動名詞taking——taking physical education才能成為a good way。之所以犯錯是中文「上體育課」的「上」省略之故。

6-31. 良好教育和財富可以確保人們長壽。

【正】：Both ***getting*** a good education and ***being*** wealthy can ensure that people live longer.

【誤】：Good education and wealth can ensure that people live longer.

【解說】：【誤】句中以education和wealth當主詞不合慣用法，應該以動名詞片語getting（或having）a good education和being wealthy來當主詞。

6-32. 對這些學生來說，分數就是一切。

【正】：***Getting*** high marks is everything to these students.

【誤】：Marks are everything to these students.

【解說】：【誤】句以marks 當主詞不合慣用法。

6-33. 限速可降低車禍。

【正】：***Having/ Imposing*** speed limits can reduce the number of car accidents.

【誤】：Speed limits can reduce the number of car accidents.

【解說】：【誤】句的主詞speed limits本身不會降低車禍。加上Having或Imposing成為動名詞片語即正確。

6-34. 去年打工大大影響了我的功課。

【正】：***Taking/ Having*** a part-time job negatively affected my studies last year.

【誤】：A part-time job negatively affected my study last year.

【解說】：

(1)【誤】句中的主詞a part-time job本身不會影響我的功課。Taking／Having a part-time job當主詞，才合邏輯。

(2)當「學習、功課」解時，study一般要用複數。

6-35. 我夢想擁有像超模一樣的完美身材。

【正】：*Having* a perfect body like that of a super model is my dream.

【誤】：A perfect body like a super model is my dream.

【解說】：

(1)【誤】句的主詞a perfect body前要加Having，成為動名詞片語當主詞，才合邏輯。

(2)【誤】句like之後要加上that of才正確。that＝body.

6-36. 醫生在社會上是個最重要的職業之一。

【正】：*Being* a doctor is one of the most important professions in our society.

【誤】：A doctor is one of the most important professions in our society.

【解說】：【誤】句不合邏輯，是因為主詞A doctor是「人」，不是profession。句子前加上being成為動名詞片語，being a doctor就是一種profession了。

6-37. 我們都知道健康很重要。

【正】：We all know that *staying* healthy is very important.

【不佳】：We all know that health is very important.

四、主詞累贅

英文寫作，除了要正確外，用字貴在簡潔。學生習作中，容易由中文句型逐譯成英文，而成主詞累贅的毛病，例如「對那些有錢人來說，他們不在乎這些費用」很容易逐譯成For people who are rich, they do not care about the expenses. 句中people等於they，造成句子用詞累贅，不夠精簡。正確說法為：Those people who are rich/ Those rich people do not care about the expenses. 以下是一些錯誤例子：

6-38. **在某些人心中，他們認為獨自學習比群體學習要有效率。**
【正】：Some people think that studying alone is more efficient than studying in a group.
【不佳】：In some people's minds, they think that studying alone is more efficient than studying in a group.

6-39. **對那些心中擁有明確目標的年輕人來說，他們應該上大學進修。**
【正】：Those young people who have a clear goal should go to university.
【不佳】：For those young people who have a clear goal, they should go to university.

6-40. **絕大多數的大城市裡，市中心總會備有必要設施。**
【正】：The central areas of most large cities are always equipped with necessary facilities.
【不佳】：In most large cities, their central areas are always equipped with necessary facilities.

6-41. **一個沒有接受大學教育的人，他的事業也許要從最底層開始。**
【正】：A person who does not receive a college education may have

to start his/her career from the very beginning.

【不佳】：For a person who does not receive a college education, he/she may have to start his/her career from the very beginning.

6-42. 住在鄉村的窮苦人家付不起子女的高昂大學學費。

【正】：Those poor people who live in rural areas cannot afford the high college tuition of their children.

【不佳】：For those poor people who live in rural areas, they cannot afford the high college tuition of their children.

6-43. 六十五歲以上的計程車司機，每年要做身體檢查。

【正】：Taxi drivers who are over 65 years of age should have annual physical checkups.

【不佳】：For taxi drivers who are over 65 years of age, they should have annual physical checkups.

第六章　練習題

選擇題：下列各題，請選出一個或兩個正確答案。

（　）1.　這個新圖書館計畫購買大量圖書。（請參考**6-1/6-8**）
  ⓐ The new library plans to buy a large amount of books.
  ⓑ The new library plans to buy a large number of books.
  ⓒ The new library plans to buy a huge amount of books.
  ⓓ The new library plans to buy a huge number of books.

（　）2.　無數的發明與發現，使現代生活複雜化。（請參考**6-1/6-8**）
  ⓐ Inventions and discoveries in countless numbers have complicated modern life.
  ⓑ Inventions and discoveries in countless amounts have complicated modern life.
  ⓒ Inventions and discoveries in countless number have complicated modern life.
  ⓓ Inventions and discoveries in countless amount have complicated modern life.

（　）3.　這位新員工的工作態度不好。（請參考**6-9**）
  ⓐ The new employee's work attitude is bad.
  ⓑ The new employee's working attitude is bad.
  ⓒ The new employee has a bad work attitude.
  ⓓ The new employee has a bad working attitude

（　）4.　學生評鑒老師，在美國很普遍。（請參考**6-14**）
  ⓐ Student evaluation of teachers is very common in the U.S.

ⓑ Students' evaluation of teachers is very common in the U.S.

ⓒ The student evaluation of teachers is very common in the U.S.

ⓓ The students' evaluation of teachers is very common in the U.S.

( ) 5. 此次高峰會，政府將採取嚴厲的安全措施。（請參考**6-16**）

ⓐ The government will take rigorous safe measures at this summit meeting.

ⓑ The government will take rigorous safety measures at this summit meeting.

ⓒ The government will adopt rigid security measures at this summit meeting.

ⓓ The government will adopt rigid secure measures at this summit meeting.

( ) 6. 住在學生宿舍比住在公寓便宜。（請參考**6-20**）

ⓐ Living in the students' dormitory is less costly than living in an apartment.

ⓑ Living in the student dormitory is less expensive than living in an apartment.

ⓒ Living in the student's dormitory is less expensive than living in an apartment.

ⓓ Living in the students' dormitories is less costly than living in apartments.

( ) 7. 體重過重對健康有害。（請參考**6-23**）

ⓐ Overweight is bad for health.

ⓑ Overweightness is bad for health.

ⓒ Being overweight is bad for health.

ⓓ Having overweightness is bad for health.

（　）8. 我們都知道健康很重要。（請參考**6-21/ 6-36**）

    ⓐ We all know that a strong body is very important.

    ⓑ We all know that being healthy is very important.

    ⓒ We all know that staying healthy is very important.

    ⓓ We all know that having a strong body is very important.

（　）9. 更多的人提出意見，會使問題變得更複雜。（請參考**6-25**）

    ⓐ More people put forth their opinions will make the problem complicated.

    ⓑ Having more people to put forth their opinions will make the problem complicated.

    ⓒ Having more people put forth their opinions, the problem will be more complicated.

    ⓓ If more people put forth their opinions, the problem will become complicated.

（　）10. 十個人組成的團隊，一星期可完成此項目。（請參考**6-26**）

    ⓐ Ten people work on a team will finish the project in a week.

    ⓑ Having ten people work on a team will finish the project in a week.

    ⓒ Having ten people to work on a team will finish the project in a week.

    ⓓ If ten people work on a team, they will finish the project in a week.

（　）11. 去野餐比去爬山要來得有趣。（請參考**6-28**）

    ⓐ Going on a picnic is more fun than going mountaineering.

    ⓑ Going on a picnic has more fun than going mountaineering.

    ⓒ It is more fun to go on a picnic than to go mountaineering.

    ⓓ It has more fun to go on a picnic than to go mountaineering.

（　　）12. 烹飪課可讓學生學會一些生活技能。（請參考**6-30/6-36**）

ⓐ Taking a cooking lesson enables students to learn some life skills.

ⓑ A cooking lesson enables students to learn some life skills.

ⓒ Taking a cooking lesson, students will be able to learn some life skills.

ⓓ A cooking lesson is a good way for students to learn some life skills.

（　　）13. 要求提高薪水是他們計畫明天罷工的主因。（請參考**6-30/6-36**）

ⓐ A salary raise is the major reason why they plan to go on a strike tomorrow.

ⓑ A salary increase is the major reason why they plan to go on a strike tomorrow.

ⓒ Getting a salary raise is the major reason why they plan to go on strike tomorrow.

ⓓ Increasing salary is the major reason why they plan to go on strike tomorrow.

（　　）14. 經商成功是我報答父母的最好方式。（請參考**6-30/6-36**）

ⓐ Success in business is the best way for me to repay my parents.

ⓑ Achieving success in business will be the best way for me to repay my parents.

ⓒ Becoming a successful businessman will be the best way for me to repay my parents.

ⓓ Being a successful businessman, I can best repay my parents.

（　　）15. 根據研究，交通違規告發單多，並不意味車禍會減少。（請參

考**6-30/6-36**）

ⓐ According to research, issuing more traffic tickets does not mean that car accidents will reduce.

ⓑ According to a study, more traffic tickets do not mean that car accidents will reduce.

ⓒ According to a research, issuing more traffic tickets does not mean that car accidents will reduce.

ⓓ According to studies, more traffic tickets do not mean that car accidents will reduce.

※解答請見P.295

第七章

誤用介系詞
造成的中式英文

本章重點：

一、介系詞in / on / at

二、當介系詞用的to

三、幾個容易誤用的介系詞

四、介系詞for／不定詞for

一、介系詞in / on / at

在學習英文的過程中，如何正確使用in, on, at三個介系詞，不知難倒多少華人學子。cheat in an exam或cheat on an exam？／in my computer或on my computer？／in my cellphone或on my cellphone？／in a ship或on a ship？／at Christmas或on Christmas？這三個常用介系詞傳統的英文教學與教科書都歸為「固定搭配」，要學生死記硬背。本書總結出一些規律，分別舉例說明如下：

7-1. **他是在牛津大學執教的首位黑人教授。**

【正】：He was the first black professor to teach ***on*** the Oxford Campus.

【誤】：He was the first black professor to teach ***in*** the Oxford Campus.

【解說】：「在校園」可說on campus或on the campus。凡是表示「平面」的概念，介系詞都用on，例：on earth/ on the planet/ on the ground / on the surface / on（the）campus。

7-2. **該劫機者在飛機上被擊斃。**

【正】：The hijacker was killed ***on*** the plane.

【誤】：The hijacker was killed ***in*** the plane.

【解說】：大眾交通工具，介系詞習慣用on，例：***on*** the plane /***on*** the bus/***on*** the train /***on*** the ship / ***on*** a cruise / ***on*** a ferry。如果指小型的交通工具，介系詞習慣用in，例：***in*** the boat / ***in*** the taxi / ***in*** my car。

7-3. **大半夜不要這麼吵鬧。**

【正】：Don't make so much noise ***at*** midnight.

【誤】：Don't make so much noise ***in*** midnight.

【解說】：表示時間的介系詞，長時間用in，如：*in* the morning/ *in* the afternoon/ *in* the evening，短時間則用at，如*at* noon/ *at* midnight/ *at* dawn（黎明時刻）。「在半夜」還可以說*in* the middle of the night。

7-4.　該齣新劇將在第十頻道播出。

【正】：The new drama will be aired *on* Channel 10.

【誤】：The new drama will be aired *at* Channel 10.

【解說】：表示「電視或電視頻道」介系詞用on，例：on TV／on CNN ／on ABC（美國國家廣播公司）／on Channel 10。

7-5.　這個學生擅長數學。

【正】：The student is good *at* mathematics.

【誤】：The student is good *in* mathematics.

【解說】：表示「擅長或拙劣於某事」，介系詞一般都用at，例：be good *at* / be bad *at* / be slow *at*。但是形容詞poor要與in 連用，weak則可與at或in連用，例：He is poor *in* English grammar.／She is weak *in* / *at* French.

7-6.　他數學拿零分。

【正】：He got a zero *in* math.

【誤】：He got a zero *on* math.

【解說】：表示「學科」，介系詞要用in，例：*in* math / *in* English / *in* chemistry. 但請比較：He got a zero *on* a math test. 句中用 on，是因為與test搭配。

7-7.　我父母將於聖誕節來看我。

【正】：My parents will come to see me *at* Christmas.

【誤】：My parents will come to see me *on* Christmas.

【解說】：表示「節日」的介詞，一般都用at，例：at Christmas / at

Halloween（萬聖節）/ at Easter（復活節）。但請注意：
如果說「聖誕節那天我將把禮物拆開」則要說I will open my
presents on Christmas。此處要用on，指12月25日那天。
另外，「聖誕節前夕」說on Christmas Eve，「聖誕節」
可說Christmas或on Christmas Day。注意介詞用on，凡是
以day結尾的節日，介詞都用on，例：on Mother's Day / on
Father's Day / on Valentine's Day（情人節）。

二、當介系詞用的to

當介系詞用的to是許多學英文人士深感困擾、極難突破的一環，尤其是相
關參考書籍不易查到。根據研究，大致可分為四類：a)動詞＋to＋V-ing、b)名
詞＋to＋V-ing、c)形容詞＋to＋V-ing、d）There are＋名詞＋to＋V-ing，茲分
別舉例說明如下：

a) 動詞＋to＋V-ing

7-8.　我反對被當作小孩看待。
【正】：I *object to being* treated like a child.
【誤】：I *object to be* treated like a child.

7-9.　一談到打網球，他在我們班上獨一無二。
【正】：When it *comes to playing* tennis, he is second to none in our class.
【誤】：When it *comes to play* tennis, he is second to none in our class.

7-10.　過去很少人會注意保護個人的資料。
【正】：In the past, few people *paid attention to* protecting their private information.

【誤】：In the past, few people ***paid attention to*** protect their private information.

7-11. 嫌犯供認殺死這富人。

【正】：The suspect ***confessed to killing*** the rich man.

【誤】：The suspect ***confessed to kill*** the rich man.

7-12. 他承認偷了我的自行車。

【正】：He ***admitted to stealing*** my bicycle.

【誤】：He ***admitted to steal*** my bicycle.

【解說】：本句亦可說：He admitted that he had stolen my bicycle.

7-13. 每當她被指責時，經常以哭作為手段。

【正】：She often ***resorts to crying*** when she is criticized.

【誤】：She often ***resorts to cry*** when she is criticized.

【解說】：resort to 作「採取（某種手段），訴諸……」解，例：Don't resort to violence.（不要訴諸暴力），後可接名詞或動名詞。

b) 名詞＋to＋V-ing

7-14. 接受大學教育是找到好工作的第一步驟。

【正】：Obtaining a college education is the first ***step to finding*** a good job.

【誤】：Obtaining a college education is the first ***step to find*** a good job.

【解說】：請比較Reducing the use of paper is ***a big step in protecting*** our environment.句中的in不能改為to。

7-15. **努力工作是成功的唯一途徑。**

【正】：Hard work is the only *gateway to becoming* successful.

【誤】：Hard work is the only *gateway to become* successful.

7-16. **很多大學生除了在教室上課外，也在網上修課。**

【正】：Taking a course over the Internet has become an *alternative to taking* a course in a classroom for many college students.

【誤】：Taking a course over the Internet has become an *alternative to take* a course in a classroom for many college students.

7-17. **你即將成為百萬富翁了。**

【正】：You are on your *way to becoming* a millionaire.

【誤】：You are on your *way to become* a millionaire.

7-18. **不同的人解決問題的方法不同。**

【正】：Different people have different *approaches to solving* problems.

【誤】：Different people have different *approaches to solve* problems.

7-19. **大部分公司雇用員工，會優先錄用本地人。**

【正】：Most companies tend to give *priority to hiring* local people.

【誤】：Most companies tend to give *priority to hire* local people.

7-20. **堅持不懈是解開這個奧祕的關鍵。**

【正】：Resolute persistence is the *key to solving* the mystery.

【誤】：Resolute persistence is the *key to solve* the mystery.

7-21. **要想通過考試沒有快捷方式。**

【正】：There is no *royal road to passing* the examination.

【誤】：There is no *royal road to pass* the examination.

【解說】：本句亦可說：

There is no ***shortcut to passing*** the exami-nation。

c) 形容詞＋to＋V-ing

7-22. **員警說他們快破案了。**

【正】：The police say that they are ***close to solving*** the case.

【誤】：The police say that they are ***close to solve*** the case.

【解說】：【正】句的solving也可說breaking。

7-23. **購買新車課徵特別稅，對舒緩全球暖化有幫助。**

【正】：Imposing a special tax on people who buy new cars is ***beneficial to easing*** global warming.

【誤】：Imposing a special tax on people who buy new cars is ***beneficial to ease*** global warming.

7-24. **十六歲以下的年輕人不適宜開車。**

【正】：Young people who are under 16 years of age are not ***suited to driving***.

【誤】：Young people who are under 16 years of age are not ***suited to drive***.

7-25. **寫好一張令人印象深刻的履歷表是獲得面談的關鍵。**

【正】：Having an impressive resume is ***crucial to getting*** an interview.

【誤】：Having an impressive resume is ***crucial to ge***t an interview.

7-26. **規律運動對保持健康至關重要。**

【正】：Doing exercises regularly is ***essential to staying*** healthy.

【誤】：Doing exercises regularly is ***essential to stay*** healthy.

7-27. **美國承諾協防菲律賓。**

【正】：The United States is ***committed to defending*** the Philippines.

【誤】：The United States is ***committed to defend*** the Philippines.

7-28. **合理的待遇對留住這些人很重要。**

【正】：Reasonable compensation is ***critical to attracting and keeping*** these people.

【誤】：Reasonable compensation is ***critical to attract and keep*** these people.

7-29. **坐公車有助於保護環境。**

【正】：Taking the bus is ***conducive to protecting*** the environment.

【誤】：Taking the bus is ***conducive to protect*** the environment.

7-30. **富裕並不等同於快樂。**

【正】：Being rich is not ***equal to being*** happy.

【誤】：Being rich is not ***equal to be*** happy.

7-31. **要想參加奧林匹克運動比賽，天天練習是必要的。**

【正】：Practicing daily is ***fundamental to competing*** in the Olympic Games.

【誤】：Practicing daily is ***fundamental to compete*** in Olympic Games.

【解說】：

(1) be fundamental to意為「對於……是必要的」，to是介系詞，後可接名詞或動名詞。

(2) Olympic Games前要加定冠詞the。

7-32. **他承認偷了我的車子。**

【正】：He pleaded ***guilty to stealing*** my car.

【誤】：He pleaded ***guilty to steal*** my car.

【解說】：plead guilty to 的to為介系詞，後可接名詞或動名詞，
例：He pleaded guilty to the *crime* / He pleaded guilty to
committing the crime.（他承認犯行。）

d) There are＋名詞＋to＋V-ing

7-33. 住在都市有很多優點。

【正】：There are many *advantages to living* in the city.

【誤】：There are many *advantages to live* in the city.

【解說】：本句亦可說：There are many benefits to living in the city/
Living in the city has many advantages.

7-34. 在住宅區建超市有優點，也有缺點。

【正】：There are both *pros and cons to constructing* supermarkets
in residential areas.

【誤】：There are both *pros and cons to construct* supermarkets in
residential areas.

【解說】：本句亦可說：There are both *advantages and disadvantages to constructing* supermarkets in residential areas.

7-35 一個人沒有專業知識，想找個好工作，基本上很困難。

【正】：There is a basic *difficulty to finding* a good job if a person
does not have professional knowledge.

【誤】：There is a basic *difficulty to find* a good job if a person does
not have professional knowledge.

三、幾個容易誤用的介系詞

英文寫作裡，介系詞與冠詞是學生最感頭痛的部分，其中介系詞還牽涉到受中文思維的影響而造成的錯誤，這也屬於中式英文，舉例如下：

7-36. **他對我的態度已經改變了。**

【正】：His attitude **toward** me has changed.

【誤】：His attitude **to** me has changed.

【解說】：「對……態度」介系詞一般都用toward或towards，不用to。

7-37. **小時候，如果成績不好，媽媽經常對我吼叫。**

【正】：When I was young, my mom would often **yell at** me if I received a bad score.

【誤】：When I was young, my mom would often **yell to** me if I received a bad score.

【解說】：yell與at 連用。

7-38. **上大學可以讓學生增廣見聞，建立社交網路。**

【正】：Going to college enables a student to broaden his horizons and **build** his social network.

【誤】：Going to college enables a student to broaden his horizons and **build up** his social network.

【解說】：build up 和build很容易混淆，該用build時，學生經常用build up。「建立信心」、「建造橋樑」、「蓋房子或建學校」、「建立人際關係」等等用build。而build up有如下常見用法：build up a business（創立事業）／build up wealth（積累財富）／build up a country建設國家。

7-39. 除了一張破椅子之外，那個房間空蕩蕩的。

【正】：***Except for*** a broken chair, the room is empty.

【誤】：***Except*** a broken chair, the room is empty.

【解說】：except所指的項目如果是具體的事物，主句中所指的項目也要具體。【誤】句中，except後的項目是a broken chair，而主句中卻是抽象的形容詞empty，而造成兩個不對等的概念。【誤】句如改成Except a broken chair, the room has no furniture. 就是正確的句子，因為a broken chair和furniture都是具體的東西。

7-40. 學校除了我之外，別無他人。

【正】：There is ***nobody*** in school ***except*** me.

【誤】：There is nobody in school ***except for*** me.

【解說】：【正】句中，except後的me與主句中nobody都指具體的「人」，屬同一概念。

7-41. 我被她的美所吸引。

【正】：I am attracted ***to*** her.

【誤】：I am attracted ***by*** her.

【解說】：【誤】句用by，顯然是受be動詞＋動詞過去分詞＋by的固定套路所影響。一個女孩牙齒很美，你可說：I am attracted to your teeth. 注意介詞不用by，但請注意：I am attracted by the beautiful tropical climate. 句中的by是正確的，不能用to。

7-42. 該項考試失敗多次，對我是個痛苦的經歷。

【正】：Failing the test many times is a painful experience ***for*** me.

【誤】：Failing the test many times is a painful experience ***to*** me.

【解說】：【誤】句中的to顯然是由中文「對我」直譯而來。

7-43.這個新學生留給我很好的印象。

【正】：The new student made/ left a very good impression **on** me.

【誤】：The new student left a very good impression **to** me.

【解說】：【正】句亦可說The new student **left** me **with** a very good impression.【誤】句用to顯然是由中文「給我」直譯而來。

7-44. 很多體重超重的人尋求各種方法減肥。

【正】：Many overweight people **search for** different methods to lose weight.

【誤】：Many overweight people **search** different methods to lose weight.

【解說】：「尋求」可說seek / search for / look for。

7-45. 林教授對學生很寬鬆。

【正】：Professor Lin is easy **on** his students.

【誤】：Professor Lin is easy **to** his students.

【解說】：老師對學生寬鬆、家長對子女寬容要說be easy **on**，這個介系詞on很多人會受中文「對……」的影響而用to。注意：be easy **on**的相反詞是be hard **on**或be strict **with**（對……嚴格），介系詞均不能用to。

7-46. 在我印象中，他是個好學生。

【正】：It is my impression that he is a good student.

【誤】：**In** my impression, he is a good student.

【解說】：【誤】句的in my impression是由「在我印象中」直譯而來。

四、不定詞／介系詞for

7-47. **我們都很用功，以便通過考試。**

【正】：All of us worked hard *to pass* the examination.

【誤】：All of us worked hard *for passing* the examination.

【解說】：【正】句中的to pass前省去in order表示目的，所以本句要用不定詞。【誤】句用for passing可能是受中文「為了通過考試」的「為了……」影響。

7-48. **現今越來越多的學生上大學學習專業知識。**

【正】：Nowadays, more and more students are attending college *to acquire* professional knowledge.

【誤】：Nowadays, more and more students are attending college *for acquiring* professional knowledge.

【解說】：與上句一樣，【正】句的to acquire前省去in order，表示目的。

7-49. **大部分學生參加這項考試，以便進入好大學。**

【正】：Most students take this test *to apply to* a good university.

【誤】：Most students take this test *for applying* a good university.

【解說】：【正】句用不定詞to apply的理由如上。

7-50. **青少年應該擁有自己做決定的自由。**

【正】：Teenagers should be given the freedom *to make* their own decisions.

【誤】：Teenagers should be given the freedom *for making* their own decisions.

7-51. **參加這項考試，對測試學生的英文程度很重要。**

【正】：Taking the test is important *for testing* the English language level of a student.

【誤】：Taking the test is important *to test* the English language level of a student.

【解說】：【正】句的important for表「對……很重要」之意；如果用不定詞表示目的，邏輯不通。

7-52. **對開進市中心車輛課徵特別稅，在降低交通擁擠來說，是個好政策。**

【正】：Imposing a special tax on vehicles driven into the city center is a good policy for reducing traffic congestion.

【誤】：Imposing a special tax on vehicles driven into the city center is a good policy *to reduce* traffic congestion.

【解說】：【誤】句用不定詞to reduce表目的，邏輯不通。如果要用不定詞to reduce，全句要改成：The purpose of this policy is to reduce traffic congestion. 但與原句意思不同。

第七章 練習題

選擇題：下列各題，請選出一個或兩個正確答案。

（　）1. 我們在半夜聽到呼救的尖叫聲。（請參考**7-3**）

ⓐ We heard a scream for help in the middle of the night.

ⓑ We heard a scream for help at midnight.

ⓒ We heard a scream for help in midnight.

ⓓ We heard a scream for help on midnight.

（　）2. 這部戰爭片將於聖誕節上映。（請參考**7-7**）

ⓐ The war movie will be shown on Christmas.

ⓑ The war movie will be shown in Christmas.

ⓒ The war movie will be shown at Christmas.

ⓓ The war movie will be shown during Christmas.

（　）3. 他數學差，但擅長英文。（請參考**7-5**）

ⓐ He is weak in mathematics, but good at English.

ⓑ He is weak at mathematics, but good in English.

ⓒ He is bad in mathematics, but good at English.

ⓓ He is bad at mathematics, but good in English.

（　）4. 海倫考試作弊，老師在卷子上打了零分。（請參考**7-6**）

ⓐ The teacher put a zero on Helen's paper because she cheated in the exam.

ⓐ The teacher put a zero in Helen's paper because she cheated on the exam.

ⓑ The teacher put zero on Helen's paper because she cheated

in the exam.

c The teacher put zero on Helen's paper because she cheated on the exam.

( ) 5. 你們要注意把所聽到的每一個字都記錄下來。（請參考**7-10**）

a You should pay attention to put down every word you hear.

b You should pay attention to putting down every word you hear.

c You should pay attention to write down every word you hear.

d You should pay attention to writing down every word you hear.

( ) 6. 這個小偷承認偷了我的車子。（請參考**7-12**）

a The thief admitted that he stole my car.

b The thief admitted to steal my car.

c The thief admitted to stealing my car.

d The thief admitted that he had stolen my car.

( ) 7. 擴大詞彙量是精通英文的第一步驟。（請參考**7-14**）

a Enlarging your vocabulary is the first step to master English.

b Enlarging your vocabulary is the first step to mastering English.

c Increasing your vocabulary is the first step to mastering English.

d Increasing your vocabulary is the first step to master English.

( ) 8. 定期保養是讓你的車子免於拋錨的關鍵。（請參考**7-20**）

a Regular maintenance is key to keep your car running.

b Regular maintenance is key to keeping your car running.

c Regular maintenance is the key to keep your car running.

d Regular maintenance is the key to keeping your car running.

（　）9. 做生意要想成功沒有捷徑。（請參考**7-21**）

ⓐ There is no shortcut to achieve success in business.

ⓑ There is no shortcut to achieving success in business.

ⓒ There is no royal road to achieve success in business.

ⓓ There is no royal road to achieving success in business.

（　）10. 青少年不適宜喝酒。（請參考**7-24**）

ⓐ Teenagers are not suitable for drinking alcohol.

ⓑ Teenagers are not suited to drink alcohol.

ⓒ Teenagers are not suited to drinking alcohol.

ⓓ Teenagers are not suitable to drink alcohol.

（　）11. 水對種植這些熱帶作物是必不可少的。（請參考**7-26**）

ⓐ Water is essential to growing these tropical crops.

ⓑ Water is essential to grow these tropical crops.

ⓒ Water is essential for growing these tropical crops.

ⓓ Water is essential in growing these tropical crops.

（　）12. 學生住在校園有許多優點。（請參考**7-33**）

ⓐ There are many advantages for students to live on campus.

ⓑ There are many advantages to students living on campus.

ⓒ There are many advantages of students living on campus.

ⓓ There are many advantages if students live on campus.

（　）13. 市政府已計畫新蓋三所中學。（請參考**7-38**）

ⓐ The city government has planned to build three new high schools.

ⓑ The city government has planned to build up three new high schools.

ⓒ The city government has planned to construct three new high schools.

d The city government has planned to develop three new high schools.

( ) 14. 你的文章還不錯，只是有幾個拼寫錯誤。（請參考**7-39**）

a Your essay is not bad except for a few spelling mistakes.

b Your essay is not bad except a few spelling mistakes.

c Your essay is not bad besides a few spelling mistakes.

d Your essay is not bad except that you have a few spelling mistakes.

( ) 15. 這所學校留給我不可磨滅的印象。（請參考**7-43**）

a The school made an enduring impression on me.

b The school left an enduring impression on me.

c The school left me an enduring impression.

d The school left an enduring impression to me.

( ) 16. 你應該尋求不同方法來解決此問題。（請參考**7-44**）

a You should look for different methods to solve the problem.

b You should seek for different methods to solve the problem.

c You should search for different methods to solve the problem.

d You should search different methods to solve the problem.

( ) 17. 父母親對我們很嚴格。（請參考**7-45**）

a Our parents are strict to us.

b Our parents are strict with us.

c Our parents are hard with us.

d Our parents are hard on us.

( ) 18. 該市為了舒緩交通擁擠，決定對開進市中心的車子徵收特別

税。（請參考**7-51**）

ⓐ The city has decided to impose a special tax on vehicles driven into the city centre for easing traffic congestion.

ⓑ The city has decided to impose a special tax on vehicles driven into the city centre to ease traffic congestion.

ⓒ The city has decided to levy a special tax on vehicles driving into the city centre for easing traffic jams.

ⓓ The city has decided to levy a special tax on vehicles driving into the city centre to ease traffic jam.

※解答請見P.295

第八章

誤用形容詞
造成的中式英文

本章重點：

一、修飾語誤置（misplaced modifier）

二、表示必要性或迫切性的形容詞

三、修飾「人」或「事物」的形容詞

四、人稱代名詞＋形容詞

五、幾個容易誤用的形容詞／形容詞片語

一、修飾語誤置（misplaced modifier）

英文的修飾語，應該離被修飾的字詞越近越好，不能由中文逐譯，否則會造成邏輯不通或意思不清的結果。但是如果句子不長，修飾語簡短，不會造成語意不清，則置於句尾亦可，如8-1，8-2，8-3。以下是學生習作的錯誤例子：

8-1.　現今越來越多的人意識到健康的重要，包括我在內。

【正一】：Nowadays, more and more people, including me, are starting to realize the importance of staying healthy.

【正二】：Nowadays, more and more people are starting to realize the importance of staying healthy, including me.

8-2.　在非洲，很多人患營養不良症，尤其小孩。

【正一】：Many people in Africa suffer from undernourishment, especially children.

【正二】：Many people in Africa, especially children, suffer from malnutrition.

【解說】：「患營養不良症」說suffer from malnutrition/ undernourishment均可。

8-3.　絕大多數的駕駛人不知道超速的嚴重後果，尤其是十八歲以下的人。

【正一】：The majority of drivers, especially those under 18, do not understand the serious consequences that speeding can have.

【正二】：The majority of drivers do not understand the serious consequences of speeding, especially those under 18.

8-4. **現今穿戴名牌產品是一種社會地位的象徵，就像香奈兒服飾、愛馬仕皮帶等等。**

【正】：Nowadays, wearing brand-name products, such as Channel clothes and Hermes belts, is a sign of social status.

【不佳】：Nowadays, wearing brand-name products is a sign of social status, such as Channel clothes, Hermes belts and so on.

【解說】：

(1) such as所連接的片語，是修飾brand-name products，所以要置於其後。【不佳】句將它置於句尾，是由中文逐譯過來的結果，宜避免。

(2)用such as舉例時，後面不可接and so on。

8-5. **現今越來越多的人選擇三十出頭結婚、生子。**

【正】：Nowadays, more and more people are choosing to get married and have their children when they are in their 30's.

【誤】：Nowadays, more and more people are choosing to get married and have their children in their 30's.

【解說】：【誤】句中的in their 30's置於children之後變得邏輯不通，因為哪有小孩子會三十多歲的？正確的說法可在in their 30's前加上when they are。

8-6. **三十多歲的人比二十多歲的人成熟，錢也賺得比較多。**

【正】：People in their 30's are more mature and are likely to earn more money than people in their 20's.

【誤】：People are more mature and are likely to earn more money in their 30's than people in their 20's.

【解說】：【誤】句中的in their 30's是修飾主詞people，所以應置於people之後。

8-7.　**全班同學都無法解答的一道數學題，當老師叫他幫忙，他一分鐘就想出來了。**

　　【正】：When the teacher asked him to work out a difficult math question that no one else in his class could figure out, he did it in one minute.

　　【誤】：When the teacher asked him to work out a difficult math question that no one else could figure out in his class, he did it in one minute.

　　【解說】：【誤】句中的in his class是修飾no one else的，所以應該緊接一起，不要被could figure out分開。

8-8.　**由於現代電腦效率高，已經取代了許多用手操作的例行工作。**

　　【正】：Thanks to their high efficiency, modern computers have taken over many routine tasks done by human labor.

　　【誤】：Modern computers have taken over many routine tasks done by human labor, thanks to their high efficiency.

　　【解說】：【誤】句中的thanks to their high efficiency修飾主詞computers，所以應置於句首。置於句尾的問題出在thanks to their high efficiency中的their指涉不清。

8-9.　**我們必須開發新科技來降低污染，以便更有效的保護環境。**

　　【正】：In order to effectively protect the environment, we need to develop new technologies to reduce pollution.

　　【誤】：We need to develop new technologies to reduce pollution in order to effectively protect the environment.

　　【解說】：in order to所引導的不定詞片語，是用來修飾主句中的主詞we，所以要置於句首。

8-10.　**很多不是當地居民的人，在外國擁有房子和車子等財產。**

　　【正】：Many people who are non-residents own property, such as

houses and cars, in foreign countries.

【誤】：Many people who are non-residents own property in foreign countries such as houses and cars.

【解說】：such as houses and cars是修飾property的，所以應置於其後。

8-11. **由於人口快速增加，過去十年來,消費者對農產品與肉類等食物的需求急遽上升。**

【正】：Due to a rapid increase in population, consumer demands for food, such as produce and meat, have risen dramatically over the past ten years.

【誤】：Due to a rapid increase in population, consumers' demand on food has risen dramatically in the past ten years such as produce and meat.

【解說】：

(1)作「需求」解時，demand後接介系詞for；作「要求」解時，demand後接on。例：a demand for skilled workers（對熟練技工的需求）／Doing it places a great demand on my time.（做此事需要花我許多時間）。

(2)「消費者需求」要說consumer demands，就像「消費者信心」說consumer confidence一樣的複合名詞，不用所有格形容詞consumers'。

(3) such as produce and meat是修飾food的，要置於其後。【誤】句將其置於句尾，成為修飾語誤置，是許多人易犯的錯誤。

(4)「過去十年來」可說over/ during the past ten years，介系詞不能用in，另外，動詞要用現在完成式。

8-12. **毫無疑問，大部分父母都希望子女能接受大學教育。**

【正】：Most parents hope, without a doubt, that their children will get a college education.

【誤】：Most parents hope that their children will get a college education without a doubt.

【解說】：「毫無疑問」說without a doubt或without doubt均可，在本句是用來修飾hope，所以要置於hope之後。

8-13. 假如一個三口之家去中餐館吃晚餐，加上稅金和小費，他們可能要花上七十美金。

【正】：If a family of three goes to a Chinese restaurant for supper, they may have to spend around US$70, including taxes and tips.

【誤】：If a three-people family goes to a Chinese restaurant for a supper, plus taxes and tips they may have to spend around US$70.

【解說】：

(1)「一個三口之家」不能直譯成a three-people family，要說a family of three（people）。

(2) supper, lunch, breakfast前均不用冠詞。

(3)【誤】句中的plus要改成including，而且including taxes and tips要置於US$70之後。

8-14. 解決市中心交通擁擠問題，政府不該全面禁止鬧區行車，而是要採取適當措施，例如：改善公共交通設施與限制進入市區的車輛。

【正】：To solve the traffic congestion problems in downtown areas, the government should take proper measures, such as improving public transportation facilities and limiting the vehicles that come downtown, instead of banning the use of vehicles downtown.

【誤】：To solve the traffic congestion problems in downtown areas, the government should take proper measures instead of banning the use of vehicles to downtown. For instance,

improving public transportation facilities and limiting the
vehicles that come into downtown.

【解說】：

(1) such as所引導的舉例用的片語such as improving public
transportation... 用來說明措施(measures)，因此必須置於take
proper measures之後，語義才連貫得起來。而且，For instance後
應該接句子，不接片語。

(2) banning the use of vehicles to downtown中的to要刪去。

(3) limiting the vehicles that come into downtown中的into也要刪去，因
為downtown在此是副詞。

8-15. 很多人喜歡買像炸薯條、可樂、漢堡等速食供作派對上食用。

【正】：Many people like to buy junk food, such as fries, cola, and
hamburgers, to serve at their parties.

【不佳】：Many people like to buy junk food to serve at their parties,
such as fries, cola and hamburgers.

【解說】：such as fries, cola, and hamburgers是用來修飾junk food的，
所以要避免置於句尾。

二、表示必要性或迫切性的形容詞

一些表必要性或迫切性的形容詞，例如necessary, important, vital,
essential, urgent, advisable, mandatory 等等，句中that引導的子句要用簡單
式，因為should省略之故，例：

8-16. 每個人都應該有權選擇在何處接受教育，此事至關重要。

【正】：It is *important* that everyone *have the right* to choose where
they want to be educated.

【誤】：It is *important* that everyone *has the right* to choose where
they want to be educated.

【解說】：【正】句用have the right，因為have 前省略should。

8-17. **一個人終身為同一公司做事非明智之舉。**

【正】：It is not *advisable* that a person *work* for the same company all his/her life.

【誤】：It is not *advisable* that a person *works* in the same company all of his/her life.

【解說】：

(1)【正】句的work不加-s，是因為前面省去should。

(2)「在某公司工作」說work for或work at，介系詞不能用in。

(3) all his life和all of his life 均正確。

8-18. **員工上班時心情好很重要。**

【正】：It is *essential* that workers *be* in a good mood when working.

【誤】：It is *essential* that workers *have* a good mood when working.

【解說】：【誤】句have不對，是因為「心情好」要說be in a good mood，不能說have a good mood。

8-19. **高速公路速限絕對不該解除。**

【正】：It is *vital* that speed limits not *be* removed from the highways.

【誤】：It is *vital* that speed limits *are* not removed from the highways.

【解說】：【正】句的not be removed 前省去should。

8-20. **人人都能接受教育，此事非常重要。**

【正】：It is *necessary* that every individual *get* an education.

【誤】：It is *necessary* that every individual *gets* an education.

【解說】：【正】句的get前省去should。

8-21. **對於一個發展中的國家來說，擁有充足的廉價勞動力至關重要。**

【正】：It is *mandatory* that a developing country *have* sufficient labor at a low cost.

【誤】：It is ***mandatory*** that a developing country ***has*** sufficient workers with a low cost of labor.

【解說】：【正】句的have前省去should。

三、修飾「人」或「事物」的形容詞

a)「人」＋ed，「事物」＋ing

　　過去分詞用於修飾「人」，例如：I am interested in playing tennis. 現在分詞用於修飾「事物」，例如：Playing tennis is interesting. 這是最簡單的規則，學生一般不會有問題。常見的例子還有：frightened / frightening, excited / exciting, frustrated / frustrating, embarrassed / embarrassing等等。

　　以下四種修飾「事物」的形容詞是學生習作時常犯的錯誤。

b)「人」＋ed，「事物」＋ful

8-22. 考試這麼多，我感受到壓力。

　　【正一】：Having so many exams, I feel ***stressed***.

　　【正二】：Having so many exams is ***stressful***.

　　【誤】：Having so many exams, I feel ***stressful***.

8-23. 醫師每天要面對許多痛苦的病人。

　　【正】：Doctors have to face many patients ***in pain*** every day.

　　【誤】：Doctors have to face many ***painful*** patients every day.

　　【解說】：「痛苦的病人」要說patients in pain，不能說painful patients，因為painful用來修飾事物，例如：「托福考了五次不及格，對我是個痛苦的經驗」要說 Failing the TOEFL test five times is a painful experience for me.

c)「人」＋ed，「事物」＋ive

8-24. **他看電視上癮。**

He is addicted to watching TV.

8-25. **看電視容易上癮。**

Watching TV is addictive.

d)「人」＋ed，「事物」＋tory

8-26. **我對考試結果感到滿意。**

I am satisfied with the test results.

8-27. **考試結果似乎令人滿意。**

The test results seem to be satisfactory.

e)「人」＋介系詞或介系詞片語，「事物」＋ful / ous

8-28. **我非常痛苦。**
【正】：I am *in* great *pain*.
【誤】：I am very *painful*.
【解說】：painful 修飾「事物」，例：a painful experience/ a painful wound。

8-29. **病人現在已脫離險境了。**
【正】：The patient is *out of* danger now.
【誤】：The patient is not *dangerous* now.
【解說】：dangerous用於修飾「事物」，例：The tiger is dangerous/ It is dangerous to approach the tiger.

四、人稱代名詞＋形容詞

　　某些形容詞或形容詞片語，要以「人」當主詞，學生受中文思維的影響，容易以「事物」為主詞，而造成邏輯不通，這也屬於中式英文，舉例如下。

8-30.　在現代社會，大部分人的生活比以前忙碌。
　　【正】：In modern society, most people are busier than they were previously.
　　【不佳】：In modern society, most people's lives are busier than they were previously.
　　【解說】：be busy要以「人」當主詞，避免以lives當主詞。「我生活忙碌」要說I am busy，避免說My life is busy。

8-31.　他飲食喝酒都很節制。
　　【正】：He is temperate both in eating and drinking.
　　【誤】：His eating and drinking are temperate.
　　【解說】：be temperate in要以「人」當主詞，「人」才能節制，eating and drinking不能。

8-32.　他游泳比我好很多。
　　【正】：He is head and shoulders above me in swimming.
　　【誤】：His swimming is head and shoulders above me.
　　【解說】：be head and shoulders above others in... 意為「……方面比別人好很多」，一定要以「人」當主詞，【誤】句以swimming當主詞不通。

8-33.　跟這些人打交道要小心。
　　【正】：You should be careful in dealing with these people.
　　【誤】：Dealing with these people should be careful.

【解說】：「人」才能be careful；【誤】句顯然由中文逐譯，以動名詞dealing with... 當主詞，而造成的以「事物」為主詞。注意：【正】句的主詞也可用we/ a person。造成這種錯誤，主要在於中文句子省略主詞，英譯時要補上，例如「過馬路時要小心」不能直譯成Crossing the street should be careful. 應該把主詞補上：We/You should be careful when crossing the street.

8-34. **獨自學習較能專注於我的課業。**
　　【正一】：I can be more focused on my work when studying on my own.
　　【正二】：Studying alone, I can be more focused on my work.
　　【誤】：Studying on my own can be more focused on my work.
　　【解說】：be focused on要以「人」當主詞；【誤】句與上句一樣，以動名詞studying on my own當主詞，造成以「事物」為主詞的錯誤。

五、幾個容易誤用的形容詞 / 形容詞片語

a）compared / comparing
　　用現在分詞comparing時，後面一定要接兩個被比較的人或事，例：

8-35. **比較Tom和Peter後，我發現Tom較為聰明。**
　　【正】：*Comparing* Tom and Peter, I have found that Tom is smarter.
　　【誤】：*Compared* Tom and Peter, I have found that Tom is smarter.
　　【解說】：【正】句的現在分詞comparing後面接兩個被比較的Tom和Peter。

8-36. **比較獨自做功課和一群人一起做，我寧願獨自做。**
　　【正】：*Comparing* doing assignments alone or in a group, I prefer doing the former.

【誤】：***Compared*** doing assignments alone or in a group, I prefer doing the former.

【解說】：【正】句的現在分詞comparing後面接兩個被比較的doing assignments alone或in a group。

8-37. **和妹妹比起來，Helen比較高。**

【正】：***Compared*** with her sister, Helen is taller.

【誤】：***Comparing*** with her sister, Helen is taller.

【解說】：【誤】句錯誤，因為comparing後面沒有兩個被比較的人。
　　　　　【正】句的compared前省去When she is。

8-38. **和二十出頭的人比起來，三十幾歲的人因為收入穩定，當父母比較稱職。**

【正】：***Compared with*** people in their 20's, people in their 30's make better parents because they have a stable income.

【誤】：***Comparing with*** people in their 20's, people in their 30's make better parents because they have a stable income.

【解說】：【誤】句錯誤，因為comparing後面沒有兩個被比較的人。

8-39. **與當醫生比起來，我寧願做個平凡的公司員工，因為壓力較小。**

【正】：***Compared with*** being a doctor, being an ordinary employee in a company is better because I would be under less pressure.

【誤】：***Comparing with*** being a doctor, being an ordinary employee in a company is better because I would be under less pressure.

【解說】：【誤】句錯誤，因為comparing後面沒有兩個被比較的人。

8-40. **教育是通往成功的快捷方式；接受過良好教育的人比未受過教育的人更可能成功。**

【正】：Acquiring an education is a shortcut to success; a well-educated person is *more* likely to succeed *than* those people who do not have an education.

【誤】：Education is the shortcut to succeed; a well-educated person is more likely to succeed *compared to* those who do not have an education.

【解說】：

(1)【誤】句以education當主詞，是受中文直譯的影響。以動名詞片語當主詞acquiring / getting / obtaining an education才合慣用法。

(2)「成功的快捷方式」說a shortcut to success。注意用不定冠詞a；另外，因為to是介系詞，所以後接名詞success。

(3)【誤】句中more likely... 後接compared to... 也是受中文直譯的影響，要改為than，注意more... than的連用法。要用compared to，前面不能有more / less / fewer等等的比較級用法，例：Canada's population is small compared to America's.

b）fewer / less

大家都知道，fewer接可數名詞，less接不可數名詞，但學生習作中，不管單數複數，都習慣用less，請看下例：

8-41. **由於人口大量增加，導致動物棲息地變少了。**

【正】：There are *fewer* places for animals to live because of the huge human population.

【誤】：There are *less* places for animals to live because of the huge human population.

8-42. **一個人若未接受大學教育，找好工作的機會就變少了。**

【正】：If a person does not receive a college education, he will have *fewer* opportunities to find a good job.

【誤】：If a person does not receive a college education, he will have *less* opportunity to find a good job.

8-43. **現在的年輕人不太重視書法，因為需要用筆書寫文件的機會不多。**

【正】：Today, young people pay little attention to their handwriting because they have *fewer* opportunities to handwrite their documents.

【誤】：Today, young people pay little attention to their handwriting because they have *less* chance to handwrite their documents.

8-44. **小城鎮交通擁擠情況比大都市要少。**

【正】：There are *fewer* traffic jams in a small town than in a big city.

【誤】：There are *less* traffic jams in a small town than in a big city.

8-45. **我希望本市賭場數量可以減少，這樣沉迷賭博的人就會變少。**

【正】：I hope that there will be *fewer* casinos in our city so that *fewer* people will be addicted to gambling.

【誤】：I hope that there will be *less* casinos in our city so that *less* people will be addicted to gambling.

8-46. **缺乏良好教育的人，擁有的專業技能就少了。**

【正】：People who lack a good education will have *fewer* professional skills.

【誤】：People who are lack of a good education will have *less* professional skills.

【解說】：【誤】句除了less要改成fewer之外，are lack of要改成lack，因為lack為及物動詞，這是非常普遍的錯誤。

8-47. 如果選美比賽被禁止，人們舒壓的途徑就變少了。

【正】：If beauty contests are banned, people will have *fewer* methods of relieving their pressure.

【誤】：If beauty contests are banned, people will have *less* methods of relieving their pressure.

8-48. 世界已變得比較和平，將來戰爭將會減少。

【正】：As the world has become more peaceful than it was before, there will be *fewer* wars in the future.

【誤】：As the world has become more peaceful than it was before, there will be *less* wars in the future.

c) most / most of

most用來修飾泛指的名詞，例：Most students hate examinations. most of用來修飾特指的名詞，例：Most of the students in our class hate examinations. 學生習作中，該用most，常誤用most of，例：

8-49. 大部分人超過六十五歲之後就會視力不好，反應遲鈍。

【正】：*Most* people have poor vision and slow reactions when they are over 65.

【誤】：*Most of* people have poor vision and slow reactions when they are over 65.

8-50. 雖然大部分人同意這個想法，有些人卻持不同觀點。

【正】：While *most* people agree with this idea, some people hold an opposite opinion.

【誤】：While *most of* people agree with this idea, some people hold an opposite opinion.

8-51. **現今大多數國家都強制國民接受教育。**

【正】：Today, *most* countries have a compulsory education requirement for their people.

【誤】：Today, *most of* countries have a compulsory education
requirement for their people.

8-52. **大多數男孩認為，愛吃甜食是女孩子氣的行為。**

【正】：*Most* boys think that eating dessert is a girlish behavior.

【誤】：*Most of* boys think that eating dessert is a girlish behavior.

8-53. **大部分人中了彩券後就辭去工作。**

【正】：*Most* people would stop working if they won the lottery.

【誤】：*Most of* people would stop working if they won the lottery.

8-54. **大部分醫療費用都很高。**

【正】：*Most* medical treatments cost a lot of money.

【誤】：*Most of* medical treatments cost a lot of money.

8-55. **如果大部分學生都在網上修課，教師失業率就會上升。**

【正】：If *most* students *chose* to study online, the teacher
unemployment rate *would* increase.

【誤】：If *most of* the students *choose* to study online, the teacher
unemployment rate *will* increase.

【解說】：【誤】句除了most of要改為most之外，動詞都要改成過去
式表假設語氣。

8-56. **當今，大部分工作要求具備大學學位。**

【正】：Nowadays, *most* jobs require applicants to have a college
degree.

【誤】：Nowadays, *most of* jobs require applicants to have a college degree.

但請注意：most of除開用來修飾特指的名詞外，也可接所有格形容詞＋名詞，例：

8-57. **我的大部分同學都已通過考試了。**

【正】：***Most of*** my classmates passed the exam.

【誤】：***Most*** my classmates passed the exam.

8-58. **大學生要把大部分時間花在學習上。**

【正】：College students have to spend ***most of*** their time studying.

【誤】：College students have to spend ***most*** their time studying.

d) be able to / be capable of

be able to要以「人」當主詞，be capable of則可以「人」當主詞，也可以「事物」當主詞，例：

8-59. **電子文件可以儲存在電腦裡。**

【正】：Electronic files are capable of being stored on the computer.

【誤】：Electronic files are able to be stored on the computer.

【解說】：【誤】句的主詞是electronic files，不是「人」，所以不能用be able to。

8-60. **他可以做辛苦的工作。**

【正】：He is able to do hard work.

【正】：He is capable of doing hard work.

【解說】：be able to和be capable of均可以「人」當主詞。

e）classic / classical

8-61. 這是一本有關封建制度的經典小說。

【正】：This is a classic novel on feudalism.

【誤】：This is a classical novel on feudalism.

【解說】：classic當形容詞用時，意為「經典的，最佳的」；當名詞用
時，意為（文學、藝術上的）「經典作品」，例：Milton's
Paradise Lost is a classic.（密爾頓的《失樂園》是一部經
典作品）。 classical只能當形容詞用，意為（文學、藝術、
音樂等方面）古典的、傳統的（以別於現代的、流行的），
例：classical music（古典音樂）/classical literature（古典
文學）。

f）historic / historical

8-62. 那場戰役在歷史上很有名。

【正】：That battle was historic.

【誤】：That battle was historical.

【解說】：historic與historical均為形容詞，但意思不同；historic指歷
史上有名、重要的，或有歷史性的，例：a historic event
（歷史性事件）/a historic site（史跡）/a historic trial（歷史
上著名的審判）。historical 意為「與歷史有關的、依據歷
史的、基於史實的」，例：a historical novel（歷史小說）
/a historical film（根據史實拍成的影片）。某些情況下，
historical與當形容詞用的history可通用，例如「歷史劇」可
說a historical play，也可說a history play。

g）automatic/voluntary

8-63. **我們大家都自動幫助這個窮人。**

【正】：All of us helped this poor man voluntarily.

【誤】：All of us helped this poor man automatically.

【解說】：

(1) automatic和voluntary都是「自動的」意思，但前者指「機器運轉的自動」，不必人工作業，例如：an automatic door（自動門）；後者指「人的內心自動自發」，不必旁人催促，所以本句「自動來幫助這個窮人」要用voluntarily。

(2) ATM（自動提款機）中的A是automated的縮寫，很多人誤寫為automatic。

h）economic/financial

8-64. **我們家遭遇經濟困難。**

【正】：Our family has run into *financial* difficulties.

【誤】：Our family has run into *economic* difficulties.

【解說】：financial有二解：

(1)財政上的，金融上的，例：financial ability（財力）/ financial circles（金融界）。

(2)經濟的，例：the financial situation of a family（家庭經濟狀況）。本句的「經濟困難」應屬於第二解，不能譯成economic。很多學生一看到「經濟的」就一律譯成economic，殊不知中文裡，如果指的是「金錢或財力」就要譯成financial。例如：「有經濟困難的學生可申請補助」要說：Students in financial difficulties may apply for subsidies. 句中不能用economic。

ⅰ) domestic/internal

8-65. **他們無權干涉我國內政。**

【正】：They have no right to interfere in our ***internal*** affairs .

【誤】：They have no right to interfere in our ***domestic*** affairs.

【解說】：internal和domestic都有「國內的」之意，但請注意下列習慣用法：「國內市場」是domestic market或home market，不是internal market；「國內航線」是domestic airlines，不是internal airlines；「國貨」是domestic products，不是internal products。「內政」是internal affairs，不是domestic affairs。

ⅰ) nutritional/ nutritious

8-66. **我想要一些有關鮭魚的營養資料。**

【正】：I would like to obtain some ***nutritional*** information about salmon.

【誤】：I would like to obtain some ***nutritious*** information about salmon.

【解說】：

(1) nutrition有兩個形容詞：nutritious意為「有營養的」，例：Beef is more nutritious than other meats.（牛肉比其他肉類有營養）。而 nutritional是「有關營養的」之意。這兩個形容詞容易混淆，就連西方人也常犯錯。

(2) salmon單複數同形，注意不加 "s"。類似不加 "s" 的動物有fish, deer, sheep等。

k) false/ fake

8-67. 我們都被那個假警報嚇壞了。

【正】：We were all scared by the ***false*** alarm.

【誤】：We were all scared by the ***fake*** alarm.

【解說】：fake可作動詞與形容詞用，是「偽造，變造」之意（make something seem real）。用來修飾具體的東西，例：a fake document（偽造文件）／a fake passport（假護照）／fake money（偽鈔）。false是「不真實的」（unreal, untrue）或「錯誤的，不正確的」（mistaken, incorrect）之意，用來修飾抽象的東西，例：a false alarm（假警報）／a false impression（錯誤的印象）。

l) dual/ double

8-68. 擁有雙重國籍，生意人飛遍全世界可節省很多時間。

【正】：Owning dual citizenship, business people can save a lot of time when flying around the world.

【誤】：Owning ***double*** citizenship, business people can save a lot of time when flying around the world.

【解說】：

(1)「雙重國籍」是dual citizenship或dual nationality，此處的「雙重」不能譯成double。請注意如下用法：dual personality（雙重人格）/ double agent（反間諜）／double standard（雙重標準）。

(2) when flying＝when they are flying。

第八章　練習題

選擇題：下列各題，請選出一個或兩個正確答案。

（　）1. 現今越來越多的國家都在廢除核電廠，包括德國在內。（請參考**8-1/ 8-3**）

　ⓐ Nowadays, more and more countries in the world, including Germany, are demolishing nuclear power plants.

　ⓑ Nowadays, more and more countries in the world are demolishing nuclear power plants, including Germany.

　ⓒ Nowadays, more and more countries, including Germany, in the world are demolishing nuclear power plants.

　ⓓ Nowadays, more and more countries in the world demolish nuclear power plants, including Germany.

（　）2. 很多西非人因為沒東西吃而餓死，尤其是小孩。（請參考**8-1/ 8-3**）

　ⓐ Many people in West Africa, especially children, have nothing to eat and die from hunger.

　ⓑ Many people in West Africa have nothing to eat and die from hunger, especially children.

　ⓒ Many people in West Africa, especially children, have nothing to eat and die of hunger.

　ⓓ Many people in West Africa have nothing to eat and die of hunger, especially children.

( ) 3. 許多人生病時才知道健康的可貴，尤其是年輕人。（請參考 **8-1/ 8-3**）

⓪ Many people do not realize the importance of health until they are sick, especially young people.

⓫ Many people seldom realized the importance of health until they got sick, especially young people.

⓬ Many people, especially youngsters, do not realize the importance of health until they are sick.

⓭ Many people, especially for youngsters, did not know the importance of health until they got sick.

( ) 4. 假如你買一部車，加上維修和汽油，一個月平均要花二千元。（請參考**8-13**）

⓪ If you buy a car, you may have to spend an average of $2000 per month, including maintenance and gas.

⓫ If you buy a car, plus maintenance and gas, you may have to spend an average of $2000 per month.

⓬ If you buy a car, coupling maintenance and gas, you may have to spend an average of $2000 per month.

⓭ If you buy a car, you may have to spend an average of $2000 per month, coupling with maintenance and gas.

( ) 5. 市政府應該為窮人多蓋平價住宅，此事至關重要。（請參考 **8-16**）

⓪ It is important that the city government builds more affordable housing for poor people.

⓫ It is important that the city government build more affordable housing for poor people.

⓬ It is important that the city government should build more affordable housing for poor people.

   ⓓ It is important that the city government has to build more affordable housing for poor people.

(   ) 6.   這項建築工程一周內一定要完成。（請參考**8-18**）

   ⓐ It is essential that the construction work should be finished in a week.

   ⓑ It is essential that the construction work be finished in a week.

   ⓒ It is essential that the construction work has to be finished in a week.

   ⓓ It is essential that the construction work is finished in a week.

(   ) 7.   穿越馬路一定要小心。（請參考**8-33**）

   ⓐ When you cross the street, you have to be careful.

   ⓑ Crossing the street must be careful.

   ⓒ You should be careful crossing the street.

   ⓓ You should be careful about crossing the street.

(   ) 8.   我自己獨居比較能專注功課。（請參考**8-34**）

   ⓐ Living by my own can be more focused on my studies.

   ⓑ Living on my own, I can be more focused on my studies.

   ⓒ If I live on my own, I will be more focused on my studies.

   ⓓ If I live by my own, I will be more focused on my studies.

(   ) 9.   比較當醫生和當科學家，我寧願當醫生。（請參考**8-35**）

   ⓐ Comparing being a doctor and a scientist, I prefer the former.

   ⓑ Compared being a doctor and a scientist, I prefer the former.

   ⓒ Compared being a doctor and a scientist, I prefer to be the former.

   ⓓ Comparing being a doctor and a scientist, I prefer being the former.

（　）10. 缺乏教書經驗的老師，找到工作的機會較小 。（請參考**8-41/ 8-48**）

ⓐ Teachers who are lack of teaching experience have fewer opportunities to find a job.

ⓑ Teachers who lack of teaching experience have less opportunities to find a job.

ⓒ Teachers who lack teaching experience have fewer opportunities to find a job.

ⓓ Teachers who lack teaching experience have less opportunities to find a job.

（　）11. 我們班上的大部分學生都來自富裕家庭。（請參考**8-49/ 8-56**）

ⓐ Most of the students in our class come from rich families.

ⓑ Most of students in our class come from rich families.

ⓒ Most students of our class come from rich families.

ⓓ Most of the students of our class come from rich families.

※解答請見P.295

第九章

誤用句型
造成的中式英文

本章重點：

一、雙名主詞

二、動詞句型think / find / make＋it＋形容詞

三、不能接受詞＋不定詞的動詞

四、形容詞句型

一、雙名主詞

中文句子裡，動詞之前使用兩個名詞很普遍，例如「我胃疼」中的「我」和「胃」兩個名詞。這種雙主詞，語言學家把「胃」視為「主詞」，把「我」視為「主題」（topic）。這種主題＋主詞的句式譯成英文時，應避免出現所有格形容詞my / your / his等字，而要用「主詞＋動詞」的句式譯出，請看下例：

9-1. **我胃疼。**

【正】：I have a stomachache.

【誤】：My stomach is painful.

【解說】：中文裡這種「主題＋主詞」的句式很多，例如：我喉嚨痛／我肚子餓／他習慣不好／他身體健康。這些句子如果以所有格形容詞my / your / his開頭譯出，就會出現My throat is painful. / My stomach is hungry. / His habit is bad. / His body is healthy. 等錯誤句子。正確的說法要以「主詞＋動詞的句式譯出：I have a sore throat. / I am hungry./ He has bad habits. / He is healthy.

9-2. **湯姆的蛀牙昨天拔掉了。**

【正】：Tom had his decayed tooth pulled out yesterday.

【誤】：Tom's decayed tooth was pulled out yesterday.

9-3. **你鞋帶鬆了。**

【正】：You have a loose shoelace.

【誤】：Your shoelace is loose.

9-4. 這個病人呼吸困難。

【正】：The patient has difficulty breathing.

【誤】：The patient's breathing is difficult.

9-5. 我脖子僵硬。

【正】：I have a stiff neck.

【不佳】：My neck is stiff.

9-6. 他英文比我好很多。

【正】：He is head and shoulders above me in English.

【誤】：His English is head and shoulders above me.

【解說】：be head and shoulders above是「勝過，優於」之意，要以「人」當主詞。

9-7. 這小女孩嘴巴很甜。

【正】：The little girl has a sweet tongue.

【誤】：The little girl's mouth is sweet.

9-8. 每個人的作息都不同。

【正】：Everyone has a different daily routine.

【誤】：Everyone's daily routine is different.

9-9. 我心情不好。

【正一】：I am not in a good mood.

【正二】：I am in a bad mood.

【誤】：My mood is not good.

9-10. 他工作態度很好。

【正】：He has a good work attitude.

【誤】：His working attitude is good.

【不佳】：His work attitude is good.

【解說】：「工作態度」是work attitude，這種雙名詞片語第一個名詞當形容詞用，類似例子如：success story, adventure story, danger period, safety standard, work experience, work efficiency等等。

9-11. **我輪胎爆胎了。**

【正】：I had a flat tire.

【誤】：My tire was blown up.

9-12. **他脾氣不好。**

【正】：He has a hot/ short/ bad temper.

【不佳】：His temper is bad.

9-13. **他的職業是醫生。**

【正】：He is a physician by occupation.

【誤】：His occupation is a physician.

【解說】：「以……為業」要說be... by occupation。【誤】句顯然是由中文逐譯造成的中式英文。

二、動詞句型think/ find/ make＋it＋形容詞

英文動詞有一種句型習慣以it當先行受詞，後面接不定詞，再接easy/ hard/ difficult/ possible/ impossible/ important/ necessary等形容詞。這個it是指代後面的不定詞to do。學生容易犯錯的原因是，中文習慣以「人」當受詞，例如：「使用電腦，這項工作在十分鐘之內我就輕易完成了。」要說The computer made *it* easy for me to finish the job in ten minutes.如果按照中文直譯成The computer made *me* easy to finish the job in ten minutes. 就是中式英文了，這種錯誤非常普遍。以下是學生習作的錯誤例子：

9-14. **擁有部落格能夠更方便讓人們結交新朋友。**

【正】：Having a blog *makes it* easier for people to make new friends.

【誤一】：Having a blog *makes people* more easily to make new friends.

【誤二】：Having a blog is easy for people to make new friends.

【解說】：「讓人們能夠……」或「方便人們……」要說make it easy（或possible）for somebody to do something，不能直譯成 make people more easily to do something。

9-15. **速食含有大量油脂，很容易使人體重增加。**

【正】：Fast food contains a large amount of fat which makes *it* easy for people to gain weight.

【誤】：Fast food includes a large amount of fat which makes *people* easy to gain weight.

【解說】：

(1)「含有」要說contain，不用include。

(2)「使……易於」要說make it easy for somebody to do something，不能說make somebody easy to do something。

注意：【正】句中的it指後面的不定詞片語。

9-16. **全面資助學院和大學可以讓學生更容易接受大學教育。**

【正】：Fully funding colleges and universities makes *it* easier for students to receive a college education.

【誤】：Fully funding colleges and universities makes *students* easier to receive a college education.

【解說】：中文說「讓學生更容易接受……」，英文不能直譯成make students easier to receive... 而要說make it easier for students to receive... 這裡的it指代後面的不定詞片語for students to receive...。

9-17. 罪犯使用變造身分會使員警難以逮捕他們。

【正】：When criminals use fake identities, they will make *it* difficult for the police to catch them.

【誤】：When criminals use changed identities, they will make *the police* difficult to catch them.

【解說】：

(1)「變造身分」就是「假身分」，英文叫fake identity，不能直譯成changed identity。

(2)使「員警難以追捕」不能直譯成make the police difficult to catch...，應該說make it difficult for the police to catch...。

9-18. 把瀕臨絕種的動物圈養在動物園裡，會使他們無法培養基本的生存技能。

【正】：Keeping endangered animals in zoos makes *it* impossible for them to develop their basic survival skills.

【誤】：Keeping endangered animals in zoos makes *them* impossible to develop basic surviving skills.

【解說】：

(1)「使他們無法……」直譯成make them impossible to... 不符合英文慣用法。就像上一句一樣，一定要說make it impossible/difficult/easy for somebody to do something，這句構的it為先行受詞，後面的不定詞片語for somebody to develop... 才是真受詞。

(2)「生存技能」要說survival skills，不是surviving skills，這種用法屬複合名詞，第一個名詞在此當形容詞用。

9-19. 有了飛機，人們能夠在短期內環遊世界。

【正】：Airplanes *make it possible* for people to travel around the world in a short period of time.

【誤】：Airplanes *make people possible* to travel around the world in a short period of time.

【解說】：【正】句的it指代後面的不定詞片語。注意：【正】句的make it possible for people to travel... 亦可說allow或enable people to travel... 這個句型非常好用，讀者可多加仿習。

9-20. **網際網路使得人們購物和付帳單更加方便。**
【正】：The Internet *makes it* easy for people to purchase goods and pay their bills.
【誤】：The Internet *makes people* easy to purchase goods and pay their bills.
【解說】：【誤】句錯誤和上句一樣，以people當make的受詞。

9-21. **工作一天之後，我覺得有必要好好休息。**
【正】：After working all day, I *found it necessary to have* a good rest.
【誤】：After working all day, I found having a good rest is necessary.
【解說】：【正】句的it代替後面的不定詞*to have* a good rest。【誤】句有兩個動詞；即使把is刪去而成：I found having a good rest necessary也不合慣用法。

9-22. **他缺乏專業知識，使他無法找到好工作。**
【正】：His lack of professional knowledge *makes it impossible* for him *to find* a good job.
【誤】：His lack of professional knowledge *makes him impossible* to find a good job.
【解說】：【正】句的it指代後面的不定詞片語*to find a good job*。

9-23. **我們都知道，大部分青少年心智不成熟，這使得他們難以避免做傻事。**
【正】：As we know, most teenagers are not mentally mature. This makes *it* hard for them to avoid doing stupid things.
【誤】：As we know, most teenagers are not mentally mature. This makes *them* hard to avoid doing stupid things.

【解說】：與上題一樣，「使得他們難以……」直譯成make them hard to... 不合英文慣用法，要說make it hard for them to...。

9-24. **我相信假如太太賺的錢比先生多，這會使他們難以維持良好的夫妻關係。**

【正】：I believe if the wife makes more money than the husband, this will make *it* difficult for them to maintain a good relationship.

【誤】：I believe if the wife makes more money than the husband, this will make *them* difficult to maintain a good relationship.

9-25. **吸毒容易讓人上癮。**

【正】：Doing drugs makes *it* easy for people to get addicted.

【誤】：Doing drugs makes *people* easy to get addicted.

三、不能接受詞＋不定詞的動詞

英文大部分及物動詞都可接受詞＋不定詞，例：The manager wants John to come on time. / My father told me to wait. 但是有些動詞只能接受詞，不能接受詞＋不定詞。以下是學生習作常犯的錯誤。

9-26. **缺乏與人溝通的能力影響我交朋友。**

【正一】：My inability to communicate with other people prevents me from making friends.

【正二】：My inability to communicate with other people *affects me* adversely *in* making friends.

【誤】：My inability to communicate with other people *affects me to make* friends.

【解說】：【誤】句中的affect只能接名詞，不能接「人」再接不定詞。

9-27. **資助學生上大學有許多方式。**

【正一】：There are many ways to support students who want to obtain a college education.

【正二】：There are many ways to **support** students in **obtaining** a college education.

【誤】：There are many ways to **support** students **to obtain** a college education.

【解說】：support後面只能接名詞，不能接「人」再接不定詞。請注意，college education前面一定要用不定冠詞a。

9-28. **現在大部分家長都希望子女能夠進入好大學。**

【正】：Nowadays, most parents **hope that** their children will enter a good university.

【誤】：Nowadays, most parents **hope their children to enter** a good university.

【解說】：hope後面不接受詞＋不定詞，例：【正】I hope that you will live on campus.／【誤】I hope you to live on campus.

9-29. **我們已通知他明天來開會。**

【正】：We have **informed** him **that** he should attend the meeting tomorrow.

【誤】：We have **informed him to** attend the meeting tomorrow.

【解說】：

(1) inform後可接受詞＋that clause，但不能接受詞＋不定詞。【誤】句顯然是按照中文句型逐譯而來的。

(2)【誤】句的informed如改成asked就算正確（ask somebody to do something是正確的句型），但意思不同。

9-30. **他堅持我要跟他一起去。**

【正】：He **insisted that** I go with him.

【誤】：He ***insisted on me to*** go with him.

【解說】：

(1) insist後可接that clause，但不能用insist on＋受詞＋不定詞。

(2)注意：【正】句亦可改成：He ***insisted on my*** going with him.

9-31. 他父親建議他主修化學。

【正】：His father ***suggested that*** he major in chemistry.

【誤】：His father ***suggested him to*** major in chemistry.

【解說】：

(1) suggest後面可接名詞、動名詞或名詞子句，但不能接受詞＋不定詞，例如不可說：I suggested her to make a choice. 應該說I suggested that she（should）make a choice.

(2)類似suggest的動詞有recommend, propose, require, demand, insist, request, urge, order等等。

9-32. 我媽媽大聲叫我去做功課。

【正】：My mother ***yelled at*** me, telling me to do my homework.

【誤】：My mother ***yelled me to*** do my homework.

【解說】：yell習慣與at連用，絕對不能接受詞＋不定詞。【誤】句顯然是由中文直譯造成的中式英文。

四、形容詞句型

a）形容詞＋介系詞＋動名詞

9-33. 我有信心通過考試。

【正】：I am ***confident of*** passing the examination.

【誤】：I am ***confident to*** pass the examination.

【解說】：

(1)「對……有信心」要說be confident of或be confident that.【正】句

亦可說：I am confident *that* I will pass the examination.

(2) be confident 後不能接不定詞。

(3) be confident也可接in，例： I am confident *in* him.

9-34. 這公車可以載四十個乘客。

【正】：The bus is *capable of carrying* 40 passengers.

【誤】：The bus is *capable to* carry 40 passengers.

【解說】：

(1) be capable 與of連用，不能接不定詞。

(2)注意本句不能說：The bus is able to carry 40 passengers. 因為be able to要以「人」當主詞。

9-35. 父母教育小孩要有耐心。

【正】：Parents should be *patient in* teaching their children.

【誤】：Parents should be *patient to* teach their children.

【解說】：be patient不接不定詞，可接in＋動名詞；如果接名詞時，介系詞可用with，例：Parents should be patient *with* their children.

b）形容詞＋of＋受詞＋不定詞

9-36. 你真好，來為我送行。

【正】：It is very *kind of you to come* to see me off.

【誤】：It is very *kind for you to come* to see me off.

【解說】：

(1)這種句型都以it作為形式主詞代替句後的不定詞，注意介系詞一定用*of*，不能用*for*。

(2)這種形容詞除了kind之外，還有*brave, clever, considerate, nice, sweet , polite, wise*等等表稱讚的字詞。

9-37. **你沒把門上鎖，實在是太粗心了。**

【正】：It was *careless of you to leave* the door unlocked.

【誤】：It was *careless for you to leave* the door unlocked.

【解說】：這種句型與上句一樣，介系詞一定要用of，不能用for。唯一不同的是，這類形容詞都是表責備的字詞，除了careless之外，還有thoughtless, selfish, stupid, inconsiderate, rush, impudent等等。

第九章　練習題

選擇題：下列各題，請選出一個或兩個正確答案。

（　　）1.　他左腳是跛的。（請參考**9-1**）
　　ⓐ His left leg is lame.
　　ⓑ He is lame in the left leg.
　　ⓒ He is lame of the left leg.
　　ⓓ His left leg has a lame leg.

（　　）2.　露西上星期把頭髮剪光了。（請參考**9-2**）
　　ⓐ Lucy's all her hairs cut off last week.
　　ⓑ Lucy cut all of her hair last week.
　　ⓒ Lucy had all her hair cut off last week.
　　ⓓ Lucy cut all her hair last week.

（　　）3.　瑪麗的功課比班上的同學好很多。（請參考**9-6**）
　　ⓐ Mary's performance in class is head and shoulders above the class.
　　ⓑ Mary is head and shoulders above the rest of her class.
　　ⓒ Mary's exercise is head and shoulder above her class.
　　ⓓ Mary's homework is head and shoulder above her classmates.

（　　）4.　該嫌疑犯的職業是工業工程師。（請參考**9-13**）
　　ⓐ The suspect's occupation is an IE engineer.
　　ⓑ The job of the suspect is an IE engineer.
　　ⓒ The suspect is an IE engineer by occupation.
　　ⓓ The suspect is an IE engineer by profession.

（　）5.　她婚姻生活美滿。（請參考**9-1**／**9-13**）

　　ⓐ　Her married life is satisfactory.

　　ⓑ　Her marriage life is satisfactory.

　　ⓒ　She has a happy marriage.

　　ⓓ　She has a satisfactory marriage.

（　）6.　他以算命為業。（請參考**9-13**）

　　ⓐ　His occupation is a fortune-teller.

　　ⓑ　His profession is a fortune-teller.

　　ⓒ　He is a fortune-teller by occupation.

　　ⓓ　He is fortune-teller by profession.

（　）7.　他臉上的傷疤使警方很容易辨識他的身分。（請參考**9-14**／**9-23**）

　　ⓐ　The scar on the face makes the police easy to identify him.

　　ⓑ　The scar on the face makes the police easy to find his identification.

　　ⓒ　The scar on his face makes the police easily identify him.

　　ⓓ　The scar on his face makes it easy for the police to identify him.

（　）8.　地鐵系統讓住在郊區的人們能夠不必開車便可通勤上班。（請參考**9-14/9-23**）

　　ⓐ　The subway systems make it possible for people living in the suburbs to commute to work without driving a car.

　　ⓑ　The subway systems make people living in the suburbs possible to commute to work without driving a car.

　　ⓒ　The subway systems make people living in the suburbs can commute to work without driving a car.

　　ⓓ　The subway systems enable people who live in the suburbs

can commute to work without driving a car.

（　）9. 缺乏運動使某些女孩子難以保持身材。（請參考**9-14／9-23**）

    ⓐ Lack of exercise makes it hard for some girls to stay in shape.

    ⓑ Lack of exercise makes some girls hard to stay in shape.

    ⓒ Lacking exercise makes it difficult for some girls to keep shape.

    ⓓ Lacking exercise makes some girls difficult to keep shape.

（　）10. 有些大學生缺乏基本生活技能，難以在宿舍生存。（請參考 **9-14／9-23**）

    ⓐ Having few basic life skills makes some college students difficult to survive in the student dormitory.

    ⓑ Having few basic life skills makes it difficult for some college students to survive in the student dormitory.

    ⓒ Without basic life skills, some college students have trouble surviving in the student dormitory.

    ⓓ Lack of basic life skills, some college students cannot survive in the student dormitory.

（　）11. 現代醫療科技讓許多癌症病人得以存活更久。（請參考**9-14／9-23**）

    ⓐ Modern medical technology makes it possible for many cancer patients to live longer lives.

    ⓑ Modern medical technology makes many cancer patients possible to live longer lives.

    ⓒ Modern medical technology makes many cancer patients able to live longer lives.

    ⓓ Modern medical technology enables many cancer patients to live longer lives.

（　）12. 這陣強風使得這些船難以離港。（請參考**9-14**／**9-23**）

ⓐ The strong wind made the boats difficult to leave harbour.

ⓑ The strong wind made it difficult for the boats to leave the harbour.

ⓒ The strong wind made the boats unable to leave harbour.

ⓓ The strong wind prevented the boats from leaving the harbour.

（　）13. 現代交通工具，例如飛機和高鐵，使得人們旅行更方便了。
（請參考**9-14**／**9-23**）

ⓐ Modern means of transportation, such as planes and HSR trains, makes people convenient to get around.

ⓑ Modern means of transportation, such as planes and HSR trains, makes it convenient for people to get around.

ⓒ Modern means of transportation enables people to get around, such as planes and HSR trains.

ⓓ Modern means of transportation, such as planes and HSR trains, makes people able to get around.

（　）14. 大部分銀行讓客戶容易開設帳戶。（請參考**9-14**／**9-23**）

ⓐ Most banks make their clients easy to open an account.

ⓑ Most banks make it easy for their clients to open an account.

ⓒ Most banks make opening an account easy for their clients.

ⓓ Most banks make their clients simple to open an account.

（　）15. 經常排練使他無法準備期末考。（請參考**9-14**／**9-23**）

ⓐ Constant rehearsals made it impossible for him to study for the final exam.

ⓑ Constant rehearsals prevented him from studying for the final exam.

ⓒ Constant rehearsals made him impossible to study for the final exam.

ⓓ Constant rehearsals made him unable to study for the final exam.

( ) 16. 他堅持要付帳。（請參考**9-27**）

ⓐ He insisted to pay the bill.

ⓑ He insisted that he must pay the bill.

ⓒ He insisted on paying the bill.

ⓓ He insisted that he pay the bill.

( ) 17. 我有信心贏得這場比賽。（請參考**9-30**）

ⓐ I am confident of winning the competition.

ⓑ I have the confidence to win the competition.

ⓒ I am confident to win the completion.

ⓓ I am confident and win the competition.

( ) 18. 教師為學生解答問題時要有耐心。（請參考**9-32**）

ⓐ Teachers should be patient to answer students questions.

ⓑ Teachers when answering students questions should be patient.

ⓒ Teachers answering students questions should be patient.

ⓓ Teachers should be patient in answering students questions.

( ) 19. 你這時把房子賣掉很不理智。（請參考**9-34**）

ⓐ It was not wise for you to sell your house at this moment.

ⓑ It was not wise of you to sell your house at this moment.

ⓒ You selling your house at this time were not wise.

ⓓ You were not wise to sell your house at this time.

※解答請見P.295

第九章

誤用句型造成的中式英文

第十章

誤用連接詞
造成的中式英文

本章重點：

在學生習作中，誤用連接詞的情形屢見不鮮，
主要是由於中英文句構不同所造成，這也屬於
中式英文。茲分成六大類舉例說明如下：

一、and/ or

二、even/ even if/ even after

三、not only... but also...

四、no matter＋wh-clause

五、run-on sentences

六、than/ compared to

一、and / or

or用於兩種情況：

a) 有選擇時

例：Students go to school or study online.

b) 在否定式之後

例：There are no reports of injuries or damage.

句中的or不能改成and，因為這是否定句式：no reports of...。

以下是學生習作常見的錯誤例子：

10-1. 減肥的方法有很多種，例如慢跑、吃藥、去健身房健身等。

【正】：There are many methods of losing weight, such as jogging, taking pills *or* working out in the gym.

【誤】： There are many methods of losing weight, such as jogging, taking pills *and* going to the gym.

【解說】：

(1)有選擇性的情況用or，用and表示三種減肥方法都用，似不合常理。

(2)「去健身房健身」說going to the gym，或working out in the gym均可。

10-2. 垃圾食品流行的一個重要原因是，它比其它食品例如蔬菜、粥或麵包都要好吃。

【正】：One important reason why junk food is popular is that it tastes better than other food products such as vegetables, congee *or* bread.

【誤】： One important reason why junk food is popular is that it tastes better than other food products such as vegetables, congee *and* bread.

【解說】：【誤】句中用and不當的理由如上句。

10-3. **他不會說英文，無法從媒體或書本獲得任何資訊。**

【正】：Being unable to speak English, he could ***not*** obtain any information from the media ***or*** from books.

【誤】：Being unable to speak English, he could not obtain any information from the media ***and*** from books.

【解說】：【誤】句中的and要改成or，因為前面有否定could not。

10-4. **地震後，沒有任何受傷或損壞的報導。**

【正】：After the earthquake, there were ***no*** reports of injuries ***or*** damage.

【誤】：After the earthquake, there were no reports of injuries ***and*** damages.

【解說】：

(1)【誤】句中的and要改成or，因為前面有否定no。

(2)當「損壞」解的damage 要用單數，damages作「損害賠償金」解。

10-5. **我的朋友丹長期與父母同住，不會做家事，也不會照顧自己。**

【正】：My friend Dan, who lived with his parents for a long time, was ***not*** able to do housework ***or*** to take care of himself.

【誤】：My friend Dan, who lived with his parents for a long time, was not able to do housework ***and*** to take care of himself.

【解說】：【誤】句中的and要改成or，因為前面有否定not。

10-6. **在網上修課，學生不必為了上課早起，或者在寒冷的冬夜摸黑行走。**

【正】：Taking online courses, students do ***not*** need to wake up early for classes ***or*** travel in the dark in cold winters.

【誤】：Taking online courses, students do **not** need to wake up early for classes **and** travel in the dark in cold winters.

【解說】：【誤】句中的and要改成or，因為前面有否定do not need to。

10-7. **有了這筆額外的錢，我就不用為了學費擔心和恐慌了。**

【正】：With the extra money, I will not have to worry **or** panic about my tuition.

【誤】：With the extra money, I do not have to worry **and** panic about my tuition.

【解說】：【誤】句中的and要改成or，因為前面有否定will not have to。

10-8. **大多數人都很忙碌，所以沒有多少時間和朋友出去閒逛或是去認識新人。**

【正】：Most people are busy, so they have **little** time to hang out with friends **or** to meet new people.

【誤】：Most people are busy, so they have little time to hang out with friends **and** to meet new people.

【解說】：【誤】句中的and要改成or，因為前面有否定little。

10-9. **網上購物和在實體店購物不同，人們不需要走很長的路，也不需要擔心在哪裡停車。**

【正】：Unlike shopping at a brick and mortar store, online shopping does **not** require people to walk long distances **or** worry about where they will park their cars.

【誤】：Unlike shopping at a real store, online shopping does not require people to walk long distances **and** worry about where they will park their cars.

【解說】：

(1)【誤】句中的and要改成or，因為前面有否定does not require。

(2)「實體店」可說a brick and mortar store或a physical store。

10-10.我們被教導說不要同其他學生發生爭執，不要使用暴力，也不要在學校吵鬧。

【正】：We were taught ***not*** to argue with other students, ***not*** to use violence, ***or not*** to be noisy in school.

【誤】：We were taught not to argue with other students, not to use violence, ***and*** not to be noisy in school.

【解說】：【誤】句中的and要改成or，因為前面有否定not。

10-11.我喜歡打籃球，但是當我第一次打籃球時，我不知道怎麼玩,也不知道怎麼熱身。

【正】：I like to play basketball; however, when I first started to play basketball , I did ***not*** know how to play it ***or*** how to warm up.

【誤】：I like to play basketball; however, when I first started to play basketball, I did not know how to play it ***and*** how to warm up.

【解說】：【誤】句中的and要改成or，因為前面有否定not。

10-12.三十年前，很少專家討論全球變暖問題，並警告大家別再破壞環境。

【正】：Thirty years ago, ***few*** experts talked about global warming issues ***or*** warned everyone to stop damaging our environment.

【誤】：Thirty years ago, few experts talked about global warming issues ***and*** warned everyone to stop damaging our environment.

【解說】：【誤】句中的and要改成or，因為前面有否定few。

10-13.從事特殊職業的人，例如醫生、消防員和律師，需要有良好的職業道德。

【正】：Those people holding special jobs, such as being doctors, firemen ***or*** lawyers, are required to have good work ethics.

【誤】：Those people holding special jobs, such as doctors, firemen **and** lawyers, are required to have good work ethics.

【解說】：

(1)【誤】句中的doctors前要加being，因為doctors是「人」，being doctors才是job。

(2)【誤】句中的and要改成or，因為這屬於有選擇性：一個人不能同時當醫生、消防員和律師。

10-14. 好市民不應該做傷害國家和社會的事。

【正】：Good citizens should **not** do harm to their country **or** their society.

【誤】：Good citizens should not do harm to their country **and** society.

10-15. 生病的時候，例如咳嗽或胃痛，你應該去看醫生。

【正】：When you are sick, such as getting a cough **or** having a stomachache, you should go to see a doctor.

【誤】：When you are sick, such as getting a cough **and** having a stomachache, you should go to see a doctor.

【解說】：【誤】句中的and要改成or，因為同時咳嗽和胃痛的概率不大。

10-16.a) 現今很多人都依賴電腦、電視和電子遊戲系統。

【正】：Nowadays, many people depend on their computers, TVs **and** video gaming systems.

【誤】：Nowadays, many people depend on their computers, TVs **or** video gaming systems.

【解說】：本句用and表示同時依賴三種科技產品，比用or表示依賴單一項更合邏輯。

b) 有些人喜歡選擇住在沒有電腦、電視和電子遊戲系統的地方。

【正】：Some people like to choose to live in places where there are *no* computers, TVs *or* video gaming systems.

【誤】：Some people like to choose to live in places where there are *no* computers, TVs *and* video gaming systems.

【解說】：【誤】句中的and要改成or，因為前面有否定no。

10-17. 這些學生沒有機會去探索外面的世界和發掘他們的興趣。

【正】：These students do *not* have a chance to explore the outside world *or* to discover their interests.

【誤】：These students do not have a chance to explore the outside world *and* to find out their interests.

【解說】：【誤】句中的and要改成or，因為前面有否定not。

10-18. 英文不好的移民很難找到工作、融入社會以及與其他人好好交流。

【正】：Immigrants who are not good at English are *unable* to find a job, integrate into society *or* communicate well with other people.

【誤】：Immigrants who are not good at English are *unable* to find a job, integrate into society *and* communicate well with other people.

【解說】：【誤】句中的and要改成or，因為前面有否定are unable to。

10-19. 很多青少年選擇用蹺課、嗑藥甚至自殺的方式來處理壓力。

【正】：Many teenagers choose to deal with stress by skipping school, taking drugs *or* even committing suicide.

【誤】：Many teenagers choose to deal with stress by skipping school, taking drugs *and* even committing suicide.

【解說】：【誤】句屬於有選擇性，所以and要改成or，因為用and表示三種方法都用，似乎不合常理。

10-20.**藉著吃速食，人們不必準備和帶自己的午餐。**

【正】：By eating fast food, people do not have to prepare *or* bring their own lunches.

【誤】：By eating fast food, people do not have to prepare *and* bring their own lunches.

【解說】：【誤】句中的and要改成or，因為前面有否定not。

10-21.**有錢人不用擔心食衣住行問題。**

【正】：Wealthy people do not need to worry about food, shelter *or* clothing.

【誤】：Wealthy people do not need to worry about food, shelter *and* clothing.

【解說】：「食衣住行」要說food, shelter and clothing，但本句為否定，所以and要改or。

二、even/ even if/ even after

even是副詞，沒有連接詞的功能，不能用來連接兩個子句。學生習作中，容易受中文思維的影響，一想到「即使」，立刻譯成even，這並沒有錯，例如：即使小孩也能回答這麼簡單的問題。可以說：Even a child can answer such an easy question. 因為這裡的even是副詞，但是even 不能用來連接兩個子句。例：

10-22.**即使你的想法比主管的好，你還是要聽他的。**

【正】：You have to follow the ideas of your supervisor *even if* your ideas are better.

【誤】：You have to follow the ideas of your supervisor *even* your ideas are better.

【解說】：【誤】句中的even是副詞，不能連接兩個子句。

10-23.即使我們到國外，也可使用網際網路，上網學習。

【正】：***Even if*** we go abroad, we can still access the Internet and take our lessons.

【誤】：***Even*** we go abroad, we can still access the Internet and take our lessons.

10-24.窮苦人家小孩，即使中學成績優秀，也無法上大學。

【正】：Children from poor families are unable to attend college ***even if*** they have good grades in high school.

【誤】：Children from poor families are unable to attend college ***even*** they have good grades in high school.

10-25.體育課程對學生很重要，就算他們離開學校之後也一樣。

【正】：Physical education is an important program for students ***even after*** they have left school.

【誤】：Physical education is an important program for students ***even*** they have left school.

【解說】：【誤】句中的even 是副詞，應改成even if 或even after才能連接兩個子句。

10-26.越來越多的人找不到工作，即使大學畢業後也一樣。

【正】：More and more people are having trouble finding a job ***even though*** they have graduated from university.

【誤】：More and more people are having trouble finding a job ***even*** they have graduated from university.

10-27.現今手機已成為人們的必須品，即使小孩也不例外。

【正】：Nowadays, cellphones are a necessary accessory for people, including children.

【誤】：Nowadays, cellphones are a necessary accessory for people, even children have no exception.

【解說】：【誤】句中的even children have no exception是由中文逐譯過來，除了文法錯誤之外，也不合慣用法，說including children即可。

三、not only... but also...

「非但……而且……」這種句構，在學生腦海中根深蒂固，因此習作時很本能的拿來套用，可惜經常犯錯。使用這種句構要注意以下各點：

a) 要注意平行

not only 所接的單字或片語一定要與but also所接的單字或片語平行，例：Providing free English training will not only benefit immigrants, but also the government. 本句的not only置於動詞benefit之前，而but also置於名詞the government之前，就造成不平行的問題了。正確的說法是把benefit置於will之後即可。

以下是一些不平行的例子：

10-28.私校學生不只要遵守穿著規範，也要嚴守校規。

【正】：Students in private schools need to follow not only their dress code but also their strict rules.

【誤】：Students in private schools need to not only follow their dress code but also   their strict rules.

【解說】：【誤】句中的not only置於動詞follow之前，而but also卻置於名詞their strict rules之前，就變得不平行了。正確的說法是把follow置於not only之前。

10-29.降低合法喝酒年齡不僅傷害青少年健康，也威脅到公眾安全。

【正】：Lowering the legal drinking age not only harms teenagers' health but also threatens public safety.

【誤】：Lowering the legal drinking age harms not only teenagers' health but also threatens public safety.

【解說】：【誤】句中的not only置於名詞之前，but also卻置於動詞之前，而成為不平行的句子。

10-30. 建造賭場不僅有利於經濟，對人們舒解壓力也有幫助。

【正】：Building casinos makes a great contribution not only to our economy but also to the relief of people's pressure.

【誤】：Building casinos makes a great contribution to not only our economy but also to the relief of people's pressure.

【解說】：【誤】句中的not only置於to之後，但but also卻置於to之前，顯得不平行。

b) not only和but also如果接子句時，除開要注意平行外，but also所連接的子句中，主詞不能省略。

例一：

【正】：Animals are our friends because they not only live with us peacefully on earth, but they also act as medicine testers.

【誤】：Animals are our friends because not only they live with us peacefully on earth, but also act as medicine testers.

【解說】：【誤】句中not only置於主詞they前，but also卻在動詞act之前，造成不平行。另外，but之後主詞they不能省略。

例二：

【正】：Playing team sports not only teaches people how to get along with others, but it also improves their social skills.

【誤】：Playing team sports can not only teach people how to get along with others, but also improve their social skills.

【解說】：【誤】句中can not only teach people要改為not only teaches

people，才能與後半句平行。另外，but之後的主詞it不能省略，it指playing所引導的動名詞片語。

例三：

【正】：Working with others not only helps students solve difficult problems, but it also enables them to build their social networks.

【誤】：Working with others not only helps students solve difficult problems, but also helps them to build their social networks.

【解說】：【誤】句中後半句but之後缺少主詞it，it係指working with others的動名詞片語。

c) not only置於句首時，主動詞要顛倒。

· 團體運動不僅較有競爭性，也可增進團隊精神。

【正】：Not only are team sports more competitive, but they can also improve team spirit.

【誤】：Not only team sports are more competitive, but they can also improve team spirit.

【解說】：

(1)【誤】句錯誤，是因為動詞are未置於主詞team sports之前。

(2)本句如果不用倒置句型，亦可說成：Team sports are not only more competitive, but they can also improve team spirit.

四、no matter＋wh-clause

大家都知道，no matter中文意為「不論」，所以「不論晴雨」就說no matter rain or shine，「不論男女老幼」就說no matter men and women, young and old，這些都是想當然爾的Chinese English。請注意：no matter 不能單獨存在，一定要接who, what, where, how, when等等所謂wh－clause，

作連接詞用，成為一個子句。

例：No matter what he says, I will not believe him./ No matter where you go, I will follow you./ No matter how difficult it is, you should finish the job by tomorrow.

但請注意以下事項：

a) 中文裡的「不論」，並非一定要譯成no matter，例如「不論男女老幼」要說regardless of age and sex；「不論晴雨」要說rain or shine；「不論飲食喝酒都要節制」要說：We should be temperate both in eating and drinking.句中的both... and... 即隱含有「不論」之意。

注意：本句不能說成Both eating and drinking should be temperate.因為be temperate要以「人」當主詞。

b) no matter＋wh- clause之後即成為連接詞，主句中不能再用連接詞but。

例：不論再怎麼努力，然而他總是考不上托福。

【正】：No matter how hard he tried, he still failed the TOEFL test.

【誤】：No matter how hard he tried, but he still failed the TOEFL test.

五、run-on sentences

所謂run-on sentences就是在兩個獨立子句中間用逗點，這在學生習作中非常普遍。究其原因，主要在於中文裡「因為」「所以」一般省略不用，而英文中兩個獨立子句間用逗點就算大錯，例：

【正】：It is raining now, so I don't want to go out.

【正】：Because it is raining now, I don't want to go out.

【誤】：It is raining now, I don't want to go out.

解決之道就是要加上連接詞或用分號 (;)，請看下例：

10-31.**學習不是學生在校唯一的任務，學會與同學互動也很重要。**

【正】：Studying is not a student's only job at school; learning how to interact with his/ her classmates is also important.

【誤】：Studying is not a student's only job at school, learning how to interact with his/ her classmates is also important.

【解說】：【誤】句中，兩個獨立子句之間用逗點不正確，改用分號就
　　　　　對了。

10-32. **減肥有許多方法，有些方法很好，但有些不好。**

【正】：There are many ways to lose weight; some are good, but others are not so good.

【誤】：There are many ways to lose weight, some are good, but others are not so good.

10-33. **任何事情都有優缺點，網際網路也沒有例外。**

【正】：Everything has its advantages and disadvantages; the Internet is no exception.

【誤】：Everything has its advantages and disadvantages, the Internet is no exception.

10-34. **時代不同了，我們生活中每天都有許多新的事情發生。**

【正】：Times have changed; there are many new things happening in our lives every day.

【誤】：Times have changed, there are many new things happening in our lives every day.

10-35. **很多人喜歡吃垃圾食物，事實上，垃圾食物已變得越來越普遍了。**

【正】：Many people like eating junk food; in fact, junk food is becoming more and more popular.

【誤】：Many people like eating junk food, in fact, junk food is becoming more and more popular.

【解說】：【誤】句中的in fact是介系詞片語，不是連接詞，所以前面
　　　　　要用分號。

10-36.時間就是金錢，因此當人們忙碌時，就選擇吃速食。

【正】：Time is money; hence, when people are busy, they choose to eat fast food.

【誤】：Time is money, hence, when people are busy, they choose to eat fast food.

【解說】：【誤】句中的hence是副詞，不是連接詞，所以前面要用分號。類似hence這樣的conjunctive adverb有therefore, thus, instead, however等等。

10-37.你鬧胃痛並不令人驚訝，畢竟你吃得太多了。

【正】：It is not surprising that you have got a stomachache; after all, you have eaten too much.

【誤】：It is not surprising that you have got a stomachache, after all, you have eaten too much.

【解說】：after all 是副詞，不是連接詞，所以前面若不用分號，就變成了run-on sentence了。

10-38.賭博和吸毒一樣容易上癮，青少年一旦賭上癮，就難以戒除。

【正】：Gambling is as addictive as doing drugs; once teenagers are addicted to gambling, it is hard for them to get rid of it.

【誤】：Gambling is as addictive as doing drugs, once teenagers are addicted to gambling, it is hard for them to get rid of it.

【解說】：

(1)【誤】句中的once是副詞，不是連接詞，所以是個run-on sentence. 只要把once前的逗號改為分號即正確。

(2)once也可當連接詞用，但一般 要置於句首，例：Once you talk to him, you will know he is a good person.

六、than / compared to

一想到「比較」，學生腦海裡浮現的英文對應詞不是than，就是compared to。但這兩個用法有別：要用than，前面一定要有比較級的詞，如more, fewer, less, -er, would rather等。以下是學生習作常犯的錯誤。

10-39.鄉村環境比都市環境要安寧。

【正】：The environment in rural areas is **more** peaceful **than** that in urban areas.

【誤】：The environment in rural areas is **more** peaceful **compared to** rural areas.

【解說】：【誤】句的more後要接than，不能接compared to。另外，【正】句than之後的that指代先行詞environment，很多學生容易忽略。

10-40.青少年駕車致死率，為其他年齡層之冠。

【正】：**Compared to** any other age category of drivers, teenagers are the number one cause of death in car accidents.

【誤】：Teenagers are the number one cause of death in car accidents **than** any other age category of drivers.

【解說】：【誤】句than之前沒有比較級的字詞，如more, less, fewer等，所以要改用compared to。

10-41.比起十年前，現在大學學費高出許多。

【正】：Nowadays, college tuition has become much **more** expensive **than it** was ten years ago.

【誤】：Nowadays, college tuition has become much **more** expensive **compared to** ten years ago.

【解說】：【誤】句的compared to ten years ago是由中文「比起十年

前」直譯過來的錯誤，要改用than，因為句前有more。

10-42.網上修課，學生所學的知識不如傳統學校學生。

【正】：Students who take online courses may not acquire *as much* knowledge *as* students who go to a traditional school.

【誤】：Students who take online courses may not acquire *as much* knowledge *compared to* students who go to a traditional school.

【解說】：【誤】句的compared to不能與前面的as much連用。

第十章　練習題

選擇題：下列各題，請選出一個或兩個正確答案。

（　）1. 這麼多人支持他，這位候選人不必擔心和恐慌落選。（請參考 **10-7**）

　ⓐ With many people supporting him, the candidate does not have to worry and panic about losing the election.

　ⓑ With many people supporting him, the candidate will not have to worry and panic about losing the election.

　ⓒ With many people supporting him, the candidate will not have to worry or panic about losing the election.

　ⓓ With many people supporting him, the candidate does not have to worry or panic about losing the election.

（　）2. 這些退休員工很窮困，沒有錢供自己花用，也無力資助子女教育。（請參考**10-8**）

　ⓐ These retired employees are so poor that they have little money to spend with themselves or with their children's education.

　ⓑ These retired employees are so poor that they have little money to spend with themselves and with their children's education.

　ⓒ These retired employees are so poor that they have no money to spend with themselves or with their children's education.

　ⓓ These retired employees are so poor that they have no money to spend with themselves and with their children's education.

（　）3.　在現代社會，寫信或打電話與朋友交流的人越來越少了。（請
參考**10-12**）

ⓐ In modern society, fewer and fewer people are communicating with friends by writing letters and making phone calls.

ⓑ In modern society, fewer and fewer people are communicating with friends by writing letters or making phone calls.

ⓒ In modern society, fewer and fewer people are communicating with friends by writing letters and telephone.

ⓓ In modern society, fewer and fewer people are communicating with friends by writing letters or telephone.

（　）4.　未接受大學教育的人無法找到高薪工作和獲得升遷。（請參考
10-18）

ⓐ People who do not obtain a college education are unable to find a high-salary job and get a promotion.

ⓑ People who do not obtain a college education are unable to find a high-paying job and get a promotion.

ⓒ People who do not obtain a college education are unable to find a high-salaried job or get a promotion.

ⓓ People who do not obtain a college education are unable to find a high-pay job or get a promotion.

（　）5.　即使他向我道歉，我也不原諒他。（請參考**10-22**）

ⓐ I will not forgive him even if he apologizes.

ⓑ I will not forgive him even he apologizes.

ⓒ Even if he apologizes, I will not forgive him.

ⓓ Even he apologizes, I will not forgive him.

（　）6.　團隊運動不只教導隊員學會如何相處，還可以改進他們的社交

技能。（請參考**10-29**）

ⓐ Not only does playing team sports teach people how to get along with others, but it also improves their social skills.

ⓑ Playing team sports not only teaches people how to get along with others, but it also improves their social skills.

ⓒ Not only playing team sports teach people how to get along with others, but it also improves their social skills.

ⓓ Playing team sports not only teach people how to get along with others, but they also improve their social skills.

（　）7. 他畢竟是個外國人，不會用筷子。（請參考**10-31**）

ⓐ After all, he is a foreigner, he does not know how to use chopsticks.

ⓑ After all, he is a foreigner, therefore, he does not know how to use chopsticks.

ⓒ After all, he is a foreigner; he does not know how to use chopsticks .

ⓓ He after all is a foreigner, so he does not know how to use chopsticks.

（　）8. 任何事情都有優缺點，建核電廠也不例外。（請參考**10-32/10-38**）

ⓐ Everything has advantages and disadvantages, the same is true with constructing nuclear power plants.

ⓑ Everything has advantages and disadvantages, constructing nuclear power plants is no exception.

ⓒ Everything has its advantages and disadvantages; constructing nuclear power plants is no exception.

ⓓ Everything has its advantages and disadvantages, including the construction of nuclear power plants.

（　）9. 他昨天並未生病，事實上，他是假裝生病。（請參考**10-35**）

    ⓐ He was not sick yesterday; in fact, he was pretending to be sick yesterday.

    ⓑ He was not sick yesterday, in fact, he was pretending to be sick yesterday.

    ⓒ He was not sick yesterday. In fact, he was pretending to be sick yesterday.

    ⓓ He was not sick yesterday, as a matter of fact, he was pretending to be sick yesterday.

（　）10. 臺北的天氣比溫哥華熱。（請參考**10-39**）

    ⓐ The weather in Taipei is warmer than in Vancouver.

    ⓑ The weather in Taipei is warmer compared to Vancouver.

    ⓒ The weather in Taipei is warmer compared to the weather in Vancouver.

    ⓓ The weather in Taipei is warmer than that in Vancouver.

※解答請見P.295

第十一章

誤用所有格形容詞
造成的中式英文

本章重點：

中英文的差異林林總總，其中困擾國人最大的莫過於所有格形容詞my, your, his, its, their, one's等等。中文的所有格形容詞在動詞後面一般都省略，而英文則不能省，例如「我洗手」，絕對不能說「我洗我的手」，但英文I wash my hands. 中的my則非要不可。「我用手遮臉」I cover my face with my hands. 句中的兩個my缺一不可，但中文絕對不說「我用我的手遮我的臉」。這道理看似簡單，但在學生的習作中，誤用所有格形容詞的例子卻屢見不鮮，這種錯誤也屬於中式英文。

11-1. 速食的優點之一是方便。

【正】：One of the advantages of fast food is *its* convenience.

【誤】：One of the advantages of fast food is convenience.

【解說】：【誤】句中缺少所有格形容詞its，之所以犯錯是由中文直譯造成的。

11-2. 與家人同住比獨自住在公寓要安全。

【正】：Living with *one's* family is safer than living alone in an apartment.

【誤】：Living with family is safer than living alone in an apartment.

【解說】：【誤】句缺少所有格形容詞one's，之所以犯錯是由中文直譯造成的。

11-3. 薪水不該是選擇職業的主要考慮因素；興趣亦應列入考慮。

【正】：Salary should not be the main basis for choosing a job; *a person's* interests should also be taken into consideration.

【誤】：Salary should not be the main basis for choosing a job; interests should also be taken into consideration.

【解說】：【誤】句缺少所有格形容詞a person's 或one's，造成語意不清。

11-4. 雖然廣告有缺點而時遭批評，我認為它還是有優點的。

【正】：Although advertising is often criticized for *its* negative aspects, I think it has positive sides.

【誤】：Although advertising is often criticized for negative aspects, I think it has positive sides.

【解說】：【誤】句缺少所有格形容詞its，造成語意不清。

11-5. 私立學校一直以良好的學習環境聞名。

【正】：Private schools have always been known for *their* good

learning environments.

【誤】：Private schools have always been known for good learning environments.

11-6. **由於缺乏練習，學生寫作能力難以提高。**

【正】：Because of ***their*** lack of practice, students are unable to improve their writing skills.

【誤】：Because of the lack of practice, students are unable to improve their writing skills.

11-7. **男孩子體能消耗量大，所以比女孩子更容易保持身材。**

【正】：With ***their*** expending large amounts of energy, boys stay in shape more easily than girls.

【誤】：With expending large amounts of energy, boys stay in shape more easily than girls.

11-8. **我想當瑞士公民，因為它的生活步調緩慢。**

【正】：I want to be a citizen of Switzerland because of ***its*** slow tempo of life.

【誤】：I want to be a citizen of Switzerland because of the slow tempo of life.

11-9. **人容易受周圍環境的影響。**

【正】：People are easily influenced by ***their*** environments.

【誤】：People are easily influenced by ***the*** environment.

11-10. **小時候，父母親經常幫我們做決定。**

【正】：When we were young, ***our*** parents always made decisions for us.

【誤】：When we were young, parents always made decisions for us.

11-11. 別浪費父母賺的辛苦錢。

【正】：Don't waste *our* parents' hard-earned money.

【誤】：Don't waste parents' hard-earned money.

11-12. 政府應該鼓勵市民使用公共運輸系統。

【正】：Governments should encourage *their* citizens to use public transportation.

【誤】：Governments should encourage citizens to use public transportation.

11-13. 這隻狗看見主人就搖尾巴。

【正】：The dog wags *its* tail when it sees *its* master.

【誤】：The dog wags tail when it sees master.

11-14. 政府的所有稅收都是由國民徵收而來的。

【正】：All the government's revenue comes from *its* citizens.

【誤】：All the government's revenue comes from citizens.

11-15. 許多醫院病床不夠。

【正】：Many hospitals do not have enough sickbeds for *their* patients.

【誤】：Many hospitals do not have enough sickbeds for patients.

【解說】：【正】句亦可說Many hospitals are short of sickbeds. 句中就不必用their。

11-16. 據說出生排行會影響到一個人的性格。

【正】：It is said that the order of *a person's* birth can affect one's personality.

【誤】：It is said that the order of birth can affect one's personality.

11-17.校園生活也許是一個人一生中最快樂的時光。

【正】：A person's time on campus may be the happiest days of his/her life.

【不佳】：Campus life may be the happiest time for a person.

11-18.飲食習慣是影響體重的一大原因。

【正】：*A person's* eating habits are one major factor that may affect his/her weight.

【不佳】：Eating habits are one major factor that may affect people's weight.

11-19.缺乏自制力是造成不良飲食習慣的主要原因。

【正】：*A person's* lack of self-control is the main cause of his/her unhealthy eating habits.

【誤】：Lack of self-control is the main cause of unhealthy eating habits.

11-20.喝酒有害健康。

【正】：Drinking alcohol is harmful to *a person's* health.

【誤】：Drinking alcohol is harmful for health.

【解說】：【正】句中的a person's亦可說one's或our。另外，harmful後接to，不接for。

11-21.由於不同的文化背景，移民對社會有很大的貢獻。

【正】：With *their* different cultural backgrounds, immigrants make huge contributions to their society.

【誤】：With different cultural backgrounds, immigrants make huge contributions to society.

11-22.心理健康對一個人的長壽有幫助。

【正】：***A person's*** mental health can contribute to his/her longevity.

【不佳】：Mental health can contribute to a person's longevity.

11-23.由於現代電腦效率高，已經取代了許多用手操作的例行工作。

【正】：Thanks to ***their*** high efficiency, modern computers have taken over many routine tasks done by human labor.

【誤】：Thanks to high efficiency, modern computers have taken over many routine tasks done by human labor.

【解說】：【正】句中的their是指主句中的主詞computers。

11-24.一生當中在同一公司工作的好處是方便。

【正】：The advantage of working for the same company all ***one's*** life is ***its*** convenience.

【誤】：The advantage of working for the same company all one's life is convenience.

【解說】：【正】句中的its是指working for the same company all one's life。

11-25.除開方便外，廣告也可以用來服務大眾。

【正】：In addition to ***its*** convenience, advertising can be used to serve the public.

【誤】：In addition to convenience, advertising can be used to serve the public.

【解說】：【正】句中的its指advertising。

11-26.為了多賺錢以提高生活水準，越來越多的人搬到大都市居住。

【正】：In order to earn more money to improve ***their*** standards of living, more and more people are moving to big cities.

【誤】：In order to earn more money to improve living standards, more and more people move to big cities.

【解說】：【誤】句除了缺少所有格形容詞their之外，主句的動詞習慣
用現在進行式。

11-27.溫哥華以美麗風景出名。

【正】：Vancouver is famous for *its* beautiful scenery.

【誤】：Vancouver is famous for beautiful sceneries.

【解說】：【誤】句除了缺少所有格形容詞its外，scenery不用複數。

11-28.有些人喜歡在大都市找高薪工作，有些人為了方便選擇住在都市。

【正】：Some people like to find a high-paying job in a big city, while others choose to live in a big city for *its* convenience.

【誤】：Some people like to find a high-paying job in a big city, while others choose to live in a big city for convenience.

【解說】：【誤】句中缺少所有格形容詞its，its是指a big city。

11-29.開車要全神貫注。

【正】：Driving requires *your* full concentration.

【誤】：Driving requires full concentration.

11-30.挖鼻子是不好的習慣。

【正】：Picking *your* nose is a bad habit.

【誤】：Picking nose is a bad habit.

第十一章　練習題

選擇題：下列各題，請選出一個或兩個正確答案。

(　) 1. 快時尚的優點之一是價格低廉。（請參考**11-1**）
ⓐ One of the advantages of fast fashion is its low prices.
ⓑ One of the advantages of fast fashion is low prices.
ⓒ One advantage of fast fashion is low prices.
ⓓ One of the advantages of fast fashion is cheap prices.

(　) 2. 網上修課最大的優點是方便。（請參考**11-1**）
ⓐ The greatest advantage of taking a course on the Internet is convenient.
ⓑ The greatest advantage of taking a course on the Internet is convenience.
ⓒ The greatest advantage of taking a course on the Internet is its convenience.
ⓓ The greatest advantage of taking a course over the Internet is that it is convenient.

(　) 3. 該城市一直以美麗風景出名。（請參考**11-5**）
ⓐ The city has always been famous for its beautiful scenery.
ⓑ The city is always famous for beautiful scenery.
ⓒ The city has always been famous for beautiful sceneries.
ⓓ The city is always famous for its beautiful sceneries.

(　) 4. 由於缺乏練習，該足球隊吃了敗仗。（請參考**11-6**）
ⓐ Because of their lack of practice, the football team lost their

games.

ⓑ Because of the lack of practice, the football team lost their games.

ⓒ Because of lack of practice, the football team lost.

ⓓ Because of lack of practice, the football team lost the battle.

( ) 5. 由於缺乏運動，這些學生身體不健康。（請參考**11-6**）

ⓐ Because of lack of exercise, these students are not physically healthy.

ⓑ Because of their lack of exercise, these students are not physically healthy.

ⓒ Because of their lacking of exercise, these students are not physically healthy.

ⓓ Because of the lack of exercise, these students are not physically healthy.

( ) 6. 由於努力與堅持不懈，這位科學家獲得了諾貝爾物理獎。（請參考 **11-6**）

ⓐ Because of hard working and resolute persistence, the scientist won the Nobel Prize for physics.

ⓑ Because of his hard work and resolute persistence, the scientist won the Nobel Prize for physics.

ⓒ Because of hardworking and resolute persistence, the scientist won the Nobel Prize for physics.

ⓓ Because of his hardworking and resolute persistence, the scientist won the Nobel Prize for physics.

( ) 7. 那家公司福利好，吸引許多人去應徵兩個經理職缺。（請參考 **11-7**）

ⓐ Because of its good fringe benefits, the company attracted many people to apply for two managerial positions.

ⓑ Because of good fringe benefits, the company attracted many people to apply for two managerial positions.

ⓒ Because of its good welfare, the company attracted many people to apply for two managerial positions.

ⓓ Because of good welfare, the company attracted many people to apply for two managerial positions.

（　）8. 市政府應該鼓勵市民減少使用塑膠袋。（請參考 **11-12**）

ⓐ The city government should encourage the citizens to reduce the use of plastic bags.

ⓑ The city government should encourage that the citizens reduce the use of plastic bags.

ⓒ The city government should encourage its citizens to reduce the use of plastic bags.

ⓓ The city government should encourage that its citizens reduce the use of plastic bags.

（　）9. 這隻狗看見那小偷就張牙警告。（請參考**11-13**）

ⓐ The dog bared its teeth as a warning when it saw the thief.

ⓑ The dog bared teeth as a warning when he saw the thief.

ⓒ The dog bared teeth to warn the thief whom he saw.

ⓓ The dog showed its teeth as warning when he saw the thief.

（　）10. 警告！抽菸可能有害健康。（請參考 **11-20**）

ⓐ Warning! Smoking may be hazardous to your health.

ⓑ Warning! Smoking maybe cause harmful to your health.

ⓒ Warning! Smoking may cause harm to health.

ⓓ Warning! Smoking may hurt health.

（　）11. 由於驚人的工作效率，這些人十天內就完成該項大計劃。（請參考**11-23**）

   ⓐ Because of their amazing work efficiency, these people finished the big project in 10 days.

   ⓑ Because of amazing working efficiency, these people finished the big project in 10 days.

   ⓒ Because of their amazing working efficiency, these people finished the big project in 10 days.

   ⓓ Because of amazing work efficiency, these people finished the big project in 10 days.

（　）12. 乘坐公共交通工具最明顯的優點是便宜。（請參考**11-24**）

   ⓐ The most obvious advantage of taking public transportation is low cost.

   ⓑ The most obvious advantage of taking public transportation is its low cost.

   ⓒ The most obvious advantage of taking public transportation is that it is inexpensive.

   ⓓ The most obvious advantage of taking public transportation is inexpensive.

（　）13. 除開方便外，使用信用卡還相當安全。（請參考**11-25**）

   ⓐ In addition to convenience, using credit cards is quite safe.

   ⓑ In addition to having convenience, using credit cards is quite safe.

   ⓒ In addition to its convenience, using credit cards is quite safe.

   ⓓ In addition to be convenient, using credit cards is quite safe.

（　）14. 為了取得更好的成績以便進入理想的大學，這些學生日以繼夜

的努力用功。（請參考**11-26**）

ⓐ In order to get better grades to enter the ideal universities, these students worked hard day and night.

ⓑ In order to get better grades to enter ideal universities, these students worked hard day and night.

ⓒ In order to get better grades to enter their ideal universities, these students worked hard day and night.

ⓓ In order to get better grades to enter an ideal university, these students worked hard day and night.

※解答請見P.295

附錄一

代名詞it／
指示代名詞this

記得2015年美國總統歐巴馬曾說，如果美國犯了錯誤，就應該承認。電視上的原文是：If we make mistakes, we have to admit ***them***. 一般人也許會認為這是一句平淡無奇的話，但對我這個學英文、教英文數十年的人來說卻感慨萬千。這是因為這句話要是出自國人之口，十之八九會說：If we make mistakes, we have to admit ***it***. 即使英文再好的人，也會犯這種語言學上叫performance error的毛病。

也就是說，你知道文法上要用複數形的them來指代mistakes，但是真正使用，卻常會用it，尤以口語為然。這種偏愛it的現象，在學生習作中屢見不鮮，請看以下實例：

1. **再生能源很天然，不會對環境造成傷害。**
   【正】：Renewable energy sources are very natural, so ***they*** will not do any damage to the environment.
   【誤】：Renewable energy sources are very natural, so ***it*** will not do any damage to the environment.

2. **一個人一生當中要在不同公司做事，因為這樣可增廣見聞。**
   【正】：People should work for different companies all their lives because ***this*** can broaden their horizons.
   【誤】：People should work for different companies all their lives because ***it*** can broaden their horizons.
   【解說】：【正】句的this指代People should work for different companies all their lives.這件事。

3. **受訓員工支領薪水，這會鼓勵他更勤奮工作。**
   【正】：If a worker in training is paid a salary, ***this*** will encourage him/her to work harder.
   【誤】：If a worker in training is paid a salary, ***it*** will encourage him/her to work harder.

4. 大學生不應該與父母同住，最重要的原因是，這樣他們可以學會獨立。

【正】：The most important reason why college students should not live with their parents is that *this* can cultivate their independence.

【誤】：The most important reason why college students should not live with their parents is that *it* can cultivate their independence.

5. 現在有些公路、圖書館和公園實施用戶付費，有些人認為這個做法很好。

【正】：Nowadays, some highways, libraries and parks charge user fees. Some people think that *this* is a good idea.

【誤】：Nowadays, some highways, libraries and parks charge user fees. Some people think that *it* is a good idea.

6. 假如高速公路取消速限，將會增加車禍發生率。

【正】：If speed limits were removed from the highway, *this* would increase the rate of car accidents.

【誤】：If speed limits were removed from the highway, *it* would increase the rate of car accidents.

7. 很多人把個人資料發在社交網站，但這樣可能導致個資外洩。

【正】：Many people post their private information on social networking sites, but *this* may lead to the leakage of their private information.

【誤】：Many people post their private information on social networking sites, but *it* may lead to the leakage of their private information.

8. **有些女孩子定期做瑜伽，但這尚不足以消耗能量。**

【正】：Some girls do yoga regularly, but ***this*** is not sufficient to consume their energy.

【誤】：Some girls do yoga regularly, but ***it*** is not sufficient to consume their energy.

9. **我喜歡坐公車的主要原因是便宜。**

【正】：The main reason why I like taking the bus is that ***it*** is inexpensive.

【誤】：The main reason why I like taking the bus is that ***this*** is inexpensive.

【解說】：【正】句的it指代動名詞片語taking the bus。

10. **「你長大後要做什麼？」這是自從上幼稚園至今我經常被問到的問題。**

【正】："What do you want to be when you grow up?" ***This*** is a question that I have been asked since kindergarten.

【誤】："What do you want to be when you grow up?" ***It*** is a question that I have been asked since kindergarten.

【解說】：【正】句的This指代前面的整個問句。【誤】句的it指涉不清。

11. **上大一時，我覺得凡事都很陌生，一時還難以調適。**

【正】：When I was a freshman, everything seemed to be strange to me, and I found ***it*** difficult to adapt to ***it***.

【誤】：When I was a freshman, everything seemed to be strange to me, and I found ***it*** difficult to adapt to ***this***.

【解說】：【正】句的第一個it指代後面的不定詞to adapt；第二個it指everything。

12. **他病得嚴重，所以沒來開會。**

【正】：He was seriously sick. ***This*** is why he was absent from the meeting.

【誤】：He was seriously sick. ***It*** is why he was absent from the meeting.

【解說】：【正】句的This指代前面的整個句子，【誤】句的It指代不清。

13. **假如太太賺得比先生多，夫妻之間會很難維持良好關係。**

【正】：If the wife makes more money than the husband, ***this*** will make it difficult for them to maintain a good relationship.

【誤】：If the wife makes more money than the husband, ***it*** will make it difficult to maintain a good relationship between them.

【解說】：【誤】句的it指涉不清。【正】句的this是指if所引導的句子。

14. **我贊成成立一個世界政府的原因是，這樣可導致資源的更有效分配。**

【正】：The reason why I agree with forming a world government is that ***it*** would lead to a more efficient allocation of resources.

【誤】：The reason why I agree with forming a world government is that ***this*** would lead to a more efficient allocation of resources.

【解說】：【正】句的it指forming a world government。

附錄二

容易誤用的副詞

表「頻率副詞」（adverbs of frequency）的always頻率最高，意為「總是……，每次都是……」，下來就是usually，接著是often或frequently。學生習作中，濫用always的例子屢見不鮮。

一、always/usually/often

1. **我開車時經常聽收音機。**

   【正】：I *often/frequently* listen to the radio while driving.

   【不佳】：I *always* listen to the radio while driving.

   【解說】：always含沒有例外之意，用often//frequently比較合邏輯。

2. **他上學經常遲到。**

   【正】：He was *often* late for school.

   【不佳】：He was *always* late for school.

   【解說】：不能用always的理由如上句。

3. **我們對別人要親切。**

   【正】：We should *always* be kind to other people.

   【誤】：We should *often* be kind to other people.

   【解說】：「對別人親切」應屬沒有例外，所以要用always。

4. **任何時候打604-315-9857這個電話都可以找到我。**

   【正】：You can *always* reach me at 604-315-9857.

   【誤】：You can *often* reach me at 604-315-9857.

   【解說】：【正】句的always表示沒有例外。

5. **女孩子通常喜歡吃甜食。**

   【正】：Girls *usually* like sweets.

   【誤】：Girls *always* like sweets.

【解說】：【誤】句中用always表示沒有例外，不合常理，因為不是每個女孩子都喜歡甜食。

6.　　**年長者比年輕人有經驗，但他們經常做過時的決定。**

【正】：Elderly people are more experienced than young people, but they **often** make outdated decisions.

【誤】：Elderly people are more experienced than young people, but they **always** make outdated decisions.

【解說】：【誤】句中用always 表示沒有例外，不合常理，因為不是每個年長者都會做過時的決定。

7.　　**我一直想去做身體檢查。**

【正】：I **have always wanted** to have a physical checkup.

【誤】：I **always want** to have a physical checkup.

【解說】：always作「總是，經常，一直」解時，動詞要用簡單現在式，例：I always go to school by bus.／The trains are always crowded during rush hours.但是如果要表示「一直想做，但尚未做」時，動詞要用現在完成式，不能用簡單現在式，如【正】句。另外，always如果與進行式連用時，則表示某種不良習慣一再重複，說話者感到不耐煩、驚訝、或者困惑，例：You are always finding fault with me.（你老是挑我毛病。）／She was always talking about her ex-boyfriend.（她老是談論前男友。）

二、sometimes/sometime/some time

這三個都是副詞，但用法不同，請看下例：

8.　　**他有時坐公車上學，有時坐捷運。**

【正】：**Sometimes** he goes to school by bus and **sometime**s by MRT.

【誤】：**Sometime** he goes to school by bus and **sometime** by MRT.

【解說】：sometimes作「有時」解，可置於句首，如【正】句。也可置於be動詞之後，例：He is **sometimes** not responsible for what he does. 也可放在動詞之前，例：She **sometimes** goes to see her parents in the U.S.

9. **我父母將於十一月間來看我。**

【正】：My parents will come to see me **sometime** in November.

【誤】：My parents will come to see me **some time** in November.

【解說】：sometime 用以指未來的某一不確定時間（an uncertain time in the future），要置於表時間的年、月、日或者星期之前，例：I will let you know **sometime** next week.

10. **我記得去年曾經見過她。**

【正】：I remember seeing her **sometime** last year.

【誤】：I remember seeing her **some time** last year.

【解說】：sometime 亦可用於指「過去的某一不確定時間」，例：The author died **sometime** around 1980.（那位作家在1980年左右去世）。

11. **他不在此地已有一段時間了。**

【正】：He has been away for **some time**.

【誤】：He has been away for **sometime**.

【解說】：分開寫的some time 用以表「一段時間」，可置於句尾（合起來的sometime不能置於句尾），亦可置於副詞ago之前，例：He went to the U.S. **some time** ago. 幾天前/幾星期前，他去了美國。

三、especially/especially for

中文的「尤其對……來說」相對應的英文到底要用especially或especially for，學生經常混淆。其實規則很簡單：especially前有介系詞for，後面就要用for，以便平行，否則就不用for。請看下例：

12. **很多人付不起帳單，尤其是住在大都市的窮人。**

【正】：Many people have trouble paying their bills, ***especially*** those poor people who live in the big city.

【誤】：Many people have trouble paying their bills, ***especially for*** those poor people who live in the big city.

【解說】：【誤】句的especially前沒有for，其後就不該加for，以便平行。

13. **通過該項考試對中學生很困難，尤其對亞洲來的國際學生。**

【正】：Passing the test is difficult ***for*** high school students, ***especially for*** those international students from Asia.

【誤】：Passing the test is difficult for high school students, ***especially*** those international students from Asia.

【解說】：【誤】句的especially前有for，其後也要加for，以便平行。

14. **獨居的人，尤其是老年人，應該雇用僕人來照顧他們。**

【正】：People who live alone, ***especially*** elderly people, should hire servants to take care of them.

【誤】：People who live alone, ***especially for*** elderly people, should hire servants to take care of them.

【解說】：【誤】句中的especially前沒有for，其後就不該加for，以便平行。

四、關係副詞where

表示地點的關係子句中，where一般只跟house/ place/ town/ village/ city 等等名詞，例如：This is the place where I was born. 但是關係副詞where也可與case/ incident/ situation/ instance/ exception等等非表示「地點」的名詞連用，請看下例。

15. **在現代社會，有錢人家庭不幸福的例子很多。**

   【正】：In modern society, there are many **cases where** rich people do not have a happy family.

   【誤】：In modern society, there are many **cases which** rich people do not have a happy family.

16. **通常丈夫賺的錢比太太多，然而也有太太賺得比丈夫多的例外。**

   【正】：It is common for the husband to make more money than the wife. However, there are exceptions **where** the wife makes more money.

   【誤】：It is common for the husband to make more money than the wife. However, there are exceptions **that** the wife makes more money.

17. **青少年在某些情況可以不聽從父母。**

   【正】：There are some **situations where** teenagers do not have to listen to their parents.

   【誤】：There are some **situations which** teenagers do not have to listen to their parents.

18. **在網上繳學費比去銀行辦理方便，只要填妥電子申請表即可。**

   【正】：Going to the bank to pay one's tuition is not so convenient as using online banking *where* one just needs to fill out an application online.

【誤】：Going to the bank to pay one's tuition is not so convenient as using online banking *which* one just needs to fill out an application online.

19. **有些情況，員警搜索嫌犯要做得很徹底。**

【正】：There are some *incidents where* the police have to search thoroughly for a suspect.

【誤】：There are some *incidents that* the police have to search thoroughly for a suspect.

20. **人們經常忘記某事，最終要吃到苦頭，這種例子很多。**

【正】：There are many *instances where* people often forget to do something, and they end up reaping the consequences.

【誤】：There are many *instances which* people often forget to do something, and they end up reaping the consequences.

練習題答案

第一章

1.a   2.b   3.b,d   4.b,c   5.b,c   6.a   7.a   8.a,c   9.a,d
10.a   11.a,d   12.b   13.a,c   13.a,c   15.d   15.d   17.b

第二章

1.b,d   2.b,d   3.a,b   4.a   5.c   6.b   7.a,b   8.a,b   9.a
10.b,c   11.a   12.a   13.a,d   14.a

第三章

1.b   2.b   3.c,d   4.a,b   5.b,d   6.b,c   7.a,b   8.a,c   9.b
10.b   11.a,c   12.a   13.a   14.a,b   15.a   16.a,c   17.b,c
18.b   19.b   20.b,c

第四章

1.a   2.a   3.b   4.a,c   5.b,d   6.b,c   7.a   8.a,c   9.b,d
10.a,c   11.b,c   12.a   13.a,d   14.c   15.a,d   16.b   17.a,c   18.a,c
19.a,d   20.a,d

第五章

1.d   2.d   3.a   4.d   5.a   6.c   7.c   8.a   9.c
10.c   11.b   12.a   13.a,d   14.b   15.a,d   16.a,d   17.c

第六章

1.b,d 2.a 3.c 4.a 5.b 6.b 7.c 8.b,c 9.c,d
10.b,d 11.a,c 12.a,c 13.c 14.b,c 15.a

第七章

1.a,b 2.c 3.a 4.a 5.b,d 6.c,d 7.b,c 8.b 9.b,d
10.c 11.a 12.b 13.a,c 14.a,d 15.a,b 16.a,c 17.b,d 18.b

第八章

1.a,b 2.a,b 3.a,c 4.a 5.b,c 6.a,b 7.a 8.b,c 9.a,d
10.c 11.a

第九章

1. b,c 2.c 3.b 4.c,d 5.c 6.c,d 7.d 8.a 9.a
10.b,c 11.a,d 12.b,d 13.b 14.b 15.a,b 16.c,d 17.a 18.d
19.b

第十章

1.c 2.a,c 3.b 4.c 5.a,c 6.a,b 7.c 8.c,d 9.a,c
10.d

第十一章

1. a 2.c 3.a 4.a 5.b 6.b 7.a 8.c 9.a
10.a 11.a 12.b 13.c 14.c

PSJ0032

中式英文面面觀

英漢辭典主編用近 1000 則例句，教你全面破解中式英文的謬誤

作　　者—簡清國
主　　編—林潔欣
企　　劃—王綾翊
美術設計—江儀玲
內頁排版—游淑萍

董 事 長—趙政岷
出 版 者—時報文化出版企業股份有限公司
　　　　　108019 臺北市和平西路 3 段 240 號 3 樓
　　　　　發行專線—（02）2306-6842
　　　　　讀者服務專線—0800-231-705・（02）2304-7103
　　　　　讀者服務傳真—（02）2306-6842
　　　　　郵撥—19344724　時報文化出版公司
　　　　　信箱—10899臺北華江橋郵局第99信箱
時報悅讀網—http://www.readingtimes.com.tw
法律顧問—理律法律事務所　陳長文律師、李念祖律師
印　　刷—勁達印刷股份有限公司
初版一刷—2021 年 1 月 22 日
初版二刷—2021 年 11 月 24 日
定　　價—新臺幣420 元
（缺頁或破損的書，請寄回更換）

時報文化出版公司成立於一九七五年，
並於一九九九年股票上櫃公開發行，於二〇〇八年脫離中時集團非屬旺中，
以「尊重智慧與創意的文化事業」為信念。

中式英文面面觀：英漢辭典主編用近1000則例句,教你 面破解
中式英文的謬誤 / 簡清國著. -- 一版. -- 臺北市：時報文化出
版企業股份有限公司, 2021.1
面；公分. -
ISBN　978-957-13-8518-1（平裝）
1.英語 2.語言學習 3.學習方法
805.1　　　　　　　　　　　　　　　　　　　109021054

ISBN　978-957-13-8518-1
Printed in Taiwan